The Xenobiotic Invasion

The Xenobiotic Invasion

by
Théo Varlet

translated, annotated and introduced by
Brian Stableford

A Black Coat Press Book

Visit our website at www.blackcoatpress.com

ISBN 978-1-61227-054-8. First Printing. November 2011.
Published by Black Coat Press, an imprint of Hollywood
Comics.com, LLC, P.O. Box 17270, Encino, CA 91416. All
rights reserved. Except for review purposes, no part of this
book may be reproduced or transmitted in any form or by any
means, electronic or mechanical, including photocopying,
recording, or by any information storage and retrieval system,
without permission in writing from the publisher. The stories
and characters depicted in this novel are entirely fictional.
Printed in the United States of America.

Introduction

La Grande Panne [The Great Breakdown or, in this case, The Great Shutdown] by Théo Varlet, here translated as *The Xenobiotic Invasion*, was first published by Les Editions des Portiques in 1930, and reprinted in 1936 by Publications de l'Amitié par le livre. It was the second scientific romance that Varlet wrote from scratch, although he had written three earlier volumes based on first drafts by other writers, which he had been hired to revise. Like *Le Roc d'or* [The Golden Rock] (1927), *La Grande Panne* takes its initial inspiration from the author's fascination with astronomy—he was a keen amateur observer—and, more specifically, with cosmobiological speculations about the distribution of life in the universe. His primary literary endeavors had always been poetic, and from the late 1920s onwards, cosmobiological themes acquired a considerable prominence in his work, in such collections as *Paralipomena* (1926), *Ad Astra* (1929) and *Florilège de poésie cosmique* [An Anthology of Cosmic Poetry] (1937).

Léon-Louis-Etienne-Théodore Varlet was born in 1878 in Lille. His father was a lawyer, but the family was unusually well-off, by virtue of having property and business interests in Russia, and he grew up with a private income, feeling that there was no particular need for him to make a living. He decided, instead—following in the footsteps of many other fashionably disenchanted sons of the *bourgeoisie*—to dedicate himself to a literary vocation. He published poetry and criticism in a wide range of literary periodicals and, like almost every other person of similar inclination, founded a couple himself—*L'Essor* and *Les Bandeaux d'or*—in collaboration with various friends. His first collection of poetry, *Heures et rêves* [Hours and Dreams], appeared in 1898. He was also an inveterate traveler, and spent a decade roaming Europe by train and bicycle before marrying in 1909 and settling in Cassis in the south of France, not far from Marseilles. He continued to travel on vacation, however, and visited Paris on a regular basis, where he maintained numerous friendships and placed work in various periodicals—although the fact that so much of his work appeared in provincial periodicals, in his native north as well as his adoptive Midi, impeded the growth of his reputation somewhat.

Although he arrived on the literary scene too late to participate in the Decadent Movement, the work of Charles Baudelaire was the most obvious influences on Varlet's early poetry, and served as a role-model in other ways. Varlet cultivated a quasi-Baudelairean reputation as a resolutely determined non-conformist, making a particular point of attempting to follow up Baudelaire's "research" in the use of drugs to attain "artificial paradises;" he reported extensively on his own experiments with hashish, opium and—most dangerously— ether. In *Au paradis du haschisch; suite à Baudelaire* (1930), he catalogued more than 100 such experiments conducted between 1908 and 1914, including illusory out-of-body experiences that took him into remote regions of outer space and illusions of existing in another person's body. He caused some slight scandal in Cassis by virtue of his dedication to naturism—practiced in the secluded coves that figure prominently in the work of the protagonist of *La Grande Panne*—and his careful cultivation of an all-over suntan, and also courted controversy with his determined pacifism. He was acquainted with several of the Symbolist writers who continued experimenting with "decadent style" in the early 20th century, and contributed to memorial volumes dedicated to Pierre Louÿs and Henri de Régnier.

Varlet published three further collections of poetry during the first phase of his career and one collection of short stories, *Le Dernier Satyre* [The Last Satyr] (1905), but the advent of the Great War in 1914 proved to be a crucial and damaging interruption, as it did for virtually every writer in France. As a pacifist, he was not required to bear arms, but nor was he allowed to remain idle. In 1917, the Russian Revolution destroyed the family fortune, which had provided his living expenses while he made very little money as a writer, and when the war eventually ended, he was confronted by the necessity of making a living from his pen. His primary source of income from 1920 onwards was literary translation, mostly from English. He made a particular specialism of the work of Robert Louis Stevenson, but he also translated several volumes of Rudyard Kipling's later work and was the French translator of John Buchan's *The Thirty-Nine Steps* and J. K. Jerome's *Three Men in a Boat*.

Varlet supplemented this income as best he could with journalism, but seems always to have had difficulty in finding publishers in Paris. For some years, his principal publisher was Edgar Malfère, based in Amiens, who issued his second short story collection, *La Bella Venere* [the Italian title is the name of a boat] (1920) in his "Bibliothèque du Hérisson" [Hedgehog Library] and then commissioned him to recast a number of poorly-written but highly imaginative scientific romances handed to him by a local author, Octave Joncquel. The first appeared as *Les Titans du ciel* [Titans of the Heavens] in 1921, and its sequel, *L'Agonie de la Terre* [The Earth's Death-Throes] followed in 1922, but the arrangement then broke down when Joncquel sued Malfère for unpaid royalties, the publisher apparently having diverted the lion's share of the proceeds from the second book to Varlet because only one scene from Joncquel's original text had survived into the published version. The lawsuit failed, and the rest of Joncquel's allegedly-prolific oeuvre was lost to history; the two published items, collectively making up *L'Épopée martienne*,[1] suggest that the loss is a cause for some regret on the part of lovers of imaginative fiction.

Malfère published another collaboration whose final draft was presumably Varlet's—a timeslip romance co-signed by André Blandin, *La Belle Valence* [Valencia the Beautiful] (1923)—and he recycled Varlet's short fiction in *Le Dernier*

---

[1] Translated as *The Martian Epic*, Black Coat Press, ISBN 978-1-934543-06-1.

Satyre in 1922, as well as publishing the poetry collection *Aux libres jardins* [In the Free Gardens] (1922) and Varlet's first solo novel, *Le Démon dans l'âme* [The Demon in the Soul] (1923). It seems highly probable, however, that none of these books made much money, and they cannot have contributed much to the soothing of the author's financial woes. When he reverted to the production of scientific romance in the Vernian *Le roc d'or*, he was probably trying to produce something a little more commercial, and the same is true of *La Grande Panne*, but a sequel to the latter novel, *Aurore Lescure, pilote d'astronef* [Aurore Lescure, Starship Pilot], failed to sell during his lifetime and was published posthumously in 1943, when it sank without trace in the midst of World War II.

Varlet did not live to see the outbreak of that war, dying in Cassis in 1938 after being plagued by sciatica for some years. He was in such dire straits by 1936 that his friends formed an organization, Les Amis de Théo Varlet, to raise funds for his support, issuing appeals for assistance in numerous French and English periodicals and publishing a regular *Bulletin* from 1936-39; it is possible that the 1936 reprint of *La Grande Panne* and his final poetry collection—which appeared from the same publisher—were, in essence, charitable gestures.

Although Varlet's poetry continued to enjoy a certain reputation, and his experiments with drugs retained some notoriety, his prose fell into obscurity until it began to attract attention from fans of the American genre of science fiction, imported into France on a large scale during the post-World War II "coca-colonization" of Europe. *Le Roc d'or* was reprinted as an sf novel, and the Amiens-based firm Encrage reissued the three collaborative novels in a handsome omnibus edition compiled by Alfu and Joseph Altairac, *Oeuvres Romanesques I* (1996), advertised as the first volume of a projected series, although no others have appeared as yet. The volume includes a number of essays on the Martian Epic, and Varlet's work in general, and constitutes a fitting tribute to his endeavors as a genre pioneer.

Although the association might have been accidental to begin with, Varlet certainly took to scientific romance with a will, and evidently had a considerable knowledge of French scientific romance; one of his acquaintances in Paris was J.-H. Rosny Aîné, whose work in the genre he admired greatly. *La Grande Panne* shows the influence of Rosny's classic disaster story *La Force mystérieuse* (1913)[2] and probably also drew some inspiration from Henri Allorge's award-winning *Le Grand Cataclysme* (1922)[3]. It does not, however, merely recycle ideas from those earlier novels, but extrapolates them with considerable care, verve and polish. Although it probably did not have much direct influence on later works of scientific romance, it does have interesting affinities with the British school of "ambiguous disaster stories" pioneered by Gerald Heard's "The Great Fog" (1944) and H. de Vere Stacpoole's *The Story of my Village* (1947). At any rate, it fully deserves to be reckoned a classic of the French genre; it remains eminently readable today.

This translation is taken from the second edition of the novel, issued in 1936 by Publications de l'Amitié par le livre, and includes the preface added to that second edition.

Brian Stableford

---

[2] Translated as the title-story of the collection *The Mysterious Force and Other Anomalous Phenomena*, Black Coat Press, ISBN 978-1-935558-37-8.
[3] Translated as *The Great Cataclysm*, Black Coat Press, ISBN 978-1-61227-026-5.

Preface
(to the Second Edition)

The present novel, *La Grande Panne*, appeared for the first time from Les Éditions des Portiques in October 1930. A year later, in October 1931, a short story signed Rowley Hilliard, "Death from the Stars," whose initial idea is singularly reminiscent of that of *La Grande Panne*, appeared in an American magazine, *Wonder Stories*. Two scientists, Julius Humboldt and George Dixon, discover a mysterious powder in a meteorite. That mysterious powder is an elementary life-form. It grows at the expense of terrestrial life. Vegetation is consumed, its foliage blackened. Humans initially experience itching, then burns. Dixon dies after atrocious suffering. Humboldt realizes the danger, but is affected himself, to the extent that he can scarcely move. He finds the strength to douse Dixon's corpse in kerosene, however, along with his bed, cottage and garden, and the entire contaminated zone; then he locks himself in and sets fire to it. His suicide is attributed to madness.

This short story enjoyed considerable success; readers demanded a sequel. Mr. Hilliard gave them satisfaction, and the second story appeared a few months later in the same magazine. Although they were very evidently inspired by my novel, the two stories have a typical Yankee crudity, and both incline toward the macabre.

Given the present state of American legislation, I would have very little chance of obtaining any pecuniary compensation for this act of "piracy." As the master J. H. Rosny Aîné did with respect to his novel *La Force Mystérieuse*,[4] however,

---

[4] Rosny added a preface to the book version of the novel in order to emphasize that its serialization in *Je Sais Tout* had begun before the serialization in *The Strand Magazine* of Ar-

I thought I ought to establish my priority here, by reporting these facts in a preface to this new edition of *La Grande Panne*. I thank my worthy collaborator in anticipation Régis Messac,[5] novelist, translator and historian of the literature of the scientific imagination, who was kind enough to draw my attention to this plagiarism.

Théo Varlet

P.S. A novel entitled *Les Naufragés d'Éros*, forming a sequel to *La Grande Panne*, will appear imminently from a publisher who remains to be found.[6]

---

thur Conan Doyle's The *Poison Belt*, whose opening sequence has strong (but presumably coincidental) similarities to it.

[5] From 1924 to 1929, Régis Messac was a professor at McGill University in Canada, where he must have made the acquaintance of US pulp magazines, notably those in the genres in which he was interested as a historian and critic—crime fiction and what the pulps in question soon dubbed "science fiction." He maintained his interest after returning to France, after which he published several translations of works by the pulp sf writer David H. Keller. It is not impossible that David Lasser, the managing editor of *Wonder Stories*, was aware of the existence of *La Grande Panne* in 1930, given that he serialized several translations of French and German sf novels and that he had a strong interest in what Varlet calls "astronautics," but the basic idea is by no means so exotic that two writers could not have come up with it independently. Varlet is, however, correct about the crudity of the two pulp stories, which were actually signed A. Rowley Hilliard, and contrast strongly with his far more sophisticated development of the premise.

[6] Varlet was unable to find a publisher for the sequel before he died in 1938; it is obviously the novel published posthumously in 1943 as *Aurore Lescure, Pilote d'astronef.*

THE XENOBIOTIC INVASION

I. In the Ruins of Tauroëntum

There is no doubt that if, on returning from that excursion, I had climbed into Géo's car and not Dr. Alburtin's, my entire life would have been changed, and probably the future of the world too.

That is why the conversation that I, Géo, his sister Luce, their mother and the doctor had that afternoon—October 15—before the ruins of Tauroëntum and the azure of the Mediterranean, began the adventure for me.

First, though, let me introduce myself: Gaston-Adolphe Delvart, born in Lille, aged 27, a respectably talented painter—if I can believe the opinion of my friends and, especially, the prices that dealers and collectors pay for my canvases. I am no prouder of them for that, however, for some daubs executed by jokers devoid of any merit attain much higher sums per square decimeter—but at least I earn a living and am conscious of making true art, which is already not that common.

But let's pass on; my art is only indirectly concerned with the present story. It is more relevant to remark that I was, at the time of which I speak, a bachelor, flirting superficially with Mademoiselle Luce de Ricourt, the sister of my friend Géo, a former school-friend turned engineer, of whom I had lost sight and rediscovered a fortnight before in Cassis, where I had come to take a vacation, to paint and to deliver myself to the pleasures of the baths and moderate nudism.

Luce de Ricourt, 24 years of age, her hair an ardent shade of red, who puts me in mind of Titian's Danae in the Museum of Naples, has an esthetic attraction for me, impeded by an evident and undeniable moral incompatibility. An authentic Baronne, but penniless, she is as modern as possible and regrets not having been born American. Money is the most important thing in life, she affirms. She has sworn to attain wealth, knows the influential businessman Rosenkrantz, and indulges in fruitful operations on the Bourse—which does not prevent her from having a fairly considerable, but purely utilitarian, artistic flair. She holds my canvases in esteem, and has confidence in a future rise in their market value, but she is openly scornful of my lack of shrewdness, which holds back that elevation.

"Tonton," she says to me, repeatedly—for she has made that gracious diminutive of my forename, and addresses me as "tu" although she used to tear out my hair for fun ten years ago—"you're not up to date. You might consider yourself young, but you're as fossilized as my noble mother, with your antediluvian prejudices."

Or: "Poor old chap! How the two of us would quarrel, if ever I took it into my head to marry you!"

That's certainly my opinion. But there's no chance, for-tunately; being in no hurry to marry, she mocks sentimentality, regrets being unable to follow Professor Morton's courses in New York in order to become an accomplished "vamp," and will only ever marry a "money-making man"—an American, at least at heart, like her. With me she's content to flirt, and take advantage of the times when I allow myself to be half-taken in order, to buy—or force me to sell, as her mother puts it—my best canvases at a discount price; they are, she be-lieves, gilt-edged investments. And that opinion flatters my self-respect sufficiently for me to pardon the maneuver, which borders on sentimental fraud.

Even her brother jokes, on occasion: "Oh, Lucy, you have no sense of morality!"

Géo has one, or thinks he has—the moral sensibility of the second quarter of the 20th century. He does not disdain the small profits, commissions, percentages and discounts he ob-tains by virtue of his position as an engineer in the factories of the important aircraft-manufacturer Hérault-Feltrie, at Saint-Denis. His passion is automobiles. He has recently equipped his car with a new device that he calls a "turbo-compressor" and he is exceedingly pleased with it.

"With that gizmo in my vulgar little Renault, I can match any branded rattletrap. The other day, coming from Paris with Mama and Luce on the road between Arles and Miramas, in the Crau—a straight stretch of 30 kilometers on the level—I caught up with a big Hispano that was cruising at 50. They let me get to ten meters behind them, but just as I was about to overtake them they pressed the accelerator. *Pfft!*—up to 80. Me, I opened up my turbo—vroom! Like an aircraft engine. A blast of the horn, and I passed them at 140. My fellows sat there flabbergasted."

At the memory of this exploit of her son's, which still gives her goose-pimples retrospectively, Madame de Ricourt murmurs: "The horror of it! 140! You could have killed all three of us, Géo!"

Madame de Ricourt, who is Luce at 50, has a chestnut-colored complexion. Plump and puffed up, she straps herself up and strangles herself to "make herself young." By virtue of the snobbery of believing that she is "up to date," she plasters herself with make-up and smokes cigarettes, but makes her outdatedness obvious at every moment.

These remarks are being exchanged near the ruins of Tauroëntum, which are on the edge of the beach at Saint-Cyr-sur-Mer. In an excavation there, one can see the remains of a scarcely-recognizable mosaic and three enormous earthenware jars, like some that can still be found in the homes of Provençal peasants: the vestiges of a Gallo-Roman villa. They have left me rather cold, and the Ricourts too. Dr. Alburtin, who took the initiative in bringing us here, is apologetic; by way of compensation, he invites us to take tea at the little hostelry on the beach, where our two cars are parked: the turbo in which I came from Cassis with Géo and his sister, and Alburtin's roadster, to which Madame de Ricourt gave preference "because the doctor drives like a sage"—which is to say that he never exceeds 60.

I would have thought Dr. Tancrède Alburtin a very pleasant fellow were it not his mania for engaging you in long conversations by clapping you on the shoulder and leaving his hand stuck there in an affectionate and exasperating fashion. The tall quadragenarian, broad in the face, with blond hair and a fair complexion, went to war as a military surgeon. Far from bragging about it and posing as a hero, he makes his exploits into amiable tall stories—but relates them all the same. We became friends two years earlier, during my first sojourn in Cassis, where he practices medicine while directing a radiotherapy clinic that he neglects slightly in order to devote himself to his personal research. He's a convinced scientist, and also has a hobbyist interest in the curiosities of the region.

The failure of his Tauroëntum is forgotten before tea and cake. The enthusiastic eulogy Géo has offered to his turbo has steered the conversation toward the speed of present and future transport. Luce evokes her memories of a trip in an aircraft: London to Paris in an hour and a half: 260 kilometers an hour.

"At Hénault-Feltrie's," her brother declares, proudly, "We're perfecting a metallic monoplane with a turbocompressor, which will give it a cruising speed of 350 kph."

In order to seek forgiveness for his failed antiquities, Alburtin joins in and stimulates the new conversation: "And when the astronautical rocket enters into everyday use, it will no longer be in hundreds of kilometers an hour that we'll be counting, but thousands."

"The horror of it!" exclaims the modernist dowager. "Fortunately, that's not for our time. I won't live to see it—and neither will you. Perhaps in a century or two..."

"Is that, Mama," Luce jokes, severely, "what you call being up to date? Don't you read the newspapers anymore?"

I was, in fact, about to cite the departure of the American rocket, but Alburtin has got in ahead of me. Facing the blue sea, upright in his wicker armchair, he is pontificating amiably:

"Interplanetary voyages? But we're almost there—we *are* there! Within ten years, Hénault-Feltrie—your boss, Géo, one of the donors of the Rep-Hirsch prize and a great champion of astronautics in France—affirmed in 1929. After the aircraft, the rocket: that's natural; it's the curve of inevitable progress. Think of the acceleration of scientific progress and the multiplication of discoveries. The 19th century alone realized more than the 2000 years preceding it. The beginning of the 20th century, up to the war, has made as much ground as the entire 19th century. Ever more rapidly, ever further, ever higher! Rockets to the Moon and the planets? That will be child's play as soon as we've discovered—in atomic disintegration, for example—more powerful sources of energy. With those presently at our disposal, it's already possible, just about. People have only been devoting themselves to it seriously for two or three years, and it's making progress— opinion is excited, impassioned; one senses that the moment has come. In 1929, a German launched the first automatic rocket at 200 an hour…which exploded after a few kilometers, along with its passenger, a cat—but that doesn't master. In 1930, the rocket-plane manned by the aviator Espenlaub[7] made a tour of the aerodrome at Lohenhausen, near Dusseldorf. It was recently announced that a professor from Budapest, Doctor Oberth,[8] has invented a rocket-shell with which he

[7] Gottlob Espenlaub (1900-1972) had been experimenting with rocket-propelled gliders since 1928.

[8] Herman Oberth (1894-1989) never got his proposed rocket into space, although he did get it on to the cinema screen in Fritz Lang's *Die Frau im Mond* (1929), for which he was hired as a technical consultant. The film appears to have been one of the primary influences on the present novel, but the actress Gerda Maurus, who played the role of the female member of the ill-fated lunar gold-mining expedition, was probably not the sole inspiration for Aurore Lescure. The American aviatrix Amelia Earhart became world-famous in 1928 after flying the Atlantic and became a familiar sight in

is planning to make a voyage to the Moon and back; 87 people, 20 of whom are women, have written to ask to company him..."

"You're forgetting the film *The Girl in the Moon*, which shows us the voyage accomplished," Luce put in, taking a long draft from the cigarette in her long jade holder, "according to the vision of its director, Fritz Lang."

"Always joking, Mademoiselle! The film was anticipation—but that's no longer the case. At present, like me, you've been able to read in the dailies of the last few days that the American scientist Professor Oswald Lescure is launching a rocket, with a passenger, into interplanetary space. And you've also been able to read in this morning's *Petit Marseillais* that the departure was due to take place today..."

"From Columbus, Missouri," I completed. "And the passenger is Professor Lescure's own daughter. He must have confidence in his invention!"

"And the girl must have a lot of pluck!" the doctor continued. "The newspapers are comparing her to an aviatrix, but her flight is much more dangerous than crossing the Atlantic by plane. Even if she doesn't get as far as the Moon, which is her intention, who knows whether she'll fall back to Earth, or whether she'll ever return here?"

"Shouldn't someone be able to follow her apparatus by telescope?" asked Madame de Ricourt, affecting a resigned expression.

"I doubt it, Madame. And anyway, there's no means of steering it, or of bringing it safely to harbor."

"It's suicide, then! The government shouldn't have permitted..."

Géo intervened. "As you can imagine, Mama, there have been test flights. One doesn't set off for the bull's-eye—the Moon—just like that, with a new machine. One must first know how to handle it. The girl has been in training, like the

the cinema, associated in the next two years with massive advertizing campaigns for clothing and cigarettes.

first aviators, the Wright brothers, at Dayton in 1903-04. Now that the doctor has reminded me about it, I've seen the name Aurore Lescure in cinema posters.

"I've seen her on the screen," Alburtin continued. "She's very pretty."

"Pooh!" said Luce, disdainfully. "An American with a PhD—a female scientist in spectacles."

"You're exaggerating Luce. She doesn't have spectacles, but she has a rather surly manner—a real tomboy…a horror. I remember now; I've seen her too—with you, Luce, and Madame Delval, at the Paramount..."

At each of these reflections, I was on the point of exclaiming: "I've seen her at the cinema too! Not once, like you, but eight or ten times, as often as I could..." But what outbursts of laughter from Géo, what jovial jest from Alburtin, what scandalized old lady's pout, and what mocking laughter from Luce I would have attracted, in making the confession it would have been impossible for me to suppress: "I've seen her…and I think she's adorable."

Wisely, I kept quiet, understanding the ridiculousness of my romantic and imaginative sentiment. To be smitten with a professional beauty of the cinema—a Rudolph Valentino if one is female, a Pola Negri if one is male—is still acceptable; there is a contagion in that, a spirit of imitation, of snobbery. One is submissive to the prestige of a face loved by thousands—but in my personal case, that explanation did not hold up. These people with cinematographic passions are predisposed to it; they are smitten in their turn by all the great film-stars. For me, on the other hand, if was sufficient for an idol of the public to appear on the screen for my individualistic instinct to raise my hackles against her; that multiplicity of homages, far from seducing me, held my sentiments below melting-point. Not once in my life had I felt the attraction of a famous face. The emotion experienced with respect to Aurore Lescure was unique in my experience.

The first time I had seen that face surge forth, after a title read with indifference, I scarcely knew who she was, and yet my gaze was caught, my attention held fast. The black-and-white image was, to me, a supernatural apparition, a revelatory upheaval. I recognized that slim young woman costumed as an aviatrix, her face made into an oval by the coarse fabric helmet, reduced to its essential features. That slightly melancholy and dolorous style, the neatly-divided mouth with the firm lips, the magnificent teeth and those limpid eyes, child-like and yet so profound, were the very synthesis of my ideal type of beauty. I had already seen it in my dreams—or in an anterior life. Who knows?

I had lashed myself with irony—in what anterior life, idiot? That young foreigner, separated from you by five or six thousand kilometers, that pioneer of a futuristic sport standing behind her rocket-ship, that shiny steel shell, with her hand on the bolt of the porthole-door that is about to close upon her when she had finished addressing her conventionally-forced smile to the camera-operator...

When her image disappeared from the screen, I felt a strange emptiness, an intimate discouragement, an immeasurable isolation...and I left the theater, refusing to watch another film, carrying the marvelous image away with me.

And, while mocking myself for that haunting, that possession, stronger and more tenacious every time, I had returned to see her, always more intimately convinced that I was recovering the image of an individual known in some anterior life, of an individual to whom I was bound by mysterious ties—but also an individual whom, in all probability, I would never meet...

Could I really allow such crazy sentiments to be suspected by my companions, even by virtue of an imprudent word of allusion, on that October afternoon, beside the ink-blue Mediterranean, in the rays of the setting Sun?

II. Aurore Lescure

Why did I get into Dr. Alburtin's little roadster in order to return to Cassis? Why did I arrange things, cleverly, so that Madame de Ricourt would take her place with Luce in the turbo, on the strength of Géo' promise that he would not exceed 30 kilometers an hour? My latent rancor in regard to the disdainful judgment passed by Luce on the American astronaut must have provoked my determination, and also the subconscious sentiment of being more in sympathy with Alburtin and the secret hope of continuing the conversation about the Rocket.

I jokingly evoked as a reason, however, that I did not want to give any offense to the doctor by seeming to scorn his modest C6.

At any rate, the decision that I made on the threshold of the Hôtel de la Plage near the ruins of Tauorëntum had, I repeat, a supremely important influence on my future, and also significantly influenced the fate of the civilized world.

If I believed in metempsychosis, I would doubtless see an occult premonition in the conversation we had just had and the image of Aurore Lescure that was haunting my mind—but I don't believe in it, and, on cool analysis, the coincidence was perfectly natural. The newspapers had announced that the flight of the interplanetary rocket would take place that day; at the same time, throughout Europe, France and America—the entire world—hundreds of thousands of men and women must have been thinking about the heroine and talking about her exploit.

The only difference there was between me and the others is that I saw her land.

The Rocket, according to the mathematicians, had an equal probability of falling at the North Pole or the middle of the Gobi desert: a simple matter of theory. If it had fallen elsewhere, it would not have had any further effect on the facts of our lives. I prefer to believe in destiny. In the real universe, of which my destiny in a part, Aurore Lecure *had* to land, inevitably, at a determined point, and I also *had* to be passing by that point at the same moment. In truth, it was all simple and natural, rather than marvelous.

It happened so rapidly that Alburtin and I scarcely had time to understand what was happening.

It was 5 p.m.; the Sun had disappeared behind the calcareous crests of the picturesque gorge that we were passing through, unhurriedly, but it was still broad daylight. Ten minutes before, at the exit from La Ciotat and the beginning of the coast, my friend Géo had afforded himself the facile pleasure of outstripping us by giving his turbo free rein, and the Ricourts ought, at that moment to have been arriving in Cassis at the Hôtel Cendrillon, where I would meet up with them again at dinner. We were within sight of the Belle-Fille pass, where two roads—the one to Aubagne and the one to Casasis—separated, when I glimpsed a light in the sky from the corner of my eye, which caused me to raise my head.

A trail of red fire, like the track of a bolide, but which was slowing as it fell vertically from the zenith…a strident fizz…

The light went out; the sound ceased—and, in the clear blue sky, a flaccid and indeterminate shape was visible, in a rapid perpendicular fall.

"An aircraft!" I exclaimed. "A plane that has caught fire and is falling!"

Keeping his hands on the steering-wheel, Alburtin took his eyes off the road for two seconds.

"A funny aircraft!" he opined. "More like a dirigible?"

In consequence of the large size of the object, it was not possible as yet to estimate its distance. In the oblique sunlight, the flaccid form of the preceding moment had taken on the clear aspect of an elongated oval and the yellowish profile of a "semi-rigid" airship. Beneath it, however, suspended by invisible wires, something metallic was sparkling.

It descended, no longer in free fall but with a regular slowness, directly toward us, on to the spur of a wooded hill that separated the two roads.

I realized what was happening and exclaimed: "A parachute descent! The plane has caught fire and the pilot has ejected."

Having arrived at the bifurcation, the automobile was close enough to the aerial object for us to be able to make out its dimensions and nature. It was not a distant large dirigible but a fairly close yellow fabric parachute supporting a canister that shone as if made of aluminum.

"What's that?" said Alburtin, perplexed, stopping at the foot of a boundary marker.

A singular anxiety invaded me; my heart was beating violently—but I dared not jump to a conclusion as yet; the parachute distracted me.

A hundred and fifty meters from us, at an equal distance between the two roads, the metallic object plunged into the pines and brushwood with a rustle of branches and foliage. The shock of impact was perceptible, and a noise of breaking glass, while the parachute settled limply on the crowns of the trees.

"Are you coming?" I said, impatiently.

"Just a minute." My companion set the car moving again, came to a stop on the edge of the road 50 meters further on, then switched off the motor and the headlights.

I had leapt to the ground, listening carefully.

The evening breeze was freshening in the great silence of those bird-free valleys, but there was no human sound—no cry for help. A profound anguish, far surpassing the anxiety that one might feel for an unknown person in danger, gripped my heart.

Through the bushes of russet rock-rose, flowering gorse and kermes oak, I drove straight toward the spot marked by the yellow festoons of the parachute's canopy, paying no heed to the gorse and goatsthorn, whose sharp needles clawed at me

23

hands and my legs, through my trousers. The plump Alburtin was panting behind me.

Finally, I made out a glint of metal in the undergrowth; a few strides further on, there was a kind of enormous shell, lying almost flat on its side, on an outcrop of rock.

A shell? No! The interplanetary Rocket! For the evocation that I had rejected a little while before as demented and absurd imposed itself upon me; I recognized the vehicle, tapered at one end, that I had seen so many times on the screen, with Aurore Lescure smiling at me, one hand on the bolt of the porthole-door.

That door, or manhole, was in front of me, but hermetically sealed by the wing-nuts and joints of an airtight shutter outlined on the wall, almost at the top of the stout recumbent cylinder.

As there were not yet two astronautical rockets in service in the world, it was undoubtedly Professor Oswald Lescure's, which had departed from Columbus, Missouri that very day. Inside it was Aurore Lescure—or her corpse.

A rapid examination of the shell showed me that the outcrop of rock on which it rested had punctured a small round hole. I bent down, to try to look inside, but there was not enough space between the limestone spur and the shards of broken glass. The disquieting odor of some chemical product was escaping from the hole.

I stood up and shouted: "Quickly, Alburtin! She's asphyxiating! Help me to open the door."

In order to unscrew it, I grabbed one of the two handles encased in cavities in the shutter of the manhole. An inscription in two languages—English and French—surmounted by the American flag and the words *MG-17 First Voyage to the Moon*, instructed: *To open, turn handle clockwise.*

"The possibility of a crash-landing was anticipated," said Alburtin, arriving completely out of breath—and he turned the other handle.

A click...

The round plate, released, fell back on its hinges to reveal a gaping opening about 50 centimeters in diameter. Avidly, I leaned into it, and glimpsed a human form, collapsed against a control panel. The figure was turned so that only the back of the helmet could be seen.

"I'm thinner than you, doctor," I declared, "and there isn't room for two."

Changing my position, I introduced myself into the hole, not without difficulty. The exceedingly small control-room was cluttered with an accumulation of levers and apparatus, on which I dared not suspend myself, and I had to set my foot on the young woman's hand, which was still clutching a handle. In spite of the two openings—the manhole and the breach in the hull—the air inside was charged with an acrid, choking odor.

I clenched my jaws in vertiginous rage. What if she were dead?

"Get ready, Doctor! I'll pass her to you."

Disengaging the fingers clenched around the ebonite handle, I lifted the inert body up by the waist. I felt its reassuring warmth through the leather costume with a surge of joy, and I raised it as best I could toward the opening.

With his professional dexterity, Alburtin first extracted the limp arms, then took hold of the young woman under her armpits and hauled her through the hole, while I followed the movement, supporting her hips. By the time I had disengaged myself, he had laid her down on the ground in a place almost devoid of pebbles, carpeted by pine-needles, and was kneeling beside her.

"No apparent wounds—a simple loss of consciousness," was his diagnosis.

"Shouldn't we take her to the car right away?" I asked, a little less anxious than before.

"Better to re-establish respiration first. A few rhythmic movements—if that doesn't work, you can help me by applying traction to the tongue."

25

Removing the unconscious young woman's helmet and unbuttoning the top of her fur-lined flying-suit, he began alternately raising and lowering her arms.

The face, in the curly shock of dark mahogany hair, cut to shoulder-length, took on the delicacy of a ball of wax, in which a residue of red in the lips might have denoted feminine coquetry as well as the warmth of life whose return I was avidly awaiting. I thought about a romance by Wells, *The Wonderful Visit*, in which an angel materializes, having emerged from "the fourth dimension." A similar marvel was realized here: the angelic astronaut had quite the fallacious domain of the screen for real existence…and I experienced a tremulous joy in recognizing, in that three-dimensional face, point for point, my black-and-white Aurore Lescure completed and made flesh.

"*Oof!* She's breathing," said Alburtin, with satisfaction, ceasing to manipulate the arms. "She's coming round now."

The eyelids fluttered, then opened wide, and her clear blue-green eyes wandered, vaguely at first, over the doctor's face, mine, and the branches of the pines. She did not see the shell, which was behind her.

With a glimmer of comprehension in her gaze, she asked: "Where am I? Did my apparatus crash?"

I knew that she was the daughter of a French-Canadian, but it was a delightful surprise nevertheless to hear her express herself in French. Her voice, still very weak, had a clear and pure tone, as enchanting as her slight accent, brisk and perfumed with ancient France. Absorbed in my delight, I left the doctor to answer her.

"You're in the south of France, Miss, between Marseilles and Toulon, four kilometers from Cassis, where I shall transport you, to my clinic. I'm Doctor Tancrède Alburtin, at your service—and this is my friend Gaston Delvart, renowned painter. Your apparatus, save for a broken window, does not seem to have suffered overmuch damage. I suppose we shall have to leave it where it is, for it must weigh several tons…"

Her brow furrowed, she was listening with an effort of concentration that was visibly exhausting her. She had difficult replying.

"No, the fuel-tanks are empty; it only weighs 400 kilograms. If you please, Messieurs, have it put in a safe place, hidden from reporters. It mustn't…and please, fetch out the green box marked *Meteorites* right away, and my pigskin valise. Oh, what luck! You're not journalists. Please, prevent the journalists from interviewing me…"

Her voice faded into an indistinct murmur. Her eyelids closed, and with a slight sigh she let her head fall back on to the carpet of pine-needles. We saw her features relax, and she lost consciousness again.

Alburtin took her pulse. Seeing that I was anxious, he said: "Don't worry, Delvart. This was predictable—the reaction. She's suffering from nervous exhaustion. It's quite natural, after her session as a interplanetary pilot. This time, though, let's not leave her here. A featherweight—I can carry her to the car by myself. You go get the green box and the valise that she was asking for. The apparatus is too heavy too cumbersome for my rattletrap; there's no great risk in letting it stay where it is until tomorrow morning. It can't be seen from the road and it'll be dark soon."

On the battlefield, Alburtin had bravely transported many a wounded man heavier than a slender young woman. Rediscovering his vigor and skill of yesteryear, he took the inert body in his arms and started walking toward the road, at a slow but sure pace, without stumbling, in spite of the pebble-strewn ground cluttered with brushwood.

After a momentary rebellion, I let him carry the precious burden away, and resigned myself to serve the castaway from space in another fashion. Returning to the shell, I plunged into its noxious atmosphere again and searched for the "green box." I discovered it lodged in the ceiling of the cockpit, held in place by spring-loaded brackets. I unhooked it. An inscription in ink left no doubt as to its identity: *Meteorites collected in the interplanetary void between 1000 and 4000 kilometers above the terrestrial surface, October 15, between 14:00 and 14:35.*

As for the pigskin valise, it was at my feet, among other objects displaced by the shock of landing and the subsequent adjustment of position. I picked it up without taking the trouble to examine the rest. I was in a hurry to get back to the woman who had fallen from the skies. I barely took time to close the round metal hatch over the manhole and screw it down. With the green box in one hand and the valise in the other I plunged into the brushwood in pursuit of Alburtin.

Loading the car wasn't easy. The doctor regretted having brought his little sports car instead of his professional saloon. The roadster had four seats, but they were arranged in individual buckets where it was impossible to lay the unconscious young woman down. After several fruitless attempts to make her comfortable, I was obliged to resolve to hold her like a child, half-extended, on my knees, with her torso against my breast and her head in the hollow of my right arm, wedged against the back of the seat—a slightly improper attitude from the viewpoint of uniformed spectators.

We only had four kilometers to travel, but dusk was only beginning to fall, and as luck would have it we encountered no less than three tourist buses whose occupants—foreigners—darted surprised, ironic or scandalized glances at us as we flew past, which clearly said: "So uninhibited, these amorous French!"

Only one acquaintance of Dr. Alburtin's—Cassis' great viticulturalist Monsieur Botin, whose Renault overtook us on the outskirts of the town—took a longer look, slowed down and asked: "An accident, Doctor?"

"Yes—I'm taking an injured woman to my clinic," the Doctor replied, evasively.

The dangerous bends as we entered Cassis saved us from having to say more and we separated from our questioner, who continued along the road to Marseilles. I could count on Alburtin to observe the discretion that the young woman had asked of us. There were, in any case, no other interrogations to deflect. The 50 meters of the Rue Droite that we had to travel were deserted, and when we arrived at the door of the clinic there was not a single human face in the vicinity.

Those few minutes since the Belle-Fille pass had passed for me like a dream, in which I forgot my role as a nurse. I held that castaway from space, that angel materialized from the screen, like a conquest, or a prey, in the intoxication of a miraculous interval, without giving any thought to the fact that the moment must eventually end. I made an effort to be as unreal myself as a character on film, to live a cinematic episode...

I came back to reality when, the car having stopped, Alburtin and a nurse took my exciting burden from my arms in order to carry her into the house. Mechanically, I leapt on to the sidewalk and prepared to follow them. Alburtin, however, who was in the lead—walking backwards along the corridor, carrying the upper part of the young woman's body while the nurse held her legs—said: "Stay and have dinner with jus, Delvart—my wife will keep you company. I'll come back down in five minutes to bring you news."

While Madame Alburtin came to the door with a welcoming smile, I hid my irritation and disappointment by taking the pigskin valise and the box labeled *Meteorites* from the car.

With regard to the doctor's wife, the habitual custodian of the clinic's professional secrets, I did not feel bound to hold anything back, and once at table with her with a glass of port, I told her about the astonishing encounter, with no other reticence than keeping quiet about my intimate sentiments.

The lady did not seem to appreciate the beauty of the adventure as I did, however. A practical and shrewd woman, she saw it primarily as a godsend for her husband, whose name would be associated in the newspapers with the landing of the interplanetary rocket.

"Let's see," she calculated, fixing her dark and pensive yes on me. "It's ten past seven, the Post Office is closed, but we can find someone to go to Marseilles. Your friend Monsieur de Ricourt won't refuse, and to draft a press release we have Monsieur Blanc, the schoolmaster, who's the regional correspondent of the *Petit Marseillais*."

The doctor's wife was speaking in such a clear and decisive tone, organizing her publicity in advance, that I was almost intimidated. Too bad, though, if I made her an enemy—Aurore's tranquility was the most important thing.

"I regret, Madame, that the principal interested party, Miss Lescure herself, asked us urgently to protect her from any interviews." By way of conciliation, I added: "Perhaps she'll lift the ban tomorrow, though—the Doctor will let us know."

I didn't have to weather the storm that I saw brewing in my companion's expression; Alburtin came into the dining-room, and I knew by his wife's resigned sigh that he was the real master of the house, and that his word would be law.

"Now let's eat!" he exclaimed. "Excuse me for having made you wait, Delvart, but I thought it best to X-ray our young miss. Nothing broken, no displacement of the internal organs, no visible fractures or lesions. As I thought, it's just nervous fatigue that caused her second loss of consciousness. She only came round to pronounce a few sentences, and fell almost immediately into a reparative sleep. She's now slumbering peacefully in the care of Madame Narinska, the chief nurse. We'll let her sleep around the clock."

"You haven't interviewed her, then, Doctor?" I asked, deliberately, with a sideways glance at his wife.

"Certainly not! Firstly, she renewed her plea that nothing should be communicated to the newspapers until further notice, and secondly, she obliged me to take a $50 banknote—'for my expenses' she specified, and for the transport of her apparatus...with which we'll occupy ourselves tomorrow, as well as her third request, to cable her father as soon as the Post Office opens."

During dinner, Madame Alburtin attempted to seize the initiative again and insidiously pronounced the names of Monsieur Blanc and the *Petit Marseillais*, but the Doctor, with a calm and implacable authority, told her the version of the story that was to be put about in order to satisfy curiosity: a simple aviation accident.

"That will also explain the transportation here of the apparatus, which can pass in a pinch for some sort of plane."

It was agreed that I would go to Belle-Fille in the morning with the local truck-driver to collect the shell and the parachute.

"As for Ricourt, if you see him this evening at your hotel, take care to feed him the same fable…and the name of the aviatrix is Aurette Constantin—that's the signature she used on her cablegram."

When we had taken coffee, the doctor's wife withdrew to make her regular tour of the clinic. In a falsely detached tone, Albertin proposed: "Suppose we cast an eye over the meteorites in the famous green box that Miss Lescure had us bring?" He anticipated my objection by adding: "Surely she wouldn't mind."

I sensed the indelicacy of the project, but if Alburtin was driven by scientific curiosity, I too was avid to see the meteorites that the young astronaut had brought back from her expedition. Without making any reply, I followed Alburtin, who led me to his laboratory.

The green box, in embossed and lacquered metal, somewhat reminiscent of a small ice-cream pail, had a lid sealed by a simple bolt, with no trick to it. At the bottom of the receptacle there was a layer of fine black granules. Alburtin picked up a pinch with a glass spatula. It was nothing much to look at: like fine coal dust whose particles were hardly visible.

"Shall we both take a look under the microscope?" the Doctor proposed.

I declined the offer. I'm not a scientist. It was sufficient for me to learn from my friend's explanations that the dust must be a specimen of the cosmic matter that drifts freely through space.

"A specimen of inestimable scientific value, for when those grains are caught by the Earth in its orbit, like a cloud of mosquitoes, friction in the layers of the atmosphere 'strikes' them like matches and volatilizes them as shooting stars. Bolides, which are heavier pebbles, probably of another sort, sometimes resist the blaze and reach the ground, but no one in the world has ever held in his hand the slightest parcel of the meteoric dust that you see here."

Alburtin, naturally, wanted to know more, and to experiment to that end. I watched him, with his index-finger at the corner of his mouth and his brow furrowed, meditatively contemplating the little spoonful of black granules. He reminded me of a difficult and suspicious patient examining a dose of a new medicine before taking it.

"You aren't going to eat it?" I joked.

Alburtin's features relaxed into a smile. "No, not eat it, but...after all, why not? A few grams more or less; the miss can easily spare me that...I want to see what happens when this meteoric dust is exposed to X-rays."

And without further ado, the radiologist proceeded to set up his experiment. He poured the pinch of black dust into a tiny porcelain cup, put it on a stand and placed it under the X-ray tube, which was as large as a football and set on an articulated pedestal. He turned a commutator; a solenoid hummed; sparks crackled; the tube lit up...

I looked on, mechanically attentive, as if watching a conjuring trick.

"Well?" I said. "Is that all?"

"That's all for the moment, I suppose. These few decigrams of meteoric dust are bathed in a torrent of X-rays, where I'll leave them all night. It's more than probable that nothing will happen, but there's one chance in ten thousand that something will. What? You're asking too much. If I knew, it wouldn't be interesting. The whole pleasure of experimentation is the revelation of something new...something unexpected. We'll see tomorrow."

I took my leave, with no suspicion of the enormous, immeasurable importance that the results of the little experiment, apparently so anodyne and insignificant, that I had seen begun before my eyes was to have. And Dr. Tancrède Alburtin had no more suspicion than I did that, in exposing those few black granules to his X-Ray tube, he was assuming a responsibility of capital importance with respect to France and the world, and triggering the explosion of a worldwide calamity—a calamity initiated by the actions of Miss Lescure, her father and, in general, everyone who had collaborated, intimately or at a distance, with the launching of Rocket MG-17 and the importation to Earth of the meteoric powder.

After leaving Alburtin's house I took the back roads in order to go directly to the harbor and the Hôtel Cendrillon, where I was staying. I thus avoided passing in front of the terrace of La Réserve, where, in view of the mildness of the evening, I would have run the risk of encountering the Ricourts with their usual gang of "Montparnos." Luce and Géo would not have failed to ask me why they hadn't seen me at dinner, and I had no desire to furnish Luce with explanations in front of those people. Besides, didn't I have to prove that I was a free man? A beach flirt ought not to become so tyrannical as to oblige one to account for one's every action!

A flirt! Luce de Ricourt! And I laughed sarcastically. Oh, Mademoiselle Lucy, you think you hold in servitude, thanks to your beauty of a red-haired Danae, the generous young painter that you bully and exploit, the Tonton around whom you run rings…but you'll see tomorrow whether he still takes any notice of you!

All Luce's teasing, the hardness of her heart, and the incompatibilities that separated us, come back to me at once during the solitary walk that I take to the end of the pier, under the stars—and I detest her, I reject her empery; for me, there is only woman in the world from now on: Aurore Lescure, the girl fallen from the sky; Aurore, the dawn of a new life…

III. A Walk to the Coves

At 7 a.m., I rang the doorbell at the clinic. In response to my inquiry, a nurse gave me a report on Miss Lescure's condition: she had spent an excellent night; no temperature; she would doubtless get up today, but she was still asleep...

"Would you like to see the doctor?" the nurse added.

"No need—don't disturb him. I'll come back later."

My expedition to Belle-Fille pass with a truck and three men was completed without any inconvenience. No one had gone into the pine-wood since the previous evening, and Rocket MG-17 was resting quietly on its bed of rock and brushwood. Transporting it to the road was relatively easy because, in spite of its dimensions—3.5 meters long by 1.2 meters in diameter, its bullet-like shape permitted it to be rolled like a barrel over the flatter sections. What gave us the most trouble was the immense parachute, spread over a dozen different trees; it was necessary to cut some of the suspension cables and abandon them, entwined in the branches.

My summary explanation—a new model of aircraft that had suffered an accident—was accepted without difficulty and satisfied the truck-driver and his assistants. More important to them were the generous gratuities I distributed to them, in addition to the agreed price, when everything had been put into a shed in the doctor's courtyard. For a tip like that, they would have picked up and transported an inhabitant of the Moon without asking too many questions.

When the truckers had gone, Albutin—who had supervised the garaging—said to me in a strange manner: "By the way, Delvart, there's news."

My heart skipped a beat. "She's taken a turn for the worse...Miss Lescure?"

"No, no! She's doing very well. She's having breakfast. I wanted to confine her to the chaise-longue for at least half a day, but no chance! She wants to get up. No, it's not her—I'm talking about my little experiment."

"The meteorites?"

"The meteorites. They've…grown. Like mushrooms. That black powder evidently includes unknown seeds, which have germinated under the influence of the X-rays. Plants, I suppose, not catalogued, of extraterrestrial origin. Botanists will erect a statue to Miss Lescure..."

We went up to the laboratory. Under the active X-ray tube the porcelain vessel that had contained a pick of meteoric dust the day before had now almost disappeared under a reddish spongy mass comparable to a polypary,[9] overflowing on to the tabletop. And the mass was active, as if seething. In places, blisters were forming, with an imperceptible effort, swelling like bubbles. Before our eyes, the two largest ones burst, with a tiny explosion, like those mushrooms known as puffballs, and a find cloud of brick-colored dust was already staining a part of the table.

"Curious, eh?" said the doctor. "And what about this?"

He pointed to the conductive wires leading to the tube. One their white silk sheath there were red patches, plaques of mould, as large and thick as lentils.

"It resembles a lichen. I'd give a great deal to have a better grasp of botany."

Even for a layman like me, the spectacle of that strange manifestation of life had an appeal to curiosity—but I was thinking primarily of the glory that the young astronaut would derive from it.

Someone knocked on the door.

"Come in!" Alburtin shouted.

His wife appeared in the doorway, pushing Aurore Lescure by the shoulder, with an affectionate gesture.

---

[9] *Polypier* [polypary] is a term, now rarely used, designating the matrix in which the polyps of corals and similar organisms are embedded.

"Tancrède, I've brought someone who's come back to life, and absolutely insisted on getting up. Good day, Monsieur Delvart—excuse me, my nurses are asking for me. Until later."

She closed the door behind her.

Bare-headed, crowned by her mahogany hair like a Botticelli page, this was another variant from the two exemplars of Aurore Lescure with which I was familiar: the pilot in the leather flying-suit with a fastened helmet circling her face, seen on the screen, and the castaway from space that I had carried here yesterday in my arms. Was this the true one, in her little cachou dress, whose long legs, clad in Havana silk, and invisibly muscular, gave an impression of discreet and supple energy?

She came toward us, holding out her slender hands, and shook ours without any conventional verbal formulae, simply pronouncing our names, but with a smile more expressive than speech. Her frank and honest gaze bathed me in a luminous vivacity. I immediately felt an intimate connection with her, like that of an old friend. And in spite of her false girlish ease she was delightfully womanly. While leaving Alburtin to joke about her rebellion against Medical Authority, I studied her as if I were seeing her gilded face, her willful chin, her slightly pronounced jaw and her broad prominent forehead for the first time. The whites of her eyes had the milky purity of the sclerotics of children, and the dazzling whiteness of her teeth formed the other pole of her adorable smile.

A decisive test. Was she what her face advertised, or was it lying, like Luce's?

"I don't have a hat! My hat-box is still in the rocket."

No—with that voice, she had to be genuinely sincere, deep down.

Seeing that she was looking at the famous green box, placed on a stool, Alburtin stopped in the middle of a sentence and blushed. Then he pulled himself together and declared, forthrightly: "I have a confession to make, Miss. The demon of scientific curiosity has driven me to commit a frightful larceny. Without asking your permission, I took a sample of your meteorites—a few decigrams—for experimental purposes."

All that was shining in the milky sclerotics was the disinterested curiosity of a scientist. "My intention was to offer you that sample. What was the result of your experiment?"

Visibly relieved, Alburtin extended his index-finger toward the spongy mass effervescing beneath the X-ray tube, and then the reddish patches on the conductive wires. "Look—this...and this."

With both hands flat on the edge of the table, absorbed in serious concentration, she leaned toward the strange vegetation for a long time. Then she straightened up.

"Here are facts that will revolutionize biology, and perhaps cosmogony. It's even more beautiful than I dared to hope. Doctor, I'm glad that you had the inspiration of experimenting on the meteorites. I intended to offer them to the University of Montreal, but who knows whether the discovery would have been made without you? I rejoice twice over that the honor will come to you, firstly because you have saved me, and secondly because it will return, via you, to my country of origin. I'm French at heart, like my late mother."

Alburtin was about to reply, but she went on, with a sudden hint of bitterness: "Perhaps you're astonished that I can dispose of this gift as I wish, but it's purely scientific and incapable of making money; it's no betrayal of the organizers of my flight. It was me, and me alone, who conceived the idea of a device designed to collect these meteorites, and who had it built and installed aboard the MC-17. My father is only interested in the Rocket as the solution to a technological problem, and his silent partner, Lendor J. Cheyne, the director of the Moon Gold Company, demands that discoveries *pay*. The solution of problems of the highest order counts for nothing in his eyes, unless they have practical results. He only wants one thing: to recover, with a fat profit, the capital invested in the astronautical rocket business. Matters of no interest to me...but to him! It's understandable, however, in a financial backer who's a businessman. Do you know how much it cost, my little four-hour excursion into space, including all the expenses of two years' research and preliminary experiments? $800,000: 20 million francs. I know that only too well! My ears have been bombarded by it." I saw her sketch a disgusted frown. "$230,000 just to pay manufacturers of laboratory equipment, and to allow me to carry the 500 kilos of liquid atomic hydrogen serving to propel the apparatus. Half as much to make an engine-tube capable of supporting the explosion of a gas raised to a temperature of 5000 degrees and ejected at a velocity of 6000 meters a second."

"I had no suspicion of these pecuniary considerations when I read about your trials in the newspapers, Miss," the doctor replied.

She gave a slight shrug of annoyance and interjected, with a smile that tempered the reprimand: "No, not 'Miss,' I beg you. Excuse me, but I've endured enough 'Misses'—let's leave that to the Yanks. In Canada we say 'Mademoiselle,' as in France."

"Mademoiselle," Alburtin repeated, bowing. "As I was saying, we were unaware of the enormity of those preliminary expenses. To consent to such sacrifices it must have been necessary from the very first day for Monsieur Cheyne—the Moon Gold Company, that is—to be certain of your eventual success. The exploitation of lunar gold will be a splendid speculation, when you have established communication with our satellite. Was that, as the newspapers said, the purpose of yesterday's flight?"

She stiffened, once again bitter and impenetrable.

"To reach the Moon is, indeed, the ultimate goal for which my father and the decors of the Moon Gold Company are aiming—a purely scientific goal for my father, a speculative goal for the Company—but..." Deliberately, she changed the subject. "By the way, Doctor, has my cablegram been sent?"

"As soon as the Post Office opened, Mademoiselle, at 7 a.m."

"I'll have a reply today, then—and if it's the one I expect, you'll be rid of me and my cumbersome apparatus tomorrow. Doctor, you're undoubtedly busy—but if you're free this afternoon, Monsieur Delvart, would you give me the pleasure of showing me around? I feel the need to breathe a little pure air—terrestrial air—after yesterday's excursion."

I accepted with a joy whose manifestations I had difficulty restricting to the simple limits demanded by politeness. It was agreed that I would come to pick her up at 2 p.m., after lunch. For the moment, though, as she was talking about going to fetch her hat-box from the Rocket, she consented, at Alburtin's request, to show us the apparatus.

Given my technical incompetence, I have no desire to risk getting lost in the details she gave us. They are, in any case, well known, thanks to numerous popularizing articles. The only advantage I have over their readers is that of having seen at close range, and touched with my fingers, that redoubtable thin "magnalium" hull, the tanks of liquefied hydrogen and oxygen, the levers and regulators controlling the take-off, acceleration and direction of the Rocket...

What excited me most was finding myself alone with the voyager for a few minutes in the cabin—which was too small to accommodate three, requiring the doctor to remain outside with his head protruding through the manhole—and to hear her evoke the fantastic hours she had spent thousands of kilometers from her native planet and human beings, in the custody of a rudimentary and unsafe apparatus, with half a ton of explosives beneath her feet, at the mercy of the slightest malfunction.

She had not had any instruments designed to measure the altitude or the distance covered; the barometer no longer functioned outside the atmosphere. There was only a "gravimeter" indicating the diminution of weight and, in consequence, the distance from the Earth, to the nearest 100 or 200 kilometers—which resulted, during the descent, in a terrible danger of smashing into the ground by virtue of deploying the parachute too late, or of being roasted by atmospheric friction by virtue of deploying it too soon after the last braking thrust of the engine...

And breathing artificial and confined air for hours on end, reeking of the caustic soda intended to "regenerate" it, the cracking of whose reservoir on impact had caused the onset of asphyxia...

And having to ensure the exactitude of every maneuver, while simultaneously gripped by migraine, limbs weakened and body drained by the atrocious malaise procured by the increase in weight during the accelerated thrust, and then its total abolition while, with the engine stopped, the apparatus ran on momentum, to collect the meteorites...a malaise that produced the dire threat of an imminent loss of consciousness, to which one did not have the right to yield, under pain of death...

As we emerged from the apparatus the young heroine saw me so emotional that she burst into valiant laughter, saying: "Bah, Monsieur Delvart, it wasn't so terrible, since I'm here, alive and ready to do it again. Besides, I'm here because of a false move; I overestimated the probable westward drift, and steered too far eastwards on the return journey. If not, I'd have landed, was planned, in the American continent. But one does better the second time around, having got used to it. Interplanetary navigation isn't very convenient, by dead reckoning, on one's own."

I uttered an exclamation of protest. "But why on your own? Why not have a companion...male or female?"

"A question of weight. It would be more convenient and safer with two, but an extra 60 or 70 kilos is too heavy. We are, after all, at the birth of astronautics, at approximately the same point as the first aerial navigators, Montgolfier or Charles and Robert. Then again, my father has so much confidence in my composure...and his discoveries."

She drew away, hat-box in hand, her mood darkened again by that allusion to her father. I was beginning to scent a mystery.

Alburtin had noticed something too. As we parted company on the doorstep, he whispered: "She hasn't been there, you know?"

"Where?"

"The Moon. That's obvious. She almost let on. That's why she dreads being interviewed. It would wound her self-esteem to admit her failure. And yet, she'll have to do it in the end. Bizarre…unless it's a matter of a stock-market coup. Perhaps she's awaiting her father's instructions."

"That would surprise me, of her," I said, simply. "Well, I'll see you later."

And with that, I went back to my hotel.

In the dining room, the boarders were already at table. I had the satisfaction of not seeing the Ricourts, all three of whom had gone out for the day in the car. I had to shake a few hands in passing, though, before arriving at my place, and I overheard an insufficiently discreet reflection behind me with regard to the "injured aviatrix."

While eating lunch, I thought that Monsieur Botin and the truckers must have been talking, and doubtless Madame Alburtin too; public curiosity had been awakened. A couple of Parisian journalists, I knew, were on holiday in Cassis. Might I have to defend "Mademoiselle Aurette Constantin" against an attempt to interview her that afternoon?

But why was Aurore so reluctant with regard to reporters? Merely out of vanity, the dread of admitting that she had not reached the Moon? That was insufficient to explain the kind of irritation and repulsion that she betrayed every time there was any mention of the director of the Moon Gold Company, Lendor Cheyne, or even her father...

I invented 20 hypotheses to account for the mystery…in she evidently could not fail to play the role of damsel in distress. And I dreamed of becoming her champion, in the manner of Don Quixote, of fighting for her, of extracting her from God only knew what web of intrigue in which she was struggling impotently, in which all her science and courage could do nothing without my help!

Those three hours spent with her that afternoon were an exquisite and seductive adventure.

She walked by my side along the Porte-Miou road with an agile and alert stride, dressed as she had been that morning but coiffed with a tightly-fastened bonnet that circled her head in the same way as a flying helmet and made her once again the Envoy, the Angel of *The Wonderful Visit*. I had assumed that it would be necessary for me to get closer to her gradually, limiting myself at first to the role of a cicerone showing off the beauties of the landscape, in order to bring our different personalities into unison, but the approximate strategy that I had prepared proved to be unnecessary.

After five minutes, before we had even got past the beach at Bestouan, where a few fanatical bathers were sunning themselves on the shingle at that unreasonable hour, the knowledgeable American scientist found herself in complete sympathy with the French painter. No educational barrier separated us any longer; we were equals, united by the delight of schoolchildren on vacation, and we were chatting freely, like old comrades.

What she told me, reported in writing, would appear insignificant and puerile, but by virtue of the delightful perfume of confidence and the candid smile of her mouth and eyes, everything she said—even anecdotes about her dogs and cats—acquired a unique sentimental value for me. I listened, with the joy of penetrating her intimate life, and she abandoned herself to her memories, associating me with them as a benevolent and wonderstruck auditor. I talked too, I believe, but mostly, I listened, untiringly to the stories that initiated me into her past, bringing me closer to her, in a quasi-fraternal fashion. With a few swords, I stimulated her to continue, uniquely avid to listen to her voice, which stirred infinite resonance within me.

I almost forgot my role as a cicerone; she forgot to "study" the landscape—but she perceived it, taking it in without paying any heed to it. With a gesture, I showed her a little inlet with white rocks, and a pine-tree leaning into the azure; or perhaps it was her, with some other gesture—and that sufficed for us to imbibe the beauty.

It was then that I committed the gaffe. I thought us so much in unison that I thought she was bathing in the same waves as me. We had been walking for an hour; we were sitting on the isthmus separating the cove of Port-Miou from that of Pont-Pin. The bulk of Cap Canaille was displaying its wild and grandiose silhouette in front of us, devoured by light, above the indigo bay, and the middle-ground there was a dazzling limestone headland. My companion was admiring it wholeheartedly with her eyes. The splendor of the decor completed, it seemed to me, the abolition of the conventional distance between us, obliging me to speak.

"Do you know, Mademoiselle, that I have known you for months?—which is a long time, in our accelerated epoch."

"Months!" And as if she read it in my gaze, she went on, with a smile in which I thought I could discern a hint of irony and weariness: "Oh yes, at the cinema. I'm a character in the world news. Who doesn't know me, on the screen? That kind of celebrity has already brought me the declarations, oral or written, of countless admirers. If I were a 'vamp,' as they say in the United States...a *femme fatale*...I'd have plenty with which to amuse myself. But I don't even want anyone to pay court to me; on the contrary, that suffices to drive me away. Do you know that in two years, I've received 1237 proposals of marriage?"

The warning was obvious, but I was stung to the quick. Was she about to confuse me with that flock of ridiculous aspirants?"

"What does that matter?" I replied. "Idleness and snobbery have nothing to do with my case. The first time I saw your image, I recognized you, as if we had already met in another, anterior existence. And today I've found you..."

She interrupted me, in a calm and indulgent one: "Monsieur Delvart, you're forgetting that I haven't seen you on the screen, so I've only known you since yesterday...or, more precisely, for an hour. I like you—quite a lot, in fact—and I'm genuinely glad the chance has brought us together. We are, I think, able to listen to one another and become good friends. I sense that you're sincere, that you mean what you say—and that's why I want to avoid a misunderstanding that might spoil everything between us."

"If I were to talk to you about love?"

"You'd be the 1238th, quite simply."

"And I'd meet the same fate as my 1237 rejected predecessors?"

"Yes. I'm already engaged." Seeing me crestfallen and discomfited, however, she added: "Engaged by the wishes of my father and the proprieties of business, to the director of the Moon Gold Company, Lendor J. Cheyne." And again I saw the painful contention appear on her face that every allusion to the astronautical company and its director provoked—but I took care not to commit a further stupidity by offering to put my Quixotic knight-errantly valor at her disposal.

I feared that I had broken the charm. For a few minutes she had ceased to be the insouciant child evoking her memories and offering them to me as playthings; she became Aurore Lescure, the first female astronaut, again, at odds with an agreeable companion that it was necessary to keep at a distance. Soon, though, deliberately at first, in order to demonstrate that she was not holding my premature declaration against me, then gradually relaxing, she became confidential again, and yielded to me once again a childish soul, the sister of my dreams.

The rebuff that I had just received, however, remained within me like a nucleus of irritation. I was overwhelmed and mollified by those delectable confidences, but even so, I couldn't help noticing that she hadn't told me anything about her father, or her fiancé, or the reasons that made her fearful of journalists...

She had given me retrospective confidences, treated me as a good comrade, yes, but not as a friend, not as a true friend.[10] Although everything about her pleased me, enchanted me, so that I clung to her with all my antennae, I did not feel the expected, hoped-for, necessary reciprocity. I was scandalized by that difference of plane between our sentiments—and yet, as she said, she had not seen me in the cinema. My amorous "crystallization" was too far ahead of hers. For her, I was not, and could not yet be, any more than a good comrade.

We had just arrived in the harbor when, in a group of idlers who were watching sardines being landed, I recognized—too late—the hideous white American sailor's cap that Géo was sporting and Luce's jade sweater. They had seen us—but so much the worse for the amenities, which I would clear up later. That hussy Luce was capable of anything, and I certainly wasn't about to introduce her to my companion. Instead of continuing along the quay, we ducked into a little side-street that led to the church. Already, Luce was peering at us with her hand shielding her eyes; I saw her say something to her brother, but the latter restrained her by the arm and addressed a conspiratorial wink to me. I repaid him with an ironic nod of the head toward my red-haired Danae, who turned away ostentatiously.

The interplay had, thank God, escaped Aurore.

At the clinic, the cablegram had arrived. As soon as we were in the vestibule, the chambermaid gave the form to "Mademoiselle Constantin," who opened it, read it and, remaining pensive and perplexed, re-read it twice more.

Finally, she said to me: "My father says that he's embarking with my fiancé on the *Berengaria*. I have to meet them in Paris on the 21st." An anxiety striped her features, an effort to understand the inexplicable.

Only one thing mattered to me, though. Affecting a placid smile, I asked: "You're not leaving immediately?"

---

[10] The French language grades degrees of intimacy in friendship in a more careful fashion than English, so I have been forced to make frequent use of a distinction between "friend" and "comrade" that sounds slightly odd in English.

I could have kissed her hand for her reply. "There's no urgency, since it's only the 16th. I have another five days. I like Cassis, and I've a right to a short holiday. But as I'm no longer an invalid, I'll leave the Doctor's house tomorrow and get a room in a hotel…yours, since you say it's a good one."

But Albertin arrived, and took us into the drawing-room. He asked about our walk, and started on hearing my answer.

"The coves! You took her to the coves, Delvart? Mercy! That's too far. I only let me patient out on the strength of her formal promise not to tire herself out."

"I'm not tired at all, Doctor."

"You might not feel it, Mademoiselle, but while you're at the clinic I'm responsible for your health. Madame Narinska will have orders to put you to bed this evening at nine on the dot." He had affected a severe tone, but then became amicable again. "Believe me, my child, don't stay up too late; you'll be more alert for it tomorrow."

I was about to take my leave, regretful about not having been invited to dinner, as I had hoped, but Alburtin gave me one of his jovial and exasperating slaps on the back.

"One moment, Delvart—come up to the laboratory…and you too, Mademoiselle. It's still growing, my little indoor horticulture."

It was, indeed, growing! As soon as we reached the door of the laboratory a slight odor of putrefying roses gripped my nostrils. Invading the table, the spongy mass born of the meteoric dust, beneath the still-active X-ray tube, was now a large, vaguely pyramidal mass the color of coffee-grounds, agitated by a seething effervescence. The swelling of blisters and the tiny explosions of fine dust were succeeding one another from second to second, in a continual crepitation. One might have though it a continuous volcanic eruption. The impalpable dust covered everything in the room with a brick-colored veil. As for the red stains on the wires of the tube, they were now tumors as large as walnuts.

So far as I was concerned, the spectacle had something disturbing and repulsive about it, but the two scientists were merely interested, and they exchanged such remarks as "Splendid!" and "Prodigious!"

"Who can tell whether what we're experiencing here is a unique phase in the evolution of the extraterrestrial seeds?" said Aurore, pensively. "Perhaps we're losing observations of inestimable value. It needs a specialist in plant biology."

"My old friend Nathan, a professor at the Sorbonne?" murmured Alburtin. He pointed at the green box and continued: "Given that the supply of meteorites isn't exhausted, we could send him a few grams tomorrow?"

As we left the laboratory, Aurore and Alburtin, who had handled the vegetation, were obliged to go into the bathroom. Being covered in dust, I too was obliged to accept a vigorous brushing by the chambermaid before leaving the clinic.

At the Hôtel Cendrillon, I confronted the mocking welcome of the Ricourts, when I asked, in the most natural tone: "How was your excursion to Saint-Maximin? Did it go well?"

"Not bad," Géo sniggered. "What happened to you, yesterday? We didn't see you in the evening."

"We were worried," said the old lady. "We thought you and Dr. Alburtin had broken down in the hills."

Luce looked me up and down with a sardonic expression. "So, Tonton, you're giving up painting for medicine...and trucking. But I don't like the way you ran away like that just now. I'd have loved you to introduce me to your pretty aviatrix."

How I detested Luce! How vulgar I found her, with her contraband Americanism, her noisy and gilded laughter! What scorn I had for her now, and what difficulty I would have had, that evening, tolerating her gibes without throwing my opinion in her face, stripped bare of all pretence. The thought of Aurore sustained me, however, and it was with brazen effrontery that I invented the necessary lies to respond to questions about "Mademoiselle Constantin," her nationality, where she had come from, and so on.

I nearly blushed, though, when Luce said: "It's curious, Tonton—she resembles that American woman we were talking about yesterday at Tauroëntum…you know, Miss…oh, yes, Miss Lescure!"

I stared at her, but she had made the reflection without attaching any importance to it, and did not insist when her brother replied, in a spirit of contradiction: "Where do you find that resemblance, Lucy? You're dreaming. Mademoiselle Constantin is visible stronger, shorter and French. Nor from the Midi, eh, Gaston?"

"No, from the North."

I was relieved when they finally went to join their friends a La Réserve.

Discontented with my evening, myself and everything, anxious for Aurore's tranquility, I spent a hour sorting out my Cassis canvases—and being harassed by itching.

"Fleas now!" I cursed. "That's the final straw! For a fortnight there hasn't been one in the hotel…and *she*'s coming to stay here tomorrow!"

IV. The America Agency's Rumor

Woken up with a start by an imperious knocking on the door of my room, I opened one eye and read on my watch, by the light of dawn: 6:15. Peevishly, I groaned: "What is it?"

The voice of the floor attendant replied: "Monsieur, it's that Monsieur le Docteur Alburtin has just phoned asking us to wake you up and tell you that Mademoiselle Constantin is leaving immediately."

"Thank you. Tell him I'm on my way."

Jerked into action as if by a cold shower, I leapt out of bed and began to get dressed, quickly but methodically, mastering the anxiety that was making my fingers tremble over the buttonholes. What was happening? What did this unexpected early-morning departure signify?

In six minutes, my chronometer on my wrist, I was ready. An inspiration: three more minutes spent stuffing a valise—and with that in hand, I ran to the doctor's house at a gymnastic pace. I would ask him to settle my bill. My canvases? Oh, they could be sent on to me. At 6:32 a.m., I was at the clinic.

I had no need to ring. The chambermaid was on the doorstep, on the lookout for my arrival. She took me through the house and into the rear courtyard, where Alburtin, in shirt-sleeves, was just closing the hood of his car, which was out of the garage, in a quasi-professional manner.

"Ah, Delvart!" he said, wiping his hands with a fistful of oakum. I knew you'd come. Read this!"

Out of his jacket pocket he took a *Petit Marseillais*, with the ink still fresh, and held it out.

As my name was pronounced, however, I saw Aurore Lescure emerge from the shed where the metallic mass of the MG-17 was gleaming vaguely. Her hands were full of packages wrapped up tightly in old newspaper; she went to deposit them in the car, while addressing a knowing smile to me, which briefly brightened her unusually grave and resolution-hardened features. Returning to the shed without pausing, she called:

"Read it, Monsieur Delvart—I'll be back."

On the first page, under the headline *AN AMERICAN HOAX? THE INTERPLANETARY ROCKET HAS REACHED THE MOON* a snapshot leapt to my eyes: the well-known photograph of "Miss Aurore Lescure" smiling at the lens in front of her apparatus.

At top speed, I read: *Stupefying news—which, however, will not seem implausible to people who have followed with some attention the progress of astronautical science in the last two years, has been transmitted to us by the America Agency. The interplanetary rocket MG-17, of which we announced the probable departure with the intention of reaching the moon, should have completed the prodigious flight. For the first time, an apparatus, piloted by a young woman only 25 years of age, the gracious and bold Miss Aurore Lescure, the daughter of the inventor Oswald Lescure, "the new Edison," has extracted itself from the Earth's atmosphere and gravitational field and, under the acceleration imparted to it by its atomic hydrogen engine, has reached the surface of our satellite in two hours ten minutes. There, still according to the America Agency's dispatch, the space pioneer, after having collected a few mineralogical specimens, including nuggets of gold, has planted in the soil of the night-star the American flag, the "stars and stripes." Then, re-embarking in her apparatus, she has made the return voyage in a lapse of time approximately equal to the outward one. Departed from Columbus, Missouri at 6 a.m., local time—noon Greenwich Mean Time—she made contact again with the Earth after only five hours of absence, at 5 p.m. "in France, in a location not far from Marseilles," which the telegram does not identify precisely, where she is being cared for in a clinic, after the shock caused by an abrupt landing.*

Assuming that the news is true, it seems astonishing, at first sight, that we have not had notification sooner of this sensational landing, but it is only fair to observe that, if the

injured astronaut has suffered a prolonged loss of conscious-
ness, her apparatus, in the absence of her explanations, might
have been mistaken for some kind of aircraft by inexpert indi-
viduals who made the discovery. At any rate, our reporters are
making inquiries at this moment, and they will soon discover
the truth.

I raised my eyes again. Aurore Lescure was standing in front of me.

"You see," she pronounced, vibrant with concentrated anger. "I can't stay here any longer. I'd be prey to journalists. I have to put them off my track."

I didn't understand. "But Mademoiselle, if it's just a rumor, why not put a stop to it right away? Establish the facts in a statement to the press, and you can rest easy thereafter."

"That's what I said to Mademoiselle," Alburtin interjected, while checking the inflation of the tires.

"It seems perfectly simple to me," I insisted.

The young woman uttered a brief laugh. "It seems that you're mistaken, my dear Monsieur. In reality, there's only one thing I can do: disappear. I didn't want to leave Cassis without saying goodbye to you, but I have to go. The doctor is being kind enough to take me to the station for the 8:15 train. I'll be in Marseilles by 9, and will take the 2 p.m. express, which will get me to Paris at 5 a.m."

While she was speaking a bell—the bell at the front door—had been rung vigorously on the far side of the house. I was about to reply to her when the door to the corridor opened and the frightened chambermaid said: "Monsieur le Docteur, it's the gentlemen from the *Petit Marseillais*. They've come by car and one of them has begun taking photographs. They insist on seeing Monsieur le Docteur and Mademoiselle, and I had to let them in. What should I say to them?"

"Zut! Zut! Zut!" groaned Alburtin. "What an idiot you are, Jeanne. I gave you orders not to let them in on any account. Well, tell them I'll be there in five minutes…that I have to carry out an operation…a childbirth…ah! Give them a glass of mulled wine. That'll help them to be patient."

The chambermaid disappeared.

"And now," Alburtin went on, "*go!* We don't have a second to lose. In five minutes they'll get impatient; in ten they'll come to see what's become of me without authority—and the interval might bring more reporters, from the *Petit Provençal*, the *Marseille-Matin* and I don't know what else. They find out about the back door; we'll be surrounded..."

And he went to open the coaching entrance that opened on to the Marseilles Road.

Aurore Lescure, standing at the car door with one foot on the running-board, offered me her hand. Without taking it, however, I raised mine in a gesture of negation to refuse the farewell she was about to pronounce.

"Mademoiselle," I said, resolutely, "permit me to accompany you. There's nothing to keep me in Cassis. I'm returning to Paris—I have my valise, as you see. We can travel together, if you don't mind."

As soon as I had spoken the first words, her smile had accepted. I put my valise in the car, on the left front seat, while she said, simply: "I don't mind, Monsieur Delvart—on the contrary."

She got in and I followed. Having opened both battens of the coaching entrance, Alburtin took his place at the steering-wheel and pressed the starter. Three turns of the wheel and the car was outside, climbing the hill in second gear—but we hadn't rounded the calvary before several passers-by—including two gendarmes—had greeted us with a "Bonjour, Doctor!"

"We've been spotted!" grumbled Alburtin, putting the car into third gear. "That was inevitable."

"Evidently, Mademoiselle can't leave from Cassis station," I declared. "The train won't pass through for half an hour. We'd have ten journalists on our back before then. If you have another hour to give us, Doctor, you need to take us to Marseilles."

"All right!" said Alburtin, laconically, without turning round.

It is three kilometers from the town to Cassis station. Half way, therefore, instead of continuing straight ahead, we turned left on to the highway that rises up in a series of sharp bends to the Gineste Pass, through a wild and grandiose land-scape: ravines with steep cliffs, bare limestone slopes cutting through the cruel azure. Idly, I thought that the landscapes of the Moon must look like that—but I refrained from imparting my reflection to my neighbor, who remained silent, absorbed in the vague contemplation of the road unrolling its tarry rib-bon beneath our wheels.

Several times since leaving Cassis, Alburtin had taken one hand off the steering-wheel to scratch the back of his neck, which caused the vehicle to serve. After one swerve more exaggerated than the rest, as we reached the Gineste Pass, he stopped the car.

"Many apologies, Mademoiselle! It's stupid, but I'm be-ing devoured by fleas. If I don't have two minutes' respite, I won't be able to drive properly during the descent." He scratched himself shamelessly, with a jovial rage. "I dread, Mademoiselle, that you might have them too? My wife com-plained of them; there must be an infestation at the clinic."

"In Cassis, rather," I interjected. "I also had them at the Hôtel Cendrillon."

The passenger's face cleared momentarily. "That's reas-suring, Doctor. When I started itching yesterday evening, I thought I was afflicted by a skin disease, and this morning, but for my precipitate departure, I'd have asked for a consulta-tion."

Cheered up by this comical episode, while we were stopped she consented to gaze at Marseilles harbor, which was visible in the distance, vaporous in the glory of the early morning light and the giant breath of the city and its docks. When we set off again, emerging from the deserted slopes, the arrival of a more rapid automobile appeared behind us, whose driver amused himself by overtaking us, returned our compa-nion to her preoccupation. She had evidently feared that it might be journalists launched in our pursuit.

The suburbs: red petrol stations; clusters of chalets buried in the pines; a tramline advertising the city limits; interminable pavements; a street bordered by oil-refineries and soap-works, plowed by thunderous lorries…and we emerged into the middle of Marseilles, in the Place Castellane, where cheerful and luminous life stages a tourney of exuberant activity around the fountain.

"Where shall I set you down?" Alburtin asked, over his shoulder, as he turned into the Rue de Rome. "It's 8:30 a.m. There's no train to Paris before 2 p.m.—but first, Mademoiselle has to deposit her parcels…after packing them up a little better."

"For that I'll have to buy a suitcase." She pointed to the packets wrapped up in old newspapers and bound with string at my feet, whose continual slippage had inconvenienced me in the course of the journey. "These are the most precious parts of my apparatus," he explained. "Doctor, I won't abuse your kindness any longer. You have to get back to Cassis. Drop me outside a shop that sells travel goods, and we'll bid you farewell."

This was done—but not content with going into one of the department stores on the Cannebière and helping in the acquisition of a small trunk in which the packages were stowed, the doctor then wanted to take us to the station in his car, to deposit our luggage, and then return us to the city and install us in the Café Riche. Finally, having drunk a toast to wish us god luck, he consented to leave.

"And have no fear for your apparatus, Mademoiselle. I'll have it packed up properly, with the parachute and send the boxes to Paris as soon as possible from the P.L.M.[11] station. I'll notify you at the Hôtel…Métropole, isn't it?"

"The Hôtel Métropole, Rue de Villiers. And don't forget to enclose a bill for your expenses. Thank you again; you've

---

[11] *Paris, Lyon, Marseille*—a fast rail link then independent of the principal network,

been extremely kind; I'll never forget the god luck that put you and Monsieur Delvart in my path."

After a final handshake, the doctor rejoined his vehicle, moved off, and was lost in the host of vehicles.

His departure left us disorientated. Now, sitting at the table in the café, in the indifferent crowd, we were truly alone. Alone…and separate.

Where, I thought, *is the insouciant intimacy of yesterday's walk to the coves? Bah! An illusory intimacy. In evoking her memories in my presence, she was treating me as a good comrade, that's all. But now, if we talk, it can only be about the secrets that she's allowed to remain between us. And I won't commit a further gaffe by stepping out of my role; I'll be the good comrade, who respects the secrets, with whom one isn't hesitant to yield to one's preoccupations.*

Aurore smoked her cigarette silently, her expression anxious, her nostrils quivering imperceptibly in nervous spasms, while I ruminated my bitterness. I respect her silence, judging myself an idiot for not being more sociable, for not knowing how to distract her with pleasant trivia. That was evidently all she could be expecting of me, since she was keeping quiet about her secrets. Not even capable of that! What a miserable companion I was, to be sure. Wasn't she regretting letting me come with her?

It did not tale long, however, for a incident to provoke the denouement of the crisis, however, by bringing matters to a head.

We had been silent for ten minutes, consuming cigarettes. Suddenly, she leaned toward me.

"Don't look now, but those two men chatting at the fourth table on my right—from the way they're looking at me, they must be journalists!"

I waited 30 seconds, and then paraded a nonchalant glance around me, without seeming to pause on anyone in particular.

Indeed, two seemingly well-to-do young men, making an awkward effort of dissimulation that only made it more manifest, were studying my companion. One of them, *Petit Marseillais* in hand, was showing the other the photograph of "Miss Aurore Lescure with her apparatus." Visibly, both were comparing the features in the picture with those of the young woman sitting beside me—and the nodding of their heads, sly glances and whispering behind their hands testified that they had perceived the astonishing resemblance

I tried to calm her down.

"Yes, they're evidently talking about you, Mademoiselle, but they're not journalists—and even if they were, even if they had the audacity to approach you, don't worry: I'm here. I'll tell them that one does not impose interviews on people who don't want give them."

"It's obvious that you don't know American journalists, Monsieur Delvart! How many times I've been obliged to furnish them with information when I had no desire to do so! I've been obsessively harassed for hours on end; one of them, in order to extort a story from me, accompanied me in an airplane from Columbus to Chicago; another dressed up as a waiter in a restaurant…and I'm convinced that reporters are just the same in France, and that they'll be even more tenacious than their colleagues in the States, now that I'm famous and have important reasons for avoiding them. Oh, look—the tall one's going into the café. That's to phone a newspaper to say that he's seen Aurore Lecscure and ask them to send a photographer. Let's go, I beg you."

Her agitation troubled me; her fear was contagious.

After all, who can tell? Perhaps she's right. I can't risk poisoning our journey with fear of reporters by keeping her there.

I call the waiter and pay him, and we leave, while the man left alone at the fourth table starts to rise to his feet and then sits down again with a gesture of annoyance.

After 100 meters of rapid walking, we turn into the Rue Saint-Ferréol and slow down.

Aurore takes me by the arm momentarily and squeezes it, in a spontaneous gesture of gratitude. "Oh, thank you, Delvart—you're very kind."

That amicable familiarity, falling on my irritation at seeing her keep secrets from me—me, who would cut off my hand for her—plays the role of detonator. So much the worse if it's a gaffe, and to hell with the "Mademoiselle"—sulky, rebellious, and desperately affectionate, I burst out: "But after all, Aurore, why are you so afraid of journalists? Forgive my brutal frankness, but it isn't possible...I have too high an opinion of you to admit that it's a question of pride...the paltry fear of having to admit that your flight wasn't entirely successful—that you didn't get as far as the Moon, as the article in the *Marseillais* claims."

"The good opinion you have of me is correct—you're not mistaken. It's by no means a matter of pride."

Overwhelmed by the flood of passers-by, we have stopped in front of a shoe-store. Aurore is no longer smiling. She looks me full in the face with her large limpid eyes, as if to read my mind. In a slightly interrogative tone, she goes on: "Delvart, you're on my side, truly? I can trust you?"

"Remember the confession I made to you yesterday, which you mocked...Mademoiselle. That's my response."

"I won't keep any more secrets from you. You ask me why I'm afraid of journalists? I'll ask you a different question: weren't you astonished to read that false information so rapidly? Or, to put it better, the intentionally-misleading fraudulent claim that I had reached the Moon?"

"I thought it was a matter of a journalist making up sensational copy...or rather, the America Agency taking advantage of the announcement of your departure from Columbus to launch the rumor. There's still time to rectify..."

"That explanation's theoretically plausible—but how could someone making things up know that I had landed near Marseilles?"

"Your cablegram..."

"It was explicitly sent from Cassis. Why keep quiet about a precise detail that would have increased its probability? No. Did you notice the detail of the gold nuggets that I'm supposed to have collected from the lunar surface? And the allusion to Moon Gold's hopes? Listen—that rumor was launched by the Company itself...by Lendor J. Cheyne, my fiancé, who had it put out by the agency in order to electrify public opinion and the shareholders. The name of Cassis isn't mentioned because Cheyne doesn't want me to be interviewed too soon...because he wants to make sure of my complicity first, with regard to journalists. That complicity was formally demanded of me, in the cable I received yesterday, to which I haven't yet replied. It was demanded of me *again*; I've always refused it until now."

"Perhaps Monsieur Cheyne believes that you did, in fact, reach the Moon?"

"He knows perfectly well, as does my father, that it would be impossible with the apparatus and fuel reserves at my disposal. He's so well aware of it that he took care to supply me, against my will, with gold nuggets, in the hope that I'd end up capitulating and making myself an accomplice to his fraud—that I'd prove flexible, at least out of filial love. My poor father, so good, so full of genius, but so fallible!"

She uttered a sob of distress; I saw that she was ready to melt into tears, right there, in the midst of the passers-by. Already, one old lady had stopped in front of the shop-window to look at us.

Gently, I placed my hand on my companion's arm, to calm her down. "Poor girl! Your pain tears me up. Pull yourself together; let's take a few steps without saying anything—come a little further on, away from the crowd, into the harbor."

I drew her away, supporting her with my arm, for she was trembling. On the Quai des Belges, I installed her on the terrace of an almost-deserted café and obliged her to drink a few drops of Madeira. Only then did I continue.

"So your father has agreed to support Monsieur Cheyne's...premature claims."

"Wait—let me tell you about him first. My father is an exceptional scientist—the new Edison, as he's recognized today, since Lendor has 'rationalized' the exploitation of his genius. But my father, a true inventor, would never have been able to profit from his discoveries on his own. He's never bothered abut that—on the contrary, his researches have swallowed up all his capital, and that which I inherited from my mother. He ended up bankrupt, two years ago, loaded with debts, worse than ruined. Them, in order to be able to continue his work, which were his very life—and, as he saw it, to remake the fortune of which he'd deprived me—renouncing his independence as a researcher, he accepted the propositions of a big businessman in the United States, Lendor J. Cheyne, who appointed himself as his 'manager.'

"You understand better now what kind of man my father is. He's purely an inventor. He sees scarcely any difference between today's reality and tomorrow's, as soon as both of them can be expressed in corrected drafts—and he'd already established those of the MG-22 rocket, which will, indeed, be capable of reaching the Moon, when we possess an explosive more powerful than atomic hydrogen—a discovery in which my father believes. Only numbers count, for him; the rest—what the vulgar call 'facts'—is unimportant. My father, I can confess to you, has no moral sensibility. Oh, don't misunderstand me, he's a kind of lay saint; his private life is perfectly innocent, but the social domain escapes him entirely; there, he loses any notion of good and evil, justice and injustice. That's why he only sees Lendor Cheyne's fraud as a legitimate anticipation...an extrapolation, as one says in the sciences...since the final result is assured and imminent.

"Lendor J. Cheyne, too, is convinced that my father's genius will overcome the final obstacles that still separate us from the conclusive success—that two or three years hence, four at the most, someone, either me or someone else, will land on the lunar surface and bring back specimens of the gold whose indisputable presence has been revealed by the spectroscope. It's only a question of money, he says—and the facts thus far have proved him right. It's by virtue of the dollars lavished on costly experiments and trials that we've already realized yesterday's flight of 1/20th of the trajectory—18,000 kilometers out of 380,000. Supported by sufficient financial resources, science and determination can do anything. But the public faith that furnishes those resources needs more vulgar bait than rational certainty. To obtain the indispensable credit from the public, one needs to nourish its faith with illusions and anticipations. One has the right to deceive it, in its own interests—that's Lendor J. Cheyne's thesis: the justification he offered for his plan, when he made me party to it.

"I ought to add one more thing, which is that my father, in spite of his fallacious title of Technical Director of the Moon Gold Company, is, by virtue of the contract that he imprudently signed with his manager, absolutely at Lendor's mercy. Lendor wouldn't hesitate to sack him coldly, like a simple foreman, while keeping his plans and taking possession of his inventions, if he doesn't find the two of us to be docile collaborators, following his orders…or if I refuse to make him, by becoming his wife, the legal co-owner of all the patents he's already using in the name of the Moon Gold Company. To be dismissed like that, at my father's age, would kill him.

"Such is my situation. Lendor J. Cheyne wants to impose on my father and me the obligation of supporting the fable that the Moon has been reached at the first attempt. My father has agreed to that. I haven't. I believe in the supreme authority of the truth…or rather, so far as I'm concerned, it's an atavistic question of moral propriety. Logically, I admit that Lendor's opinion might be tenable, and I don't condemn it, from a business viewpoint. I'm convinced that success is inevitable and imminent, that we're on the eve of making the journey. My first great flight has only reinforced that conviction—but I'd deem myself to be soiled, personally dishonored and unworthy to pilot the Rocket if I cheated, and didn't declare the actual results obtained, and nothing more...

"And yet, I love the task I've taken on—one day to be the first representative of humankind to take possession of the lunar soil; I'd be heartbroken to be replaced in that enterprise. And then again, I love my father, and wouldn't want to cause him the slightest difficulty. Now, if I talk, if I allow myself to be interviewed. I'll infallibly tell the truth, give the lie to the newspapers' fiction. The Moon Gold Company will collapse in a gale of laughter and universal scandal. To avenge himself, Lendor will, as he's threatened, sack my father, which will be the end of him...

"You see now, my dear Delvart, why I fled Cassis, and why I begged you to get us away from the Café Riche as soon as possible..."

She breathed deeply, ravaged by anxiety, but now mistress of herself. Her cheeks, beneath their pale flesh tone, had taken on a vivid redness; her eyes lost in the spectacle of the Old Port and the swing bridge, which she did not see, she considered the cruel and atrocious case of conscience momentarily. Then she looked at me, holding back her distress, as if she were glad to have confessed the truth to me, and not hoping for any help from me other than the comfort of my impotent sympathy.

I did not dare lavish banal words of encouragement upon her. In a concentrated ne, into which I attempted to inject the fervor and sincerity of my sentiments, I said: "Aurore...permit me to call you that...I can't see any remedy for the situation you've just explained to me...not yet. But if we think about it, and if we can talk about it again later, perhaps we'll find a means of getting out of it. You can count on my absolute devotion."

She listened to me gravely and stoically. "Thank you. I accept your help. But what can you and I, or anyone, do? My situation is inextricable."

In the silence that followed between the two of us, amid the racket of the traffic—the bells of the trams and the horns of the automobiles—shouts reached us: "Get the Paris newspapers, arrived his morning by airplane…*Matin, Journal*..."

The vendor advanced, his sheaf of papers under his arm. I bought two of them.

MOON REACHED…even larger letters than in the *Marseillais*; the same photograph, but more distinct, of "Miss Lescure with her apparatus," the same text, slightly expanded; a new paragraph, announcing that "the inventor of the Rocket, Oswald Lescure, and Lendor J. Cheyne, have embarked for Europe with a view to organizing astronautical exhibitions and creating a subsidiary of the Moon Gold Mining Co. Ltd."

Aurore folded up the papers, mechanically taking care to hide her portrait. She sighed. "Oh, he's clever, my fiancé. He intends to confront me with a *fait accompli*, by means of the immediate diffusion of the false news. He's counting on muzzling me until his arrival, and finding me in a few days' time resigned to support his abuse of trust. What can I do?"

"You can, at any rate, keep quiet, if you can avoid the journalists."

"And talk, if they succeed in catching up with me?"

I reflected momentarily, then said: "So talk. You do have a subject on which you can allow yourself to be interviewed, truthfully: the collection of meteorites, and the experiment carried out on them by Dr. Alburtin…while awaiting those of Professor Nathan. That's a scientific discovery of the greatest importance. You said so yourself."

I was aware of the insufficiency of the solution I was proposing, and to prevent my companion from objecting, I played for time. "By the way, what have you done with the green box? You haven't left it behind in Cassis?"

"It's in the trunk, in the left luggage office—but I also have a phial in my handbag, here, containing specimens of the vegetation generated in the doctor's laboratory."

That diversion deflected us from the hotter topic. It continued to preoccupy us, but by tacit agreement we dropped the question for the moment.

During lunch at the Restaurant Pascal—oysters, a sumptuous bouillabaisse, washed down with white Cassis wine and an old Chateauneuf-du-Pape—one point of protocol was firmly established. Once again, I had just addressed her simply as "Aurore," when I saw her frown. I was troubled.

"Excuse me—I thought you had given me permission..."

"Yes, yes...but it's because people might hear. Aurore...no. Say Aurette instead. That's what my comrades at university called me."

I breathed again. But the "comrades" depleted my pleasure slightly: that familiar appellation was not granting me any special privileges. Slyly, I offered myself a small compensation. "All right: Aurette, not Aurore. But at the École des Beaux-Arts, they called me Gaston, not Delvart."

"Gaston? Yes that's better. I didn't think of that."

Well, that's progress. If she still considers me a mere comrade, at least she's leaving me the illusion of a closer intimacy.

As for the demands she made to pay half the bill, and a little later, at the station, to reimburse me for her ticket—if he had had to pay for those two first-class tickets, the aspirant Don Quixote's wallet would have been within a few francs of running dry.

The journey from Marseilles to Paris was completed without incident—but what an awful train that 2 p.m. express is! No sleeping-cars, nor a restaurant car. We had to get pre-packed meals, which were execrable, at the Lyons-Perrache buffet. And the fleas! Our compartment must have been infested by them. The previous day's itching at the Hôtel Cendrillon took hold of me again, more violently, and Aurore was scratching too. The third passenger, a taciturn Englishman, similarly seemed prey to fleas, and he darted indignant glances at us, as if we were responsible.

And we were!

I was later to discover the origin of that epidemic of pruritus. Aurore had opened the wide-necked phial in order that we might examine the red "mold" from Alburtin's house in the palm of her hand, and the impalpable dust it expelled. That dust was made up of microscopic spores, and those spores, as the population of Paris was soon to learn from experience, constituted a redoubtable "itching powder."

Furthermore, thanks to the obstinacy of the Englishman in reading his magazines, the electric lights in the compartment had burned all night long, to add to our inconvenience—and by the time we arrived, their bulbs were covered with a sort of coral-colored lattice-work.

V. At Professor Nathan's Residence

Paris at 5 a.m., beneath pale electric lights, in darkness and—on exiting the station—rain...

"Porter!" The luggage in a taxi...

"The Hôtel Métropole!"

A somnolent clerk gave my companion a form, which she filled in, and "Mlle. Aurette Constantin of Montreal (Canada)" was allotted room 127.

"Sleep well, my dear Aurette. We'll meet at half-past eleven, at the Terminus Saint-Lazare Café!"

At the door of the elevator, she turned round once more to send me an amicable smile, and I went back to the taxi.

"Rue Cortot. Yes, behind Sacré-Coeur, off Rue Caulaincourt."

The cupolas of the Basilica had scarcely begun to stand out in the first light of dawn when I rang the bell, and the door only opened on my third attempt. It was necessary for me to negotiate with the somnolent concierge, who was not expecting my return for another fortnight, and did not want to admit that it was really me.

A sentiment of abandonment and discouragement oppressed me on finding myself back in my studio. I switched on all the lights, but the untidiness of the room, carelessly left as it was, with its scattered canvases, ended up inspiring me with disgust. Suddenly, I perceived the folly of my return. Another one of those "whims" for which my late father had so often reproached me! "Hothead!" he said, rightly. "Artistic temperament," as my mother had proffered, with more indulgence. I had never been any different, that was for sure!

After becoming infatuated with an Americanized Danae who twisted me round her little finger, to be romantically smitten with a world celebrity against her wishes, who considers me as a good comrade, and appreciates my devotion, but that's all...and who is already engaged, besides—resolved to

65

make a marriage of convenience…of cold, scientific, American convenience!

If it's true that a grand passion is one that is unrequited, here I am, on my way to being the most striking living illustration of that axiom!

In addition to all that, my canvases are still in Cassis. In what condition will they reach me, if they're packed by laymen? And I need them; I have to make some money, and it's my "coves" that sell best.

While ruminating these reflections and scratching my residual itches I went to bed and ended up going to sleep without putting out the beside lamp.

When I woke up, from a heavy sleep, more tiring than a late night, at 10 a.m., the first thing that struck my consciousness was an odor of rotting roses. I was astonished to see the bulb of the lamp clad in a thick coral-colored lattice-work, the festoons of which hung down like stalactites, like an ornament from some baroque fantasy. It took me a few seconds to comprehend that this was a new growth of the impalpable powder brought from Cassis on my clothing and my person. The flexible wire was also laden with a mushroom-growth of lenticular patches and red nodes, like those in Alburtin's house but larger, which had grown more rapidly, on which tiny blisters were already swelling, bursting one after another and each projecting a cloud of fine red dust. There was some of it on my bedclothes and on my face. My neck and shoulders were itching again, violently—and it was then that I began to establish a link between the so-called infestations of fleas and the dust of the "celestial fungus," as I then dubbed it.

That ridiculous incident, the dirt that squashed under a finger like brick-colored sweat, ended up putting me in a bad mood. Having switched off the lamp, I undertook a summary cleaning of the bulb and the wire, but I soon abandoned the task, leaving its completion to the concierge, who fulfilled the functions of a housekeeper for me.

Not being a scientist, the possibilities implicit in that invasion did not occur to me as yet. I saw it merely as a disagreeable episode; I did not even think of the possibility that it would recur as soon as I switched on the electricity again.

A bath and fresh clothes put an end to the itching, but not the bad mood. I was prickly and miserable. The rendezvous with Aurore only inspired a suspicion that I was being taken for a ride…and she would be fashionably late, the Angel!

The North-South from Lamarck to Saint-Lazare; the station clock showing 11:25…

I went into the Terminus, went on to the right-hand platform—the Le Havre side—then went back to the other…

"Gaston!"

Aurore, half standing behind her table, her hand extended! I was about to go past without recognizing her!

The mere sound of her voice, raising up a tidal wave of tenderness and marvelous hopes, restored my good humor. While sliding between the marble tabletops to sit down beside her on the bench, I considered her with my painter's eye, and I understood.

"Ah! You've bought a new hat, Aurette. Congratulations. The change is so extraordinary…"

"That you didn't recognize me. I've succeeded, then. My Havana straw bonnet, which compressed me face, bore too close a resemblance to the flying-helmet I'm wearing in my photographs—whereas with this lacy capeline with a flared brim, people can see my hair. I've fluffed it up too."

"You can rest easy. No journalist will identify you."

"The precaution's all the more useful because the newspapers have advertised my departure from Cassis. It won't take long for them to start looking for me in Paris." Observing my astonished expression, she added: "You haven't read it? Look, here's the *Matin*. In the latest news."

The items was headlined: *FROM AMERICA TO CASSIS, VIA THE MOON.*

Marseilles, October 18. It is in Cassis, a charming little port 20 kilometers from Marseilles, well-known to painters and visitors to the Côte d'Azur, that Miss Aurore Lescure, the first female astronaut, whose prodigious flight we reported yesterday, remade contact with the terrestrial globe on return-ing from her expedition to "blonde Phoebe." Picked up un-conscious in the territory of the commune by the radiothera-peutic physician Tancrède Alburtin, who was passing by in his automobile, she was transported to the doctor's clinic. The latter "judged it his duty, in view of the young astronaut's condition" to forbid any interview with her. This is the reason for the silence maintained by the dispatches published in yes-terday's editions regarding Miss Lescure's exact landing-place. It must be assumed that it was for the same reason, in order to take a few days' well-deserved rest, that she left Cas-sis this morning for an undisclosed retreat. This voluntary reclusion will be of short duration, however, and we shall soon have the privilege of offering a detailed account of her adventure in these pages, which she is in the process of writ-ing for us.

I folded up the paper, my only comment being a slight shrug of the shoulders.

"I telephoned Professor Nathan," she added. "He was in-formed of our arrival by Dr. Alburtin, and he'll see us shortly, at 2 p.m. I've brought the box and the phial."

"Ah! In that regard, I'll have news for him." And I told her about the incident of my lamp and the flex invaded by the "celestial fungus."

The North-South [12] to Rennes...the Rue de Vaugirard, facing the autumnal Jardins du Luxembourg...

Professor Albert Nathan received us in his severe study, whose walls were entirely lined with books. When we came in he nodded his head, without getting up from his armchair, and offered us two chairs with a gesture.

"Mademoiselle Aurette Constanin; Monsieur Gaston Delvart...my former pupil and friend Tancrède Alburtin tells me that you have an interesting communication to make to me. I can give you five minutes. Be brief."

---

[12] The old metro line A which became line 12 in 1930.

He was a tall, thin old man of indeterminate age, between 65 and 80, with leathery features and a forehead extended by baldness between two tufts of silvery white hair. He
fixed the Olympian gaze of his dark blue eyes upon us, as if he
doubted that people so young could have anything to teach a
scientist of his species.

I humbly admit, despite the good opinion that I had of
myself as an artist, that I felt very small in front of this superior representative of humanity, a biologist doubled with a
philosopher of universal repute. I let my companion speak.

Holding her head high and her gaze steady, modest but
confident, she said: "Monsieur le Professeur, before anything
else, I'm obliged to ask for your word as a scientist and a gentleman that you will not mention to anyone whatsoever the
object of my visit or my current address. It's imperative that
no one knows that I'm in Paris until circumstances permit me
to authorize it. Aurette Constantin is only a pseudonym."

Albert Nathan's white and bushy eyebrows frowned. "I
don't like secrecy, Mademoiselle. Out of consideration for
Tancrède Alburtin, I'll make you the promise you ask, but if
your communication were to have scientific results, I must
have authorization to publish them...if they're worth the
trouble."

"Provided that no one knows that I'm in Paris, I see no
objection to your publishing the results. As to whether they're
worth the trouble, you shall be the judge."

Bending down slightly, she picked up the green box from
the carpet, where she had deposited it on sitting down, rose to
her feet, and went to open it before the scientist's eyes.

"This is meteoric dust that I collected outside the terrestrial atmosphere, at altitudes between 1000 and 4000 kilometers. I'm Aurore Lescure."

The grand old man sketched a pale smile, which accen-
tuated the irony of his gaze.

"Mademoiselle Lescure, I believe that you are a doctor
of physical and mathematical sciences, and that Cartesian methods of rational research are familiar to you. A scientist must

always doubt *a priori*. What is the proof that this dust—which might, parenthetically, have been more appropriately submitted to my colleague Quentin-Dufour, the mineralogist—is meteoritic in origin?"

"When you have experimented with it, Monsieur le Professeur, you will observe that, at the very least, this dust behaves in a fashion very different from any terrestrial substance."

Briefly, she described the generation and the appearance of the spongy magma the color of coffee-grounds obtained under the X-ray tube, and then brought the wide-necked phial out of her handbag.

"This other red dust has been projected by the blisters that form spontaneously on the magma, and it's this, it seems, that propagates the red vegetation of which these are specimens."

"Vegetation that is generated in particular on illuminated electrical lamps and long conductive wires," I added, emboldened. "And it grows very rapidly...more rapidly at present, it appears, than at the beginning in Cassis."

I told him what had happened that very morning in my room.

Was the scientist listening to me? I don't know. While I was speaking, he leaned over the table and, with the aid of nickel-plated tweezers, took from the green box and the phial, successively, a few meteoric grains, a little impalpable red powder and a sample of coral fungus, which he deposited one by one on a piece of paper. Then, equipped with a powerful magnifying-glass, he pored over the specimens.

When I fell silent, he looked up. The skeptical smile had vanished from his face, and without even looking at me, he addressed himself to Aurore, in a deliberately cold and impassive tone in which contained emotion was detectable.

"Mademoiselle, these are indeed spores and tissue with no relationship to terrestrial plants. If the facts that you have reported are accurate—and I shall verify them soon enough— we have in these organisms the first evidence of a new creation in the process of developing on Earth and hastening to take possession of its new domain. In that event, Mademoiselle, science will owe you the solution to one of its most intriguing enigmas: the origin of life. Your meteorites are specimens of the mysterious cosmozoans,[13] or seeds of extraterrestrial life, that were purely hypothetical until now...

"I have every reason to believe that your discovery is bound to have considerable resonance, not merely within the scientific world, for the experiment will not be limited to Dr. Alburtin's laboratory and mine. It will develop outside, thanks to the extreme smallness of these reproductive spores, which renders them as mobile and diffusible as flower-pollen. You are carrying it on your persons, and have left it in the atmosphere throughout your journey. No matter how few of these seed-germs settle on electric wires through which current is passing, the insemination of Paris is assured. That will be very interesting to observe."

He fell silent, and ostentatiously consulted his watch, which he had placed on the table in front of him.

"It's agreed, then: I shall undertake a study of his knew living realm. Do you need this box and phial, Mademoiselle?"

"No, Monsieur le Professeur; they're yours. I only collected these meteorites in order to donate them to science."

"Thank you. Would you care to give me your telephone number, so that I can inform you when I have something new? Hôtel Métropole, Room 127...perfect. Now, excuse me, I have work to do. Mademoiselle, Monsieur..."

---

[13] The original version of the term translated as *cosmozoaires* in French and cosmozoans in English appears to have been coined by Hermann Richter in 1865, in an obscure essay subsequently credited by Svante Arrhenius as the origin of the theory of "panspermia," which he popularized: the notion that life is communicated to planets by spores drifting in space. Although Varlet never uses the latter term in the text, he includes a history of the notion in a later chapter.

He did not get up from his armchair, any more than he had when we arrived; nor did he offer us his hand.

We withdrew. I was furious. To think that this was a scientist of the Institut, a man of the last century, in which it is claimed that courtesy and politeness were cultivated. Not once had he addressed himself to me, and he had not invited me to return. Oh, to be sure, I had no desire to return! Evidently he considered me, in my capacity as an artist, to be a good-for-nothing. Only Aurore, the donor of his cosmozoans, had some right to his interest."

"What a boor! He wasn't even polite to you, Aurette!"

"Yes, Gaston, he was polite. If you knew what American scientists are like, you might even think that he was very polite. The essential thing, in any case, is that he has consented to study the meteorites. I feel somewhat liberated of a responsibility."

"Do you think his prognostication has any chance of being realized? The insemination of Paris, as he put it? He's exaggerating, isn't he?"

"He sees a theoretical possibility, at the very least. He's extrapolating from the laboratory to real life."

We were I agreement in concluding that the professor's observation was merely a mental vision, incapable of assuming any real importance in the domain of everyday facts. The agile and confident vertigo of Paris, the turbulent movement of the Metropolis, took hold of us as soon as we had regained the great arteries.

The spectacle of the marvelous organism that is a capital city functioning with such a complex harmony, inspires such confidence in the solidity of civilization! How could one suppose that its order might be put in peril by that pinch of dust brought back from space by my companion?

Aurore wanted to regulate our relationship immediately, in such a way as to "respect my liberty." I had made the mistake of talking to her about my art-dealers, and she wanted me to visit them that afternoon.

"What about you, Aurette? You don't know anyone in Paris. What would you do? No, I shall devote this first day to you. This is my holiday, just as it's yours."

All that I consented to do was to go into a café to write a letter to the proprietor of the Hôtel Cendrillon: I asked him to send me the bill that had been settled by Alburtin, and to send me my paintings, well wrapped-up, and the other effects I had left in Cassis.

For my part, I obtained permission from her to let me paint her portrait—but the day was too far advanced, and artificial light is worthless. She promised to do a sitting for me the following day.

After that, a stroll through Paris—still good comrades, although she yielded more of her memories to me and I recovered, momentarily, the illusion of a current of mutual sympathy.

That evening, we went to the Paramount. A surprise was reserved for us there… a documentary film with sound, transmitted by telephotography: the departure of the Rocket from Columbus three days earlier. Aurore was amused to hear and see herself pronouncing her final words and entering the apparatus—and then the surge of the shell into the Heavens, thunderously, and the cheers of the American crowd…but she was glad of the obscurity of the auditorium, which protected her from any danger of any direct confrontation by her neighbors of her living image.

VI. The Lichen Gains Ground

I got home after midnight but didn't go to bed imme-diately, thinking I was reading the memoirs of Benvenuto Cel-lini, but actually dreaming about Aurore. The concierge had shaken my bed-sheets and cleaned the lamp and its wires, but it was evident that the spores had, to use Professor Nathan's term, inseminated my apartment. I had been reading for half an hour, and was getting drowsy, with the illusion that rain was beginning to patter on the window-panes, when I noticed that the lamplight was getting weaker and redder...and there was an odor of rotting roses...and the itching!

A new network of coral lace encrusted the bulb and the wires of the flex. The little crepitation that I had mistaken for rain was nothing less than the minuscule and reiterated explo-sions of the spore-producing pustules projecting their ochreous pollen on to the night-stand, the sheets and me.

The joke was turning sour. For the first time I thought: *Science is all very well, but it would have been better to leave that box of meteorites in the woods at Belle-Fille!* Without the censorship of my subconscious, as Freud puts it, my exclama-tion might have been translated as: *Why did you take it into your head, Aurore, to collect those satanic cosmozoans?*

Reluctant to clean the bulb, disgusted by the idea of get-ting my hands dirty, I switched off the light.

My first thought on waking up is for Aurore, but it's no longer a question of addressing reproaches to her. Another two days! Yes, in two days, her father and fiancé will disembark in Paris, and then it will be over. Goodbye daily meetings with her; goodbye illusion of amorous companionship and tempting myself with the hope that eventually, by virtue of sensing my adoration nearby, she might end up seeing me as something more than a good comrade. From the way she talks about her father and her fiancé, especially her father, I understand that as soon as they're here, I'll cease to matter; she'll work with her father, not leaving him an more. Will she even make an effort to escape that monopoly and devote one hour a day to me… for which I won't ask? For I can't think of introducing myself into their company. By what right? With what excuse? I'm nothing with regard to science or business—and as for the services I've rendered Aurore, what gratitude will these people think they owe me? That I picked her up? But that honor belongs to Alburtin. That I escorted her from Cassis to Paris? That I'm keeping her company? She could easily have done without me; her fiancé might even look upon it with a jaundiced eye, if I were tempted to make use of it. I'm painting her portrait? Well, they'll pay me, and it will earn me a distracted "Thanks" with, at most, an invitation to diner...

Another two days. While going to pick up the *Excelsior* and the *Matin* that the concierge, resuming her regular routine, has deposited on my doorstep with a carton of milk, I glimpse an insidious desire in the hidden depths of my conscience: that the *Berengaria*, having suffered damage—an encounter with an iceberg—will be delayed for a day or two. But there aren't any icebergs in the North Atlantic in October.

Who was it said: "I don't know what the soul of a criminal is like, but that of an honest man is appalling!"[14]

A shiver runs along my hands and arms to my back and clutches at my heart...

AN INTERVIEW WITH MISS AURORE LESCURE, THE WOMAN WHO HAS BEEN TO THE MOON...

Poor girl! She's been discovered! The reporters have got to her. They've extracted lies from her…but when? Last night? I only left her at the door of the Métropole at 11:45 p.m.!

---

[14] The quotation that Gaston has in mind is from *Le Bourgeois* (1906) by Abel Hermant, although Hermant used *conscience* [conscience] rather than *âme* [soul] and *canaille* [rogue] rather than *criminel* [criminal].

As I read, however, the aguish ebbs away; I realize that the interview is no more authentic than the preceding article. It's Cheyne's plan, which is continuing and developing. Not a word of this has been pronounced by my Aurore of yesterday. First of all, this photograph of her in the bonnet she's no longer wearing. And where did the interview take place? Cassis? Marseilles? Paris? The reporter doesn't say. He keeps quiet "at Miss Lescure's request"—that "Miss" again, which she began by correcting to "Mademoiselle"—to avoid fatiguing her with too many visits from his colleagues, because "she is still very shaken by the shock of her abrupt landing." Oh, if the reporter had seen her trotting around Marseilles and Paris with me! Here's a photograph of the species of diving-suit that she had to put on in order to leave the Rocket and walk around on the Moon. Here are the gold nuggets collected during her "lunar landing." He thinks himself witty, the reporter who finds the phrase grotesque.[15] Three lines on the "meteorite trawl," but nothing about the harvest she reaped in actuality...the only one! Ah! And to finish, the businessman, who is showing his true colors, at arm's length:

The Moon Gold Mining Co, Ltd., founded by Lendor J. Cheyne with a capital of $30 million, is about to issue news of a prodigious means of impulsion. In spite of the doubling of the advertized capital, the shares, issued at $20 and previously quoted on the New York Stock Exchange at $40, went up to $60 yesterday. Monsieur Cheyne, who is presently sailing for France aboard the Berengaria *with Monsieur Oswald Lecure, the inventor of the Rocket and father of Miss Aurore, will disembark at Cherbourg tomorrow afternoon. He intends to organize an exhibition of the MG-17 at the Champ-de-Mars, and a new departure for the Moon as soon as the young astronaut is fully recovered. In the meantime, he informs us by radiotelephone, he is busy setting up a European subsidiary of the*

---

[15] It is more grotesque in French, by virtue of the substitution of *atterrissage* [landing, or, more literally, coming to earth] by the humorously improvised "*allunissage.*"

Moon Gold Company, based in Paris, in order to allow French investors to share in the evident dividends that the shareholders on the company will soon be receiving.

Good! The lamp in my studio, by means of which I'm reading, is beginning to darken and redden. It's quite dark—a day of Parisian "fog," and I had to switch on the light as soon as I awoke…fleeing the bedroom, where the bulb at my bed-head is still encrusted with the lichens born yesterday evening, shriveled now, which the concierge will clean up...

Here in the studio, the new lichens, of a more vivid vermilion and a further increased energy of development, are already sheathing the wires and forming a felt-like network on my lamp. There first reproductive vesicles are popping and projecting their impalpable powder…and the odor is nauseating! And I'm itching again!

There's no reason for it to stop. The only means would be for me to go without light—but I'll need it this afternoon, with that cataclysmic sky, to begin Aurora's portrait. Will I have to fish out my old oil lamp?

Oh, too bad! Too bad about that, too bad about everything! Another two days! In the meantime—in the marvelous meantime, without any hope of intimacy with Aurore...

But I don't have to meet her until 11:30, just like yesterday, at the same place. And it's only 8 a.m. What shall I do until then? Stay here in the studio? And watch the lichen grow on the lamp? Oh no—I'd go mad! Or try to work by the oil-lamp? No, I can't; I'm too impatient, too agitated. I need to go out, to walk in the streets.

Instead of going to visit my dealers, however, as I ought to do, I decide to go and see my uncle Frémiet, the photographer. I'll arrange with him to take a dozen pictures of Autrore. With those, even if she only sits for me once or twice, today and tomorrow, I'll be able to continue—I daren't say "finish"—her portrait from memory. Without being as gifted as Alma-Tadema, who painted from memory faces and locations that he'd seen several years before, I have a good visual memory, above average...

My uncle lives a long way away, at the far end of the Boulevard Saint-Michel, which means I have to spend an hour doing nothing but traveling, on the Metro and by bus...

Why did she choose the Terminus Saint-Lazare as a meeting-place again? Because she wants to visit the Galeries Lafayette again with a view to restocking her wardrobe? She doesn't neglect feminine coquetry, but makes fun of famous couturiers; the presentation of mannequins and the fittings dear to snobbery irritate her. She's rather choose a ready-made costume, and she has such a harmonious figure, such an innate elegance, that any "confection" whatsoever, which would make any other woman look a fright, suits her marvelously. Without wasting any time, or spending a great many dollars, she buys her own clothes...

I was a quarter of an hour early, and, while seeking to clear my conscience with respect to her in the café, I perceived at first glance that things weren't quite right with the electric lighting, which was all on, in view of the fog. Near the door, there was a waiter on a stepladder, in the process of furiously dusting a dirty bulb, stained with a layer of red dross. The lichen! And I could smell the characteristic odor in the air. At the back of the room to the right, two electricians were similarly perched next to an active chandelier deprived of one of its bulbs, scraping a vermilion felt off the wires with harsh straps, which was almost immediately renewed beneath their fingers. The bulbs and fittings with which they were not yet busy were in various stages of invasion. The reddish light of the worst-affected was scarcely piercing the vegetal crust.

Some of the customers—who were numerous, given that it was the hour for aperitifs and the weather was bad—were watching the operation with intrigued and disapproving eyes. Others were pretending to ignore the ill-timed cleaning work. An old military gentleman wearing medals was quarreling with a waiter and pointing above his head at lamps velveted with crimson mold, the impalpable powder from which was floating in his "mandarin."

This disturbance didn't end there though. The majority of people in the café, clients and staff alike, were scratching themselves, with varying degrees of discretion according to their temperament and level of education. They were scratching themselves while casting suspicious, anxious or menacing glances at their neighbors.

"It's disgusting!" protested one plump bearded citizen, furiously. "Manager—send for the insecticidal powder!"

A revolution was rumbling, which the managers, frightened by always dignified, were attempting to appease, helping the waiters to wipe the tales, change the bulbs and, despairing of the cause, protect the drinks with the aid of saucers inverted over the glasses.

Aurore came toward me, darting consternated glances over the agitation, and allowed herself to be conducted to a banquette.

"Here too!" she said. "Do you know, my dear Gaston, that it's the same in the Galeries Lafayette, from which I've just come? The store is full of ladders, electricians and firemen. In spite of that, one can hardly see any longer, and clouds of red dust are falling from the light-bulbs. Everyone's scratching, and the salesgirls are packing up the clothes on many of the floors. It's terrible, this invasion! It's starting at my hotel. I was able to avoid switching on the light in my room, but the lichen has manifested itself in the neighboring ones. A manager stopped me in the hallway to ask me whether I'd been inconvenienced by the "mosquitoes." Bellboys going past in the corridors were carrying fly-sprays!

"But that's not all—something more serious is happening at my hotel. Someone must suspect my identity; my effects have been searched, and the trunk."

"Which contains the pieces removed from your rocket?"

"Yes: the outlet of the ejection-pipe, the liquid hydrogen compressor and the gravimeter. For a scientist, those accessories speak volumes. There's also the trademark, *Moon Gold Patented*, on the gravimeter. It seems to me to be the prelude to an interview...not like the one in this morning's newspaper—a real one."

"Come on, Aurette, don't be so quick to get anxious..."

"Oh, I've made my decision—don't try to reassure me; it's futile. I know what I'm going to do. I'll tell the story of my voyage, but without mentioning the Moon, since that's already been done. The journalist can conclude what he likes from that. It's cowardice on my part, I know, but I'm afraid for my father. I'm too scared. Cheyne is capable of anything. I received a wireless telegram from him this morning in which he says: *Resistance futile. Be careful*. And in fact, he's found the means to break me, with that fake interview. Thanks to that, the decision has been taken away from me; I've been put out of the game. Worse still, since I've read it, it seems to me that I no longer count, that my destiny is playing out independently. The real Aurore Lescure has her own life, in the newspapers and the conversations of all the human beings on the planet; it's her that's interviewed and photographed. I almost envy her; she, at least, hasn't brought meteorites back to Earth—but she's stolen my personality. I'm no more than a myth, a vain shape sitting at this café table...a lie preparing to tell lies. I despise myself."

Her tone was distressing. Although she was trying to laugh, I sensed that she was embittered, almost demoralized.

"If you tell lies, my dear, it's out of devotion, to save your father. For me, you're the most noble of women...and the only reality that matters."

She straightened up slightly, but looked around, without appearing to have heard me.

"It's me, however, who is the origin of this calamitous disturbance—and what proves that I'm a myth is that I can't quite believe, as yet, that I'm really responsible."

The café was emptying. In spite of all the efforts of the electricians and the staff, the invasion of lichen was gaining speed, and half the light-bulbs, encased in red, were only giving out an infernal glow Weary of scratching and drinking

80

crushed-brick powder, the furious customers were decamping one after another.

Fleeing the catastrophic spectacle in our turn, I dragged my companion away.

Taxi...Poccardi's, in the Rue Favart.

Limpid and bright on immaculate tablecloths, the gilded light of lamps is already making us feel better. A bottle of Chianti and one of Capri white, finocchi, sole Milanaise, *lasagna au parmesan*, gorgonzola, *cassata siciliana*: with that menu, optimism is reborn. Everything will work out; the incidents caused by the cosmozoans will be inconsequential; Nathan or someone else will rapidly discover a means of preventing the growth of the lichen outside laboratories, where it will merely be a subject of scientific study...

And, drinking coffee amid cigarette smoke, we end up cheering ourselves up with the illusion that all those worthy people at the Terminus had, of being subject to an invasion of fleas. A trifle drunk, Aurore almost resigns herself to letting people believe that she has been on the Moon. Will she not indeed be there a few months hence—a year at the most? Even the arrival of her father and her fiancé the day after tomorrow is not such a bad omen as I imagined; it won't interrupt our friendship. Aurore will introduce me to them, and when all three of them return to America, why shouldn't I accompany them? I'll have great success over there, like so many French painters, and I'll earn a lot of dollars, which is not to be disdained...

Even the Heavens did their bit, clearing for an hour; the natural light in my studio was sufficient, and I had no need to light up for the sitting. In three hours of good work, I made a detailed sketch for Aurore's portrait. Then we went to see my uncle Frémiet to have the photographs taken.

That wasn't all—my morning visit had already produced its effect, and I observed it with a certain guilt and a fit of irritation: I was a germ-carrier! The poor fellow certainly had no suspicion of it while he carefully wiped the spotlights that modern photographers habitually use to illuminate the subject with a damp cloth. He turned the commutators while looking at his apparatus with visible apprehension.

"Damn it!" he murmured, after a minute, tugging at his long beard. "It's starting again! It's crazy! Since noon, there's been no means of keeping a bulb clean for five minutes once it's lit. Fungus is forming on them, as you can see. I've never heard mention of anything like it! And the dust! The diabolical dust that spoils the plate—I hardly dare open a shutter."

Aurore shot me an interrogative glance. Should she tell my uncle what was happening? I shook my head violently behind his back, shrugging my shoulders and raising my eyebrows to express impotence. What good would it do to tell the truth, since we had no remedy to offer?

"Let's move quickly," the photographer requested.

And, modifying the subject's pose between each shot according to my instructions, he took a dozen pictures: full face, profile, three-quarters, from various more-or-less elevated angles, as is usual in such cases.

By the tenth shot, the spotlight bulbs, invaded by the fateful coral lace, were only yielding two thirds of their luminosity.

My uncle clicked the switches angrily. "If this goes on, damn it, I'll have to close the shop!" But his natural insouciance soon got the upper hand, and, taking me to one side, he recovered his jovial bonhomie to invite me to "take pot luck."

"You're very kind, Uncle," I demurred, "but I've already invited my client, Mademoiselle Aurette Constantin, to dine with me in town..."

In spite of the material success that has made him, belatedly, the most renowned photographer on the Left Bank, Père Frémiet has always remained a trifle Bohemian and abrupt. He replied, as much for Aurore's benefit as mine: "In town! Why, Monsieur my nephew, do you think you're on the far side of Panama in my Latin Quarter? Invite Mademoiselle Constantin to share some thin soup with your old blockhead of an uncle.

Your aunt won't tolerate a refusal, and I dare say that you won't eat better at the restaurant."

The prospect scarcely filled me with joy, but Aurore, amused by my uncle's joviality and perhaps curious to see a bourgeois Parisian abode, accepted, and I had to give in.

That was how we came to dine at the Frémiets' that evening. Save for matters of politics or religion, in which she limited herself to sighing and raising her eyes to heaven in response to her husband's subversive or irreverent opinions, my aunt treated all his decisions as oracles; she welcomed the stranger I brought without any ill-grace, and did not take long to warm to her on seeing her enjoy her cuisine—for Madame Frémiet was justly proud of her cordon-bleu talents.

Scarcely half way through the meal, however, an impetuous development of lichen invaded the light-bulbs and their suspending wires, from which the red powder snowed abundantly on to the dishes; it was necessary to give up on electric lighting to light the oil-lamps kept in reserve in case of power-cuts. My uncle met the misfortune with a brave face and tried to guide his annoyance, as well as the itching by which he was devoured. Young Oscar Frémiet, a 13-year-old enfant terrible, who complained loudly about being "tortured by fleas," got a clip round the ear.

My aunt was particularly fearful for her dishes, but the cheese soufflé was no less delicious for being eaten by the light of the oil-lamp. A bottle of Heidsieck was opened in honor of my "client" and the conversation turned to current events. Naturally, there was mention of "Miss Lescure," and our hosts piled up unwitting gaffes. My aunt, a good house-wife, not knowing whether the Moon was any further away than Marseilles, believed what the papers said unquestioning-ly, but my uncle, argumentative by nature, affected skeptic-ism.

"Tall stories! Which will serve, you'll see, to extract money from credulous fools. Me, I agree with Clémentel-Vault, who said in so many words in yesterday's *Journal*: 'The nuggets don't convince me at all. Even if Miss Lescure had brought back from her lunar journey a testimonial certi-fied by a Selenite mayor, I still wouldn't believe it!'"

Aurore was embarrassed. So, even though I generally abhor the wireless, I welcomed young Oscar as a liberator when he proposed that we listen to the concert at the Eiffel Tower.[16] Even if he never acquires any other claim to glory, he will always have the honor of probably having been the first human to discover the gustatory properties of the new variety of lichen born in the long waves of the Tower. In the middle of listening to Debussy's *Jardins sous la Pluie*, we heard him cry: "Oh, Papa! It's just like raspberry jam! You ought to taste it too...and you, Tonton, and you, Mademoi-selle!"

And he scratched with the tip of his index-finger, which he had just licked, in order to offer us a little of the ruby red gelatinous substance swathing the lamps of his station.

"Disgusting child!" exclaimed Madame Frémiet. "Leave that dirt alone, Dodo—it's surely poisonous!"

More curious with regard to novelties, Père Frémiet con-sented to taste, prudently, a crumb collected by his own fin-ger-nail.

"Indeed, the stuff's not bad at all—but all the same, if it's going to grow everywhere...what can it be? What can it possibly be?"

Aurore and I had the honor of being presented with the unknown and suspect foodstuff on saucers, with silver tea-spoons

Young Oscar had said it: it was entirely similar, in both taste and consistency, to an exquisite raspberry jelly.

---

[16] In the early days of radio broadcasting, the Eiffel Tower was the site of the Paris transmitter.

VII. One More Day!

The following day—October 20—news of the inexplicable vegetal invasion was displayed in all the morning newspapers, displacing other news, including that of the voyage to the Moon and the Moon Gold Company. *Excelsior* published an entire page of particularly suggestive photographs depicting the struggle against the invasion of lamps and wires at the Galeries Lafayette, the Terminus Saint-Lazare, the Hôtel Métropole, the Paramount cinema and the Institut.

Obviously! Places in which Aurore and I had spent some time and spread spores, separately or together, since our arrival in Paris...but the Institut? Oh—Nathan, of course! He too was a germ-carrier now, as much as and more than us, since he must have devoted himself to the intensive cultivation of the lichen in his laboratory!

The greater part of the article, devoted to the detailed description of accidents that had happened in these various places, told me nothing more than I had already seen for myself. I scanned the rest:

...At the corner of the Boulevard Malesherbes and the Avenue de Courcelles, opposite the Hôtel Métropole, a proliferation of these strange plants occurred on the electrical cables of a conduit that had been exposed in order to carry out repairs. It resulted in a short-circuit and started a fire in the neighboring gas-pipe...

...We are informed shortly before going to press that a center of contamination—as the propagation of this strange epidemic what strikes electrical apparatus must be called— became manifest yesterday afternoon in the well-known photographic studio of Monsieur Marcel Frémiet in the Boulevard Saint-Michel. The appearance of the evil in a part of Paris so distant from the others listed above deprives us of the hope of localizing the invasion, the origin and mode of propagation of which remains a total mystery at this point in time. Rumors

are circulating in certain quarters, in the vicinity of afflicted buildings, attributing the responsibility for these facts to some malignant foreign power; there has even been talk of "microbial warfare." We advise our readers to be wary of fantastic interpretations of a phenomenon that will doubtless prove to be purely natural in kind when its origin is discovered, and which has thus far remained almost wholly inoffensive, with the exception of the material damage, which is not very considerable. These vegetal proliferations are more inconvenient than dangerous, and one can affirm that microbial warfare taking the form of an abrupt attack would not be limited to the use of such anodyne means.

...The Prefect of Police has opened an inquiry. The municipal laboratory charged with analyzing the substances formed on lamps and conductive wires has not yet published its conclusions.

...A telephone call received from Marseilles as we go to press informs us that analogous outbreaks have been occurring in the great marine city and its suburbs for the last two days. Will this "electrical epidemic" not be restricted to Paris, then? Judgment reserved pending further information.

As I was leaving, the concierge stopped me in the vestibule.

"So it's true, then, Monsieur Delvart, that the Boche are spreading itching-powder shells throughout Paris? It began in your apartment, then your neighbor Monsieur Noguès', but we've had it in the lodge since yesterday evening. Me, I don't feel the 'incests' but my husband is red raw because of scratching all night. Before he goes to work at the Metro I had to put talcum powder all over him, just like a little child...and if we switch on the light, there's dirt everywhere. It grows like calves' lung over the lamp and the wires. What will become of us?"

"Do as I do, Madame Taquet; don't put the electric light on any more, use oil-lamps or candles. You'll find that your husband won't itch any more, and no more calves' lung will grow on your lamps."

86

And I went out, leaving the good woman incredulous and mystified. I heard her murmur behind my back: "Always the joker, that Monsieur Delvart! Candles, fine—but that won't stop the itching-powder itching!"

Unlike the day before, it was fine October weather—a delicate blue sky, bright sunlight—which filled me with horror at the thought of plunging into the underworld of the Metro. I chose to go on foot along the Rue Caulaincourt as far as the Boulevard de Clichy. I did not see signs of any great preoccupation or real anxiety on the faces of the passers-by anywhere.

I had just stopped a taxi at the corner of the Boulevard de Clichy when I noticed a thick reddish coating enveloping the battery-container on the footplate like some old rag.

In response to my intrigued stare the driver laughed. "You can step up, Monsieur, it's not excrement; it's all over the taxis, too, this accursed Boche fungus! That stuck to my battery-box yesterday evening, and all the while I'm on the move, the more I wipe it off the more it grows back—so I'm leaving it, as you see."

I understood immediately that the spores were gaining ground from one hour to the next, and that, inevitably, all the electrical apparatus in Paris would soon be invaded by lichen. That contaminated battery-holder on the footplate suddenly gave me the impression, which I had not had thus far, of the beginning of a social catastrophe.

"Where to?" asked the driver, as I stood there in a daze, with one hand on the door handle.

I shook myself. "Hôtel Métropole."

Outside the hotel, at the corner of the Boulevard Malesherbes and the Avenue de Courcelles, a group of idlers, under the benevolent gaze of a policeman, had surrounded an electrical distribution inspection-hole, in which two electricians were working on the cable, repairing the damage caused by a short-circuit...

In the hotel there was nothing apparently abnormal except for the odor of insecticide and the anxious and agitated attitude of the staff. The lamps had been cleaned and none was lit. Nevertheless, at the desk, a fat German in gold-rimmed glasses, a green Tyrolean hat and a waterproof overcoat was setting his bill, addressing vehement reproaches to the dignified and tight-lipped cashier. As I went by I caught the word "inzegdes" repeated abundantly.

The electrical elevator was out of order. I took the stairs without asking anyone anything. I knew Aurore's room number: 127, on the third floor. As I arrived at the door, I was surprised to hear voices inside. A visitor? Without knowing why, I was gripped by anguish. I knocked. The voices fell silent; I recognized Aurore's saying: "Come in!" I obeyed.

A bizarre spectacle caused me to stammer as I greeted the young woman, who came to meet me. She was in conversation with the *valet de chambre*, and the latter, in a red-and-black striped waistcoat, with a feather duster obliquely stuck in the front pocket of his apron, and a notebook and pen in his hands, was preparing to take notes, striking the pose of a perfect reporter.

On a sideboard, a tray laden with croissants, a cup, a coffee-pot and a milk-jug was fuming. The man had just come in, on the pretext of bringing the breakfast she had ordered.

"My dear friend," Aurore said to me, "You've arrived just in time. This waiter, who claims to be a reporter, is demanding an interview..."

On seeing me, the man became anxious. I advance towards him, scarcely containing myself. "By what right...?"

He took a card from his pocket and replied, stranding up straight and attempting arrogance: "Here's my pass, which Mademoiselle has already seen...Tristan Meffray, special envoy of the America Agency."

"So what? Is it the Agency that told you to come here?"

"Y...es." I could tell that the man was lying. "I need to complete my previous interview...which only concerned Mademoiselle's lunar landing"—he emphasized the last phrase with sardonic intention—"and I've come, by means of this disguise, which I beg both of you to excuse, to ask her for a few details of the manner in which she collected the cosmozoans that are in the process of extending their benefits throughout the capital."

"Cosmozoans?" I replied, violently. "You said cosmozoans! Where did you get that term? No newspaper has so far employed it..."

"Monsieur le Professeur Nathan has had the extreme kindness to inform me about the invasion of the lichen. The article whose substance he has communicated to me is in the press at this moment. I ought to admit that he refused to give me any information regarding Mademoiselle's residence, but I learned that elsewhere. No one but an astronaut—and there's only one of them in the world—could be keeping in her room, in a trunk secured by a cheap lock, the nozzle of a pipe made of refractory material, a liquid hydrogen compressor and a patented gravimeter..."

"So you're the one who searched my luggage!" Aurore exclaimed.

"Oh, as a matter of professional duty." The fake valet smiled in a self-satisfied manner. I experienced an ardent desire to slap his face.

"Monsieur," I exclaimed, "this espionage is odious! Mademoiselle Aurette Constanin has nothing to say to you."

"But Mademoiselle Aurore Lescure has a great deal."

Aurore was about to speak, but anger carried me away; I got in ahead of her. "Mademoiselle will tell you nothing. Get out, Monsieur!"

"You're making a mistake. If it isn't me who gets Mademoiselle to talk, it will be one of my colleagues...or the employees of Monsieur le Préfet de Police—for infractions of the law concerning foreign visitors; her passport isn't in order. The customs authorities will have a word to say too, on the subject of her apparatus and the cosmozoans that were introduced into France without being declared on arrival."

I sensed that I was about to put my foot in it, since Aurore had resolved yesterday to submit to an interview, but it was too late to back off, and the man might perhaps take his revenge...

A sudden inspiration struck me.

"That's all right, Monsieur. Mademoiselle will complain tomorrow to Monsieur Cheyne. We'll see whether he approves of you overstepping your instructions."

I had hit the bull's-eye. Going pale, the fake valet put on a tight smile, which he wanted to be casual and disdainful, and bowed.

"Monsieur…Mademoiselle…since my presence is unwelcome at this moment, I won't insist. Until we meet again."

The door closed. Aurore clapped her hands girlishly and said, with a hint of sarcasm: "Admirable, Gaston! You recovered from your precipitation by means of an even greater presence of mind. Without any reproach, my friend, had it not been for your violent intervention, I would have given the man a few details about my fishing for meteorites, and he would have gone away almost satisfied—but by invoking the name of Cheyne you've prevented him from carrying out his threats. You've 'had' him, as you say in France—don't you? What gave you the idea?"

"His hesitation when I asked if he'd been sent to see you by the America Agency. I deduced that the reporter was acting on his own initiative, in the hope of getting a story out of you that he could sell to some newspaper for a high price. And as you told me that the America Agency is more or less dependent on your fiancé…"

"You concluded that the gentleman would be afraid of being severely reprimanded if he incurred my displeasure. That's true. Thanks to you, my friend, he's now out of the picture. He took his gamble and lost. Whether he's a good sport or not, he must recognize that…I don't have any more annoyances to fear until tomorrow, except the reproaches of my conscience with regard to the lichen…feeling like a criminal…"

Still that obsession! It was necessary to distract her from it at any price.

90

Without emphasizing the point, I simply proposed: "Shall we go out, Aurette? It's 11 a.m.—time for an aperitif. Where do you want to go?"

"To the Terminus Saint-Lazare." The name had sprung forth spontaneously, as if by reflex. Seeing my disapproving pout, she added, with a sort of cruel humor: "That's where I acquire the psychology of a true criminal, in its entirety. I want to return to the scene of my crime!"

"Our crime, if you please!" I replied, forcefully. "If there is a crime, I claim my share in it. I'm a germ-carrier, just as you are, and I'd like to know how many Parisians aren't, at the present moment!"

In spite of the good weather and the short distance, Aurore manifested a desire to take the Metro; she had a very American weakness for that mode of transport. Villiers station was 100 meters way.

At the entrance situated in the Boulevard de Courcelles, five or six people were slowly climbing the steps; they were arguing hotly, palpating something and passing it from hand to hand…something like a torn red rag. At the sight of it, my stomach clenched with apprehension, and Aurore uttered a kind of horrified sigh—but neither of us made any comment. At the foot of the stairs, as we passed the people coming out, we recognized between their hands the fateful coral felt born of the extraterrestrial sores. The lichen had begun to invade the Metro!

It was still a minor matter, in truth, as we were able to see on the platform while we waited for our train. Here and there, along the six rails—the two conductive rails and those of the track—were red plaques where patches of fungus were staining the shiny metal. Among the array of light-bulbs in the ceiling, only four or five were carrying the characteristic red lattice-work of the contamination.

"Who knows, Aurore!" I whispered in my companion's ear. "Perhaps the virulence of the germs is diminishing, becoming exhausted…"

She looked at me, a reproach in her frank and honest gaze. "Why are you trying to deceive me, Gaston? This is only the beginning."

That was the general opinion of the public around us. Leaning over the edge of the platform or raising their eyes toward he laps, people were pointing out the alarming stigmata to one another. In one group, a fat man was holding forth, vituperating against the Company and the Government.

"Come on, there's still hope!" joked one wag, as the train came into the station. "People are always scratching themselves in the Metro!"

In the first-class carriage into which we climbed, the lamps were still unaffected, the travelers indifferent. The tunnels were doubtless not yet contaminated in the direction of the Porte Champerret.

Europe…Saint-Lazare…the long subterranean corridor…the rotunda, with its stained-glass windows lit from within, as usual, but a few external lamps "diseased"…and the Cour du Havre staircase took us directly to the pavement of the Terminus.

Numerous idlers standing in front of the café seemed to be waiting for something, but nothing was happening. In the fine October sunshine, the terrace populated with customers had resumed its normal appearance; it was the same inside, on the wall- and ceiling-lamps; the polished and unilluminated bulbs remained clear.

But for what we had just seen in the Metro, we might have been tempted to believe that the threat had vanished…

But no! On the road, in the flood of taxis and buses, only the occasional vehicle is not dragging along, either on the battery-holder on the footplate, or the chassis underneath the engine, its ragged goiter of red fungus growths. As for the trams, every passing vehicle is stirring up between its wheels, as it passes by, a spray of dry mud…of lichen, torn up by the "plow" from the gutter supplying the current.

Not far away there is a sudden detonation, like a burst tire, and confused cries…

It's coming from the direction of the Rue de la Pépinière. At ground level, underneath a stationary tram, a white flame flashes: a short-circuit. But within a second, the spectacle is hidden from us by the compact rush of curiosity-seekers running toward it. We can no longer see anything ahead of us but the file of tram-cars immobilized by the accident. Then smoke rises up in the distance: the short-circuited vehicle has caught fire.

Many customers have deserted the terrace to go take a look, but we don't move. Aurore, very pale, gazes at me profoundly, as if she were investing her last hope in me. I attempt to distract her, affectionately, by chattering about anything at all, until the moment when, one after another, the idlers come back to sit down at her neighboring tables, and we learn—to our relief—that no one has been hurt, that the passengers were able to escape in time from the blazing vehicle.

"Get the *Paris-Midi*!"

Avidly purchased from the vendors, as if people expected to find therein the story of the accident that has just occurred before their eyes, the paper did not contain the article by Professor Nathan mentioned by the reporter from the America Agency. The only news we read there, other than that in the morning papers, was the admission of the invasion of the Metro by the lichen. The fact had been observed for the first time early last night on the North-South, between the Lamarck and Rennes stations…the one at which I embarked and the one at which I exited in order to visit my uncle. The contamination of the battery-containers, magnetos or dynamos of taxis and buses also began during the night; that of the tramways became manifest at 6 a.m., opposite the Terminus—this very spot.

In spite of this worrying diffusion, the author of the article gave evidence of a fine optimism in declaring that "measures have been taken by the authorities to put a stop to the extension of the electrical epidemic."

After that, the dispatch announcing that the *Berengaria* would be in Cherbourg at noon tomorrow took on a rather ironic flavor:

As soon as he arrives in Paris, which he intends to reach by airplane, Monsieur Lendor J. Cheyne will busy himself organizing the subsidiary of the Moon Gold Mining Co. Ltd. He has already made radiophonic arrangements with the banks in the United States and Europe. Shares in the European Moon Gold Company will be issued at a nominal value of 500 francs, half payable on subscription...

Before lunch, Aurore took care to telephone Nathan. The previous day, she had made plans to visit the biologist today, if possible, and it had been agreed that I would let her go alone, but since the declaration of the America Agency reporter, I wanted to accompany her, in order to address to Nathan the reproaches that his unpardonable indiscretion merited, in my opinion.

In spite of the regulation forbidding two people to make use of a public booth at once, I took my place at the apparatus with Aurore, in the Post Office at the Madeleine.

"Hello—yes, this is Professor Nathan. What do you want, Mademoiselle Lescure? I'm in the middle of lunch."

The curt brusqueness of his tone offended me. With an impulsive gesture, I tore the receiver from Aurore's hands and launched forth, unthinkingly: "Hello, Monsieur le Professeur—Gaston Delvart here. I'm with Mademoiselle Lescure. She has had a very disagreeable experience this morning: a journalist who came from your residence, to whom you wrongly revealed the confidences that she made to you under a seal of secrecy..."

"Monsieur Delvart, your youth alone excuses your intemperance and your stupidity. I do not recognize your right to criticize my conduct or to doubt my word. Mademoiselle Lescure only demanded secrecy with regard to her place of residence. If the reporter from the America Agency has discovered that, I can do nothing about it. To each his own: to Mademoiselle Lescure, the brute fact of the discovery of the cosmozoans; as for my conclusions on that subject, they belong to science—which is to say, to the world. You aren't going to claim the right to prevent me from making them public?"

"And what are they, pray?"

"Oh no! I've drafted a full article this morning, in order that I can be left in peace. Read it in the special edition of *L'Intransigeant*."

I was doubtless about to utter some harsh words, but Aurore made haste to take the receiver away from me.

"Monsieur le Professeur, I grant that you have every right to publish your conclusions, even if that premature revelation will cause me inconvenience. But you'll surely accord me the pleasure of seeing the results of your experiments in your laboratory?"

There was a tormented groan at the other end of the wire. Then: "So be it; I owe you that. I'm very busy; hold on which I consult my appointments. I can give you 25 minutes this afternoon, at 3:30 p.m. Be prompt."

And he hung up.

We looked at one another. A bitter rictus raised the corners of Aurore's lips.

"That scientist of the Institut de France is as bad as American scientists. They gladly forget the real author of any discovery that comes into their hands. It wouldn't take much for Monsieur Nathan to think of himself as the father of the cosmozoans." With a sigh of regret, she added: "I wish to God that were true!"

Before leaving the Post Office, I asked for Frémiet's number. His deep baritone voice answered.

"Oh, it's you, young Gaston. What's new since yesterday? You've read the papers, eh? It's amazing! I received the first journalist at six this morning—15 have come already, with photographers and cinematographers. The house is full of magnesium fumes…and it's still continuing on the lamps…and it's winning. There's only my boy who's jubilant, with his radio jam, as he calls it."

I put a brake on the old man's enthusiasm. "I only have one thing to say to you, Uncle—it's about the prints of Miss Constantin. When can I come by to pick them up?"

"With all this to-do…let's say the day after tomorrow, in the morning—hold on, let's do better. Come for lunch at noon on that day and bring your client; she's made quite a hit with your aunt…and me too." He chortled jovially. "Tee hee! Congratulations, my lad—she's a real cracker, your little…"

I interrupted hastily "Miss Constantin is here, on the other receiver; she thanks you for your kind invitation, Uncle, but she'll no longer be in Paris the day after tomorrow…"

Alas, in having recourse to that little white lie, I didn't think that I was so good at predicting the future.

We had lunch at the Taverne Royale, at the back of the room in order to avoid seeing the automobiles in the street trailing their goiters of lichen. The establishment was free of contamination, and the wall-lights above our heads were glowing clearly.

Like me, Aurore made an effort to forget the haunting, and during the meal we almost succeeded. I held forth to my companion about painting, and once again I admired in her the combination of unexpected knowledge and sound judgment, along with the ingenuous simplicity of a child. Already, in my studio the previous day she had appraised my canvases with a astonishing instinctive taste. This time, she talked about ancient and modern painters, citing their names and the works she had seen in American museums or in reproduction…

That 23-year-old knew everything: sciences and arts, Latin and Greek. She was a modern female Pico della Mirandola, with an additional intellectual modesty that as adorable. One might have thought that she was listening to herself talk—no, as if it were natural to take a just pride therein, but in a semi-indulgent, semi-irreverent fashion. She listened as a gladly-amused witness to the phenomenon of her own universality. After some dazzling flight of intellect she would fall silent with a smile on her youth and in her eyes with the milky sclerotics, as if to excuse herself and say: "Don't make too

96

much fun of me; I'm not doing it on purpose; it's not my fault if I have an infallible memory and an intelligence capable of comprehending everything!"

But Aurore, girl fallen from the sky, you also have—I sense it—a heart made to be moved in unison with mine, ready to vibrate on the same wavelength as that of your "good comrade." You're refusing to listen to it, your heart. Will the day ever come when you'll permit total accord to be established? One day? But today is the last day of out fallacious intimacy—perhaps an adventure with no tomorrow, of which al that will remain to my will be your unfinished portrait...

How shall I live on, after having verged on the possibility of happiness, of marvelous harmony...?

At 2:15, as we were finishing our coffee, the special edition of the *Intran* arrived. Professor Nathan's article!

Fallen back from out heaven into immediate reality, leaning over the paper, side by side, we read.

VIII. A Xenobiotic Invasion

Science has revealed and put at the service of human-kind, on a gigantic scale, forces that had only been fugitive or unperceived phenomena before, hidden or unutilizable, and as it makes progress, with an ever-accelerating thrust, we must expect to see the emergence more novelties foreign to our anterior notions. One may say without paradox that that the further the manifestations of science go, the more contrary they are to the natural order of things.

From this viewpoint, the cryptogamic invasion from which several parts of Paris are presently suffering must be considered in the context of the most recent scientific progress. One can safely predict that it will rapidly curb the turbulent manifestations of the "lichen" and, sooner or later, extract useful applications therefrom, as it has done with all its previous conquests.

Everyone endowed with the slightest speculative curiosity will be legitimately interested to learn that this proliferation of unknown vegetation is not a fortuitous occurrence, a *lusus naturae*,[17] but one of the results of the first astronautical expedition to have vanquished weight and surpassed the limits of the terrestrial atmosphere.

Almost all the articles that have been written about Mademoiselle Aurore Lescure's flight have dealt complacently with the nuggets of "lunar" gold collected by the young astronaut, but none has judged worthy of comment the harvest of meteoric dust carried out by her in the void of interplanetary space.

Now, for science, these nuggets are a negligible matter. For several years now, we have known for certain, by virtue of the spectroscope, about the presence of gold deposits on our satellite, and it tells us nothing more to have real specimens on

---

[17] Freak of nature

Earth, even by the kilo or the ton. Speculation alone will find its reckoning therein...in the beginning, at least, before the superabundance of the yellow metal causes its price to collapse.

For science, the only result of the expedition that counts—but a result of primordial importance—is the tangible demonstration that the existence of cosmozoans is not merely a hypothesis, but a grandiose reality. Mademoiselle Lescure's flight brings a definitive solution to one of the most anguishing problems of cosmogony: that of the appearance of life on our planet.

Let us briefly recall the history of that theory.

As early as 1821, the first person—a Frenchman, the Comte de Montlivault—had the idea that fragments of heavenly bodies, projections of lunar volcanoes charged with seed-germs, might have encountered the Earth and populated it.[18]

In 1865, a German scientist, Dr. H. E. Richter, gave substance to this hypothesis, imaging that our world was in perpetual communication with the stars via the intermediary of stones falling from the sky: bolides or meteorites. As these bolides often contain carbonaceous substances that appear to

---

[18] The reference is to Comte Éleonore de Montlivault's *Conjectures sur la réuinion de la Lune et de la Terre, et des satellites en general à leur planète principale*; Montlivault subsequently published two other works of cosmology, including his letters on that subject to Baron Fourier. In fact, earlier versions of theses regarding the interplanetary transmission of "seeds" can be found in Christiaan Huygens' *Kosmotheoros* (1698), and in Charles Tiphaigne de la Roche's eccentric scientific romance *Amilec, ou la graine d'homme* (1753; tr. in *Amilec*, Black Coat Press, ISBN 9781612270333). The well-known popularizer of science Henri de Parville also envisaged the possibility of the interplanetary transmission of living matter in his semi-documentary scientific romance *Un Habitant de la planète Mars* (1865; tr. as *An Inhabitant of the Planet Mars*, Black Coat Press, ISBN 9781934543450).

originate from the decomposition of extraterrestrial organisms, Richter thought that these celestial stones might sometimes contain whole and healthy seed-germs. These seed-germs, set free when the stones explode in consequence of the shock of their impact, could have inseminated the Earth.

The same theory was defended a few years later by the illustrious scientist Lord Kelvin; the physiologist Preyer and the physicist Helmholtz allowed themselves to be influenced by his ideas.[19] They called the concept the hypothesis of cosmozoans, a name that has survived.

In our day, the botanist Philippe Van Tieghem and the geologist Stanislas Meunier are enthusiastic supporters of this hypothesis, to which the Swedish scientist Svante Arrhenius has given a new form by supposing that the sidereal seed-germs, the cosmozoans, are not enclosed in bolides but circulate in space in a naked state in the form of meteoric dust, propelled by the pressure of light. Dr. Paul Becquerel, on the other hand, denies that these seed-germs could resist the destructive action of ultra-violet light.

The appearance of the lichen brings us irrefutable proof that there really exist, scattered in infinite space, seed-germs susceptible of giving birth to a vital creation on a heavenly body, in certain conditions.

But then, one might say, if these seed-germs exist, why is our Earth not continually inseminated by them? Why has the proliferation of this cosmic vegetation, which I shall call xenobiotic, from the Greek *xenos*, foreign—foreign to the Earth, that is—and *bios*, life, not taken place before today?

Because the atmosphere, entirely gaseous as it is, opposes an insurmountable barrier to these seed-germs, and plays

---

[19] Lord Kelvin talked about Richter's theory in his presidential address to the British Association of the Advancement of Science in 1871, which was entitled "On the Origin of Life"; that raised its profile sufficiently to interest Hermann van Helmholtz and William Thierry Preyer; the latter featured it in his *Naturwissenschaftliche Thatsachen und Probleme* (1880)

the role of a protective screen with regard to the Earth, which preserves it against the invasion of other types of life, whose seed-germs are disseminated in space. Because the cosmozoans that the Earth encounters in its course through infinite space do not reach the surface; they are stopped by the atmosphere, the friction of which "strikes" them like matches and volatilizes them; they are shooting stars.

Everything happens as if the creation that has implanted itself on our globe—the "biosphere," as cosmologists put it; which is to say, the totality of the living world, animal and vegetable—had been put into sealed jar since its origin, in order to evolve there according to its own destiny: an isolation that one can interpret, as one chooses, as a wise precaution of the Creator or as a combination of favorable and natural circumstances. For it could be—it seems highly probable—that the cosmozoans floating in space are not identical in nature in the various sectors of space.

Without going as far as to say that the essential properties of matter, such as gravitation, vary according to the zones of space, numerous scientists, invoking the Einsteinian "curvature of space," and the fact scientifically established, among others, in 1927 by Monsieur Gheury de Bray that the velocity of light diminishes,[20] have cast doubt on the assertion that natural laws, as we know them on Earth, are valid throughout the entire cosmos. It is probable that the laws regulating life in the various stellar steams are diverse, that life is manifest in forms and with modalities entirely unforeseen by us. On planets orbiting Sirius, for instance, the cosmozoans that inseminated them during their creation might give them organisms of a chemical formula in which the carbon chains that reign here

---

[20] The arguments employed to back up Maurice Edmond Gheury de Bray's assertion that the velocity of light is not constant, originally published in French in 1927 and reprinted in *Nature* in 1931, are now largely discredited, although the thesis still appeals to dissenters from Einsteinian theory.

are replaced, let us say, by compounds of silicon, or even nitrogen, as Eugène Turpin has suggested.

Admitting, with the magnificent dualistic theory of Monsieur Belot,[21] that the Earth was given birth by pulsatory waves during the penetration of the "protosun" into the Galactic Nebula, it would have captured and put in shelter beneath the bell-jar of its atmosphere the vital seed-germs harvested in that distant sector of the universe.

Since then, during the millions of centuries that separate us from life's debut on our planet, the other living seed-germs, the new cosmozoans, that the Earth has encountered in its course are, for us, as if non-existent. At the very most, one might admit that the barrier of the atmosphere has been forced, at some moment in the past by a bolide, a crack in which might have enclosed a few cosmozoans and protected them from burning. That is possible, theoretically—but the new creation must have been ephemeral, for no trace of any such event remains in the geological strata.

To any objection, therefore, to the notion that there is a great multitude of excess seed-germs, a prodigal supply of billions and trillions of stray cosmozoans, some of which might land on a star ready to receive them, we respond that nature, in its infinite exuberance, does not make paltry and utilitarian calculations. The law of least effort is an anthropomorphic invention. Even before our eyes, in the realm of terrestrial things, nature spreads its seeds, eggs and spores with an immeasurable prodigality, the vast majority being destroyed, annihilated without any profit for life. Each female cod or herring lays more than a million eggs, a termite queen hundreds of thousands, and when one things also of the winged seeds of elm-trees, the spores of mushrooms...

---

[21] The reference is to Émile Belot's *L'Origine dualiste des mondes et de la structure de notre univers* (1924, with an introduction by Camille Flammarion), also known as *Essai de cosmologie tourbillonaire.*

But how many of nature's seemingly unavoidable vetoes have already been transgressed by science? The MG-17 Rocket has infringed this prohibition and, thanks to the ingenuity of its pilot, who was able to collect them, has brought back to Earth a provision of meteoritic seed-germs.

Nevertheless, if science had not intervened once more after their arrival on terrestrial soil, the cosmozoans captured by Mademoiselle Lescure would not have developed in the present natural conditions. Just as every terrestrial seed requires a certain temperature and determined level of humidity and light, these cosmozoans need, in order to develop, radiations that only exist in the light of suns during their ardent youth; they were destined for a planet receiving torrents of X-rays from its central star, and fields of electromagnetic induction of various intensity. For millions of centuries, neither the Earth nor the Sun has answered to this definition. But is it not the prerogative of science to break the apparent course of natural conditions?

Scientific civilization has rendered possible the artificial reconstitution of these conditions at various points. Torrents of X-rays are poured forth at will by radiologists' tubes; fields of electromagnetic induction of varying intensity reign around light-bulbs, in the vicinity of conductive wires, accumulators, dynamos and so on—on condition, of course, that the apparatus is functioning and the current flowing.

My experiments, actively pursued for 48 hours—the details of which I shall spare the public, reserving them for my communication to the Académie—have demonstrated that the birth and evolution of these cosmic creatures takes place at two distinct times.

Firstly, under an X-ray tube, the meteoric seed-germs, extracted from their multimillennial inertia, begin to germinate and yield a primary rudimentary tissue, almost uniquely composed of reproductive spores that I shall call B spores. That is the primordial phase, the trigger-finger of creations, the privileged moment of the *Fiat Vita!* that cosmozoans—these cosmozoans, at least—must encounter in order to propagate on a heavenly body.

Secondly, once that initiation has been effectuated, the X-rays becme unnecessary. From the initial tissue produced under their influence the B spores are born, which disperse, and to which it is sufficient to encounter an electromagnetic field to germinate in their turn and produce the lichen, the Xenobiota, whose evolution continues indefinitely, through successive generations.

But this evolution, which occurs in electromagnetic fields, presents an exceptional characteristic that science has not yet had an opportunity to observe in our own biocosm, the *élan vital*[22] of which is depreciated, almost at the end of its course: the effervescence, the quasi-frenetic haste of this creation in its nascent state, which is rushing to the conquest of new forms.

Is this a matter of the speed appropriate to this creation—the speed at which the xenobiota reproduce, at the beginning of the evolution, on a virgin planet that they have just inseminated? That is quite possible, but we have no means of verifying it. In any case, their "time"—the rhythm that presides over their development—has nothing in common with that of the life that is familiar to us. It is the accelerated, hectic time of a creation at the debut of its conquest. Hours are, from its viewpoint, equivalent to centuries or millennia for terrestrial species. In a few hours, the successive generations of the xenobiota evolve as much as the large animal and vegetable species of our creation have evolved in the course of an entire geological period.

---

[22] The term *élan vital* [vital impetus] was coined by Henri Bergson in 1902 in association with his theory of creative evolution, but the notion that some such impetus must have declined in the course of Earth's evolutionary history is considerably older, employed by several early evolutionists to excuse the fact that evolution did not appear to be observably ongoing at present.

For the best point of comparison we can find to give some idea of that frenetic cadence it is necessary to seek in the world of micro-organisms for bacteria and protozoa that have remained similar to what they were in the beginning, whose generations succeed one another today with a fantastic rapidity, with no common measure with the order of duration that measures the development and reproduction of higher animals—mammals and humans. Certain bacteria, for example, reproduce after an hour, and compensate for their smallness with that rapidity of multiplication. At a rate of one generation per hour, two descendants per individual, and so on. Ferdinand Cohn has calculated that one bacterium, in a favorable environment, can produce several million individuals per day—and if those individuals were all to escape the causes of destruction, the geometric progression continuing, the total number of descendants would reach, in four and a half days, one decillion, 10^{38} individuals—1 followed by 38 zeroes—or, to put it another way, the volume of all the water contained in the world's oceans.

That is a calculation, but in the same order of facts, examples of abrupt explosions of life—"waves" of life as the naturalists of old used to put it—have not entirely disappeared from the present-day world, even among organisms significantly superior to bacteria. Sometimes, in a few hours, at privileged points on the Earth, myriads of algae, insects, spiders or small vertebrates are seen to appear and become abundant. Thus "ephemerae," on certain summer evenings cover the banks of rivers with their cadavers to a depth of several centimeters. One can also cite "rains" of frogs and "clouds" of locusts.

In 1889, the naturalist Dr. William Carruthers[23] observed a migration of locusts over the Red Sea, born in the space of

---

[23] Varlet has "G. Carruthers;" I have corrected several other slightly-mistaken references in this chapter without comment, but it is possible that I might be wrong in assuming that this

several hours, which flew over for the entire day of 25 November, which implies a cloud of 2.4 x 10^{12}—240 trillion—individuals, 5,967 square kilometers in extent and weighing 4.10 x 10^7—41 million—tonnes, a figure of the same order as that of all the copper, zinc and lead extracted in the course of the entire 19th century: 4.47 x 10^7.

Well, the living matter born of the cosmozoans, the Xenobiota, is, as we have observed, permanently in this phase of hyperactivity. Instead of decreasing, of attenuating, it is following an ever-increasing curve from one hour to the next. It is a new creation, crazed by the initial impulsion that is operating the primer of its reign, seeking its path in all the impetuosity of a genetic liberation. In the same way, terrestrial evolution passed thousands of species in review in order to end up with the types that took turns as monarchs of the planet: ammonites, dinosaurs, mammals. But here the research is proceeding at a accelerated pace; within a matter of hours several new species have been "invented" and tried out by the Xenobiota in progress toward the procreation of superior forms, and perhaps toward the equivalent of the supreme success that is, in terrestrial creation, Humankind.

For my experiments have permitted me to establish a fact that has escaped the public as yet: in spite of the apparent identity of the reproductive spores, the generations of the Xenobiota are polymorphic and protean. The lichen generated under an electric lamp is not the same as that on conductive wires; it is different on a battery-container and different again on a magneto. The intensity of the electrical fields appears to influence the differentiation much more than the voltage. I have, thus far, already catalogued 32 distinct species divided into seven genres; and, in spite of the increasing rapidity of reproduction in the wild, I believe that I have anticipated, in the laboratory, several dozen generations of the normal succession. I have observed the ultra-rapid development of certain

one is to William Carruthers, the then-president of the Linnean Society.

giant forms, and others corrosive to copper and aluminum, which literally devour the conducive wires to which they are attached.

I cannot write at length, in a simple popular article, about the morphological and chemical composition of Xenobiotic tissue. Suffice it to say that the Xenobiota have no analogue, whether animal or vegetable, in the organic world known thus far. Their fundamental chemical composition is of the type NO_7Ar_2 (nitrogen, oxygen, argon). They are therefore formed at the exclusive expense of the atmosphere. Under the influence of electromagnetic waves, Xenobiota assimilate gases directly from the air in order to construct their substance, rather like the way that the chlorophyll in the leaves of our plants assimilates carbon dioxide under the influence of solar light. Certain species also construct a resistant skeleton by the adjunction of Si (silicon), Cu (copper), Fe (iron), Al (aluminum) etc., appropriated for their support: the glass of a bulb; the conductive wire.

One aliment indispensable to the Xenobiota is electricity. In the absence of any induction field, the starved lichen ceases to grow, and then perishes; its excretion is no longer compensated by is nutrition and it slowly resorbs itself, volatilizing in 30 hours—without any residue, save for those varieties with a skeleton.

As for the reproductive spores—which is to say, the microscopic grains of the impalpable powder that the lichen's vesicles project and propagate it at a distance, it I remarkable that they have properties entirely different from those of the initial cosmozoans.

The cosmozoans, or meteoritic seed-germs, are designed to conserve potential life, to be the receptacle of future creation during its transference through space, so they are practically immortal and indestructible. Neither the cold nor the void of space, nor ultra-violet radiation, affects them; it requires a temperature of more than 300 degrees to kill them.

Conversely, the reproductive spores generated on Earth, whether from the initial magma or the lichen, have the role of bringing about an immediate transmission of life, and only possess a feeble resistance. A temperature above 120 degrees or below zero, or traces of chlorine, bromine or iodine, are sufficient to kill them, and it is possible that they only conserve their ability to germinate for a few days: a lack of resistance, we hasten to say, that will facilitate the battle against the lichen's expansion.

It is necessary to recognize that a new kind of life has taken up residence on the Earth and is striving, with all its youthful energy, to secure its place on our globe. But the reader, perhaps alarmed by the initial results of the invasion, may rest easy. The battle is unequal between this rudimentary, purely organic lichenoid vegetation and the active intelligence of human beings. Science, which has conquered the cosmozoans, will be able to master the Xenobiota.

In the extreme case that we did not succeed in hindering their development and they became a real inconvenience to civilization before the first frosts rid us of the new creation, it would be sufficient to starve them by cutting off the current and suspending the production and distribution of electrical energy for a few days in the contaminated zones.

But I am not addressing the subject of public utility. My role as a popularizer is limited, for the moment, to projecting the light of science on the strange and singular facts that have disconcerted the inhabitants of Paris, and to allow them to glimpse the utility that might drive from the importation to Earth of the Xenobiota, which I shall persist in calling a conquest.

The slight radioactivity with which the spores of the lichen are endowed—to which they must owe the urticarian properties that make them resemble itching-powder—and other phenomena of the same order that I have observed in some of the more highly-evolved species authorize the most considerable hopes. The study of these new facts will probably assist us to resolve, in the near future, a crucial problem of which science awaits the solution: provoking atomic dissociation at will. And that discovery, formidable in is consequences, thanks to which we will realize without difficulty something that is still only a utopian idea, "a hundred horse-power in a matchbox,"[24] will compensate abundantly for the few temporary inconveniences that Parisians will have to suffer today with regard to the comforts of existence linked to the efficient functioning of electrical apparatus.

Once again, and more magnificently than ever, science will have played its role, which is to disrupt the apparent course of natural laws, using them against themselves in order to make them finally pliant to its ends, to the utility of humankind and the greater benefit of civilization.

---

[24] The original version of this quote, in Jules Verne's *Robur le conquérant* (1885; tr. as *The Clipper of the Clouds*), is to *one* horse power "*dans un boitier de montre*" [in a watch-case]; as Professor Nathan has already modified it, it did not seem inappropriate for me to update it slightly, for the convenience of modern readers.

IX. The Accident on the North-South

The article has interested us so keenly that we almost forgot Aurore's appointment. When we finished reading it was ten past three. In order to reach Nathan's house by half past, we only just had time to take the North-South to the Madeleine station and cross the road.

On the way, we talked about it.

"You see, Aurette, you're no longer at risk of disgrace when people discover your identity. Now they'll crown you with honors. Thanks to the anticipations of this enthusiastic scientist, you've become a benefactress of humanity. It's good for you, this article—I no longer hold his rudeness against him."

"It's good for me, and for the reception that awaits my father and Lendor tomorrow…yes, but all the same, it commits an injustice that I won't forgive him. It doesn't say a word about Dr. Alburtin. To read it, one would think that it was Nathan who had the inspired idea of experimenting on the meteorites with X-rays."

We reached the Metro entrance at the junction, facing the tramway stop. A hand-written placard fixed to the double doors at the foot of the staircase announced without commentary: *The circulation of trains on line 3 (Champerret-Gambetta) is suspended between Saint-Lazare and Villiers stations. The latter station is temporarily closed to the public.*

The same idea occurred to us, provoked by the professor's commentaries on the acceleration of the lichen's growth.

"Some minor accident," I said, in a tone that attempted detachment.

"Villiers station is near the Hôtel Métropole," Aurore added, simply, without looking at me.

At the entrance to the platform, a suffocating odor of rotting flowers replaced the phenol of the corridors, which testified to an attempt at disinfection. Under the vault of the station a dull, non-human rumor was audible. One might have thought that it was the noise of a forest whose branches were cracking under a winter frost, mingled with crepitations. The lights—"diseased" for the most part, wrapped in vegetal networks—were reddening. Crowded on the platform edge, the travelers were opening their eyes wide and scratching themselves silently.

The Xemobiota had invaded the tracks—but it was no longer a timid offensive, as at Villiers that morning; a vehement thrust of the extraterrestrial creation was developing aggressive battalions of lichen on the rails, a reddish-purple coating bristling with spikes, like a giant crystallization. In the vault, packets of branched stalactites were hanging from the two trolley-wires and the three feeder cables. Here and there, new prolongations of these vegetal masses, as thick as a thumb and as long as a hand, were visibly surging forth, developing like the sections of an expanding telescope...or, better, like those party balloons into which one blows. After a brief interval, a blood-red bubble formed at the tip of the arm, which burst with a noise like a child's pop-gun, projecting its dust of spores.

The spectacle hypnotized us all. Not a word was pronounced during the four or five minutes that the train made us wait. Finally, it arrived, whistling. It stirred up a cloud of dust, noisily crushing the vegetation on the rails. The front of the engine was scared and stained with red, as if it had just cleared a path through an abattoir. Oblique traces of the same kind striped the walls of the carriages.

It was hideous, but the force of habit engulfed the passengers in the carriages. The people getting out were uttering sighs of relief and hastening toward the exit. The doors slammed. The conductor gave the signal. Slowly, the train went into the tunnel.

Our first-class carriage was moderately furnished. Aurore was able to sit down on a folding seat; I remained standing beside her. Our neighbors, afflicted with mutism, gazed apprehensively at the sick light-bulbs while scratching me-

111

chanically. Seeing one of them completely masked by its carapace of crimson lichen, a tall and gangling boy-scout took a "Swedish knife" from his belt and started scraping the bulb. His example was soon followed, and the cleaned lamps brightened, lightening the moral atmosphere of the carriage.

At La Concorde, a flood of passengers getting on jam-packed the carriage, pressing me against Aurore, who was obliged to get up from her folding seat—but I had the warmth of her body against my side and shoulder, and the communion of our gaze rid the silence of its constraint.

Meanwhile, the pause went on. On the platform, facing us, the station-master, leaning over his telephone was alternating replies directed into the apparatus with remarks to the train conductor, who was waiting at the door of his glazed cabin. Finally, the difficulty seemed to be resolved. We moved off—at reduced speed, as if the train were groping its way. Half way from Chambre-des-Députés we slowed down even more, and then stopped. After two or three minutes, there was a false start; we went forward a few meters, then stopped again, definitively.

Even though they are quite familiar to Parisians, these breakdowns in mid-tunnel are always slightly disturbing; people think about possible accidents. Today, in that carriage lit by blood-stained bulbs and surrounded by a rumor of monstrous menace, it was agonizing.

Stopped indefinitely...the impatience among all those people, in a hurry to reach their destinations, broke the silence. People murmured, in low voices at first, then loudly.

"What are they waiting for, then?" complained a man in a bowler hat and tinted spectacles—doubtless a teacher.

"Take care of the lamp above your head, then," the boy-scout said to him. "It's starting to get murky again."

Aurore raised her wrist-watch toward me, on which I read 3:27. "I won't get there by half-past."

"And he's perfectly capable of refusing to see you, if you're late!"

Silence fell again. People stopped talking, in the hope of hearing a signal outside—an order from the conductor, or the noise of an employee's footsteps on the track. In the sonorous silence of the tunnel, however, there was still nothing more than a dull rumor mingled with crackling, rustling and snapping sounds...the enormous growth of the Lichen at work...and also the purr of a violent air current, whose movement through the open ventilators was tangible.

"Can you hear it?" Aurore said to me. "That's the rush of air created by the lichen's nutrition, which is absorbing the atmosphere of the tunnel on a massive scale."

I admired her scientific presence of mind.

Behind me, though, there is a shrill, strangled scream. I turn round, as all the passengers do.

"There...there! It touched my neck! It's all warm!"

A fat woman, her features twisted in fear beneath her make-up and her eyes bulging, is pointing to an open ventilator art the top of a window, through which a hideous red thing has surged, like a flayed fist. People jostle one another trying to get a look at it. Peering more carefully, I distinguish behind the glass, among the reflections of the illuminated interior objects in the blackness of the tunnel, an enormous tentacle of lichen, whose growth has introduced its tip into the carriage.

"The fungus! The Lichen! The Xenobiota!" All the names applied to the cosmic vegetation spring forth at once. The danger has been realized: the accelerated, lightning-fast growth.

Shrill female squeals...frightened, indignant exclamations.

"They aren't going to let us go..."

A confirmed alarmist affirms: "The lichen has invaded the tunnel; the train's stuck inside; we'll be crushed, asphyxiated..."

Everyone looks at his neighbors, tensely, only waiting for a signal...and there'll be panic. I see Aurore's lips quivering, her eyes searching mine for a composure that is in the process of escaping me, under the pressure of the unanimous folly. Desperately, I take refuge in the obsessive idea of protecting Aurore at all costs. I lean toward her.

"Pay attention, my dear." She is backed up in the angle formed by a seat-back and the window of the carriage. I turn slightly and enclose her within the barrier of my arms, may hands on the aluminum bar. "Don't move. We're going to get out through this door here, since there's an emergency ladder to get down to the track."

Outside, the tunnel is filing with cries, the sound of footsteps: the gallop of a stampeding herd. The passengers in the other carriages fleeing toward the station?

In our carriage, everyone runs to the forward doors and, in the reddened penumbra of the invaded bulbs, they strike out with their fists, trying to break down the doors. In vain—they're blocked.

"What about us? Aren't they going to let us out? They're going to let us die! Guard! Here! The first-class coach! Never mind—let's get out of the windows."

The sound of breaking glass. Outside, the majority of the fugitives have gone past. Calls for help, vituperations, blasphemies from the laggards...a revolver shot resounds, close at hand.

"Ger out, quickly! Move, damn it! Damnation!"

At our end of the carriage, however, the small communication door opens, and the white beam on an acetylene lamp, brandished by a controller, leaps to my eyes. And a sub-officer commands: "Attention in there! Order to evacuate the train and proceed on foot to Chambre-des-Députés station. But the current hasn't been cut off...we haven't been able to telephone the sector. Watch out—beware of the electric rails. Walk well within the rolling trails or outside to the left. No jostling, one at a time—but hurry up!"

While everyone starts running, the man comes to the door close to which Aurora and I remain in isolation, and pulls a lever that opens the battens, through which the wind rushes in, and the tempestuous racket of the growing lichen. He hangs his searchlight on the bar of a luggage-rack, lifts the

114

chain securing the iron ladder flattened against a seat-back, rotates it on its axial support and, guiding it outside the carriage, lowers it into the retaining groove, amid a muffled sound of breaking branches.

"Exit this way!"

The man goes down first, lantern in hand—and the bright acetylene beam reveals the spiky red thicket of the lichen that is extending its tentacles underneath the carriage.

I hoped that, in view of our favorable position, Auriore and I would be the first to get down after him, but all the passengers have flooded back *en masse* toward that doorway.

The disappearance of the lantern has left us in almost complete darkness; the light-bulbs, left to their own devices, have ended up masking themselves. Clinging to a bar with one hand, holding Aurore in front of me with the other, I succeed initially in retaining our position of priority in spite of the pressure, but at the moment when, letting go of the bar, I advance my hand toward the vertical ramp at the top of the ladder, some big devil takes advantage of it to knock my hand away with a blow of his fist, pushes me back furiously, takes my place, and gets down.

For two seconds, at the very edge of the gaping opening, wedged among the frightful jostling of the front rank, in which people are using their elbows to resist he pressure, I sway, with nothing more to retain me, and with Aurore in my arms, braced with all my strength.

"Don't push, damn it! Let us get down!"

A surge shoves me…we are thrust over the edge.

Not directly on to the track; branches deaden the fall, breaking dryly like elder-twigs. I fall on my side, my companion on top of me; she hasn't even made contact with the ground. Getting to her feet first, she helps me to do likewise.

"No harm done, Aurore?"

"No harm done, Gaston?"

The ladder, a few paces away, disgorges the fugitives one by one. Hand in hand, we insert ourselves into the Indian file, for the space between the carriage and the wall of the tunnel is not wide enough to walk two abreast.

Under our feet, a path has been cleared, but the proliferation is continuing frenziedly under the carriages: a confused mass from which menacing limbs project, tentacles that brush us as we pass by. The cries of the fugitives ahead of us and behind us don't drown out the confused din of the busy lichen; it fills the tunnel with its gigantic and hectic growth. And ever stronger, the roar of the formidable flood of air that lashes our faces, and against which we labor.

Bravely, Aurore follows me; I feel her stumble.

"Am I going too quickly?"

"No, no! Go on—there's someone stepping on my heels."

And in front of us and behind us, in the trotting file, always cries of: "Faster! Get a move on!"

Surpassed, the first two second-class carriages, empty inside, with bloody light-bulbs. Now we're in the dark; in the light of the acetylene lantern, lost in the distance, red stalactites stand out. I stumble over a bush of warm tentacles; it's impossible to advance. Has the lichen suddenly blocked the passage? No—the path veers to the left to take the middle of the rails.

We go on between two confused, bristling walls full of crepitations, which rise up to shoulder-level. Above our heads hang stalactites whose tips brush us; my arms and torso bump into warm spongy tentacles, the little ones giving way elastically, the larger ones shattering…and the man in front of me is no more than five meters away! The crazy living growth is still accelerating.

In a funereal nightmare, I march hopelessly, struggling against the Niagara of air that whips us, with Aurore in tow, mute, breathless, stumbling, through that living grotto, the enchanted wood that is slyly attempting to bar our passage, to blockade us among its fronds, to swallow us…

To reach the station! Where is it? There's no more trace of light visible ahead, not even a signal. Is the tunnel already blocked by the lichen? No, the torrent of air proves that its remains free.

Cries of protest and oaths propagate behind us, getting closer—a furious stampede catches up with us...a violent impact of Aurore's hand against mine...and I fall down with her, shoved sideways by someone overtaking us in the branches of lichen.

A hideous impression, feeling those branches give way beneath one! Of being buried in a swarming mass of dry, warm tentacles, which yield beneath one's hand, slip away beneath one's feet, making me despair of ever being able to get up again. And on the path, the fugitives, who are panicking and howling in fear!

"Aurette! My Aurette!"

Her silence scares me. She has fallen down with a little groan and is still lying there, abandoned. On my knees, leaning over her, I gently palpate her face. She exhales, in a breath: "It's over. I'm going to faint. Leave me—save yourself, beloved!"

The confession fills me with a surge of triumph and desperation. She loves me! At last!

And we're doomed!

Those few seconds of immobility have sufficed for the lichen to invade us with its inexorable dust. Like those of an octopus endowed with intelligent purpose, the dry, warm tentacles have multiplied their garrotte around the recumbent body. Blindly, I tear them away in fistfuls, break them and try to free her from them—but they renew themselves constantly, and others elongate. I'm gripped myself, invaded, entangled in the multiple and disgusting embrace of those slender, dry, warm limbs...

It's over. It's death...

And, in a despairing surge of ecstasy, I deposit on the lips of my beloved the first kiss, which will also be the last...

What does that clamor of deliverance rising up in the distance of the tunnel matter to me? Those people out there, crying their joy at being saved...

Me, I shall die happy.

But what's happening? In addition to those cries, and the decreasing roar of the air-current, which is slackening, there's a kind of enormous silence in the tunnel, an incomprehensible lacuna, the stopping of something. No more crepitations, no more crackling; the enchanted forest of living and aggressive branches has been frozen in immobility, as abruptly as the flick of a switch. And the tentacles over Aurore and me are also frozen…I still remain in their grip, but the octopus seems to have been struck by catalepsy.

Suddenly, I understand the meaning of the cries that are getting closer.

"The current's been cut off! There's no more danger in walking on the electric rails!"

The lichen is paralyzed, for want of electrical nourishment; the pressure of life has paused. We're saved…saved! And Aurore loves me!"

With thrusts of the hips, feet and fists, I detach myself, breaking and tearing away the still-warm tentacles. I free Aurore, take her in my arms and pick her up…

We're alone, the last to remain; everyone else has decamped, saved. And the memory comes back to me of the occasion of our first meeting, in Cassis, when I held her in the same way in Alburtin's automobile. But this time, she loves me!

A wave of heroic vigor carries me way, and I no longer feel the weight of my cherished burden.

Ten paces, and beyond an unsuspected bend in the tunnel, the noisy platform of the station appears, where silhouettes are agitating in the light of acetylene searchlights. Others come to meet us—rescuers…

In my arms, Aurore is reborn, reanimated, and wants to be put on the ground.

"I can walk, Gaston, I assure you. That ridiculous weakness has passed."

I refuse. Triumphant, exultant, I'm about to express my joy at her confession—but a nurse comes up to me and asks:

"Is she injured? Does she need a stretcher?" And when I set Aurore on her feet in order to demonstrate that she has no need of one, the woman supports her by the other arm, and, when we reach the end of the platform, helps her climb the iron ladder.

The nurse, in her solicitude, as if she is reluctant to let go so soon of her last two refugees, insists that we drink a cordial—authentic Green Chartreuse, no less. Nurses, doctors and firemen surround us, and journalists too—but thanks to one of their colleagues, who happened to be in the train during the accident and is dictating an article to them, we're able to escape without difficulty. I even see someone make a gesture of surprise at the sight of Aurore, and take a step toward her...but I was already drawing her toward the stairway.

Once through the barrage of agents and the crowd, having covered 50 meters, we finally breathed again, on the Quai d'Orsay.

Aurore disengaged her arm, which I was still supporting.

"The air is doing me good. Shall we walk for a little while?"

Under the half-defoliated trees of the Quai, between the Seine and the road-traffic, it seemed to me that we had returned to real life. The previous minutes, spent underground, in the power of the Lichen, appeared more phantasmagorical than an opium or hashish dream. If the memory of the intimate form of address and the supreme word "beloved" had not been profoundly engraved in my heart, I would have doubted that I had heard them. In any case, I experienced a certain modesty in recalling them; I felt that she had let me glimpse, by surprise, a forbidden underside of her soul; it had been a mistake; after that confession, she *ought* to have died. Having both survived, there could be no more question of it between us—and yet, since I knew...how could I recover the simple good comradeship that she had imposed on me in the preceding days?

So be it! I could not surrender myself to the triumphant surge that had lifted me up just now, but I could at least, by means of an allusion...

119

She was walking by my side, pensively, sometimes observing me obliquely. She had guessed what was passing through my mind. She was following the course of my sentiments. At the very moment when I was about to speak, she stopped me.

"No, Gaston, my dear friend—not now. No irremediable speeches. Listen to me. Only one thing happened, in the tunnel, when I fell: that you renounced saving yourself in order to attempt to save me, or die with me. I didn't say anything. Nothing. It doesn't count, since we're here, alive. It's necessary that it doesn't count. Nothing should or can be changed between us. Except, the memory of your devotion..."

"Good comrade!" I could not help exclaiming, bitterly.

"You see? You're incapable of restraining yourself, just now. It's necessary, for the future of our friendship, that we don't stay together today. We're going to go our separate ways. Here's a taxi"—and, raising her arm, she stopped the car, which came to a stop alongside the sidewalk—"which will take me back to my hotel. I'll rest, sleep—don't worry about me. In compensation, I'll come to your studio tomorrow morning, for a sitting."

"The last..."

"And then we can talk. But I repeat, in the name of our friendship—no allusion to the forbidden word that the supreme danger extracted from me. Is that agreed?"

"Yes, Aurette. It's agreed."

"Until tomorrow, then, Gaston—9 a.m."

And, briskly saying "Hôtel Métropole" to the driver, she climbed into the cab and slammed the door—but she opened the window in order to give me, in the guise of a better farewell, a frank, honest smile of loyal friendship.

X. Enter Danae

Even in the context of my personal history, the sentiments that agitated me that afternoon and evening are of no
great importance. They only influenced the events of my life
in a negligible fashion, and it's better to pass over them in
silence. Destiny's decision was not modified in the slightest
by the follies that racked my brain during the hours I spent
walking through the city, and then in my studio: by my re-
sentment, in thinking about the separation she had imposed on
me for that exceedingly precious day; by my rebellion against
the obstacles and my resolution to vanquish them, to take Aurore away in order that she need only listen to the voice of her
heart.

During those hours, I believed in the absolute power of
the human will; I forgot my habitual belief that we are in the
hands of the gods: our interior gods and those of events...

And by virtue of an ultimate inconsequence, I went so far
as to reproach Aurore for having made me that confession, for
having let me understand that she loved me, when I was beginning to adapt myself to our reciprocal situation, when I had
resigned myself to being nothing to her but a good comrade...

How the retrospective illusion of passion can transform
and falsify the memory of our own sentiments!

But, I repeat, the moral suffering I endured that day, and
everything I promised myself to say the flowing day, during
the sitting, are of no importance. None of it was realized—
even the last part.

It's better to offer a glimpse of the situation in Paris, that
evening and the following day. That period of my life was, in
general, so intricately linked with the history of the Lichen,
that I cannot recount my memoirs of one without talking about
the other. During the 18 hours in question, however, only the
Lichen had any importance, and I can dispense with any men-

tion of my humble person; I do not routinely mistake myself for the center of the universe.

This time, instead of recording events in the order in which I found out about them, I shall anticipate the next day's news, in order to talk about the facts of communal experience.

The total stoppage of traffic throughout the Metro network, even on lines still unaffected, did honor to the discernment and decisiveness of the directors of the company, who immediately realized the urgency of that measure and dared to institute it at 7 p.m., despite of the consequences for the shareholders.

Admittedly, it required two further incidents and several more "explosions of life" analogous to that of the North-South to make the company understand that it ought not to be stubborn in maintaining the train service. At 5 p.m., the Maillot-Vincennes line was badly contaminated in its turn, the tunnels invade by an ultra-rapid growth of lichen, and two trains were blocked as ours had been, one at the Champs-Élysées station and the other near Bastille—but the current was swiftly cut off and there were no victims. A little later, an obstruction occurred between the Gare du Nord and Les Halles, but the trains were wisely retained in the stations.

From 4 p.m. onwards the tramway authority adopted an identical measure for the tramways, after a dozen incidents analogous to the one we had seen in the Rue de la Pépinière at various points of the network: short-circuit and overheated motor, with or without a consequent fire in the car.

Only then did Parisians understand that it was getting serious. Until then, even in the worst-affected quarters of Paris, everything had been limited to domestic inconveniences, tolerated with more or less good humor—but on learning about that series of accidents, one after another, then the stoppage of the trams and that of the Metro, there was a general stir of emotion.

The users of various tram lines, for want to being able to get home after a day's work by their usual means of transport, fell back on the nearest Metro station, but even though the official cessation of traffic was only ordered an hour late, by 6 p.m., the rains were only running on truncated lines. At the Gare Saint-Lazare, the Invalides and the Quai d'Orsay, people living in the suburbs ran into a complete disruption of electrically-powered train services, by virtue of short-circuits, as on the tramways. The remaining means of transport: buses and taxis, were overwhelmed, and their insufficiency obliged a large number of suburbanites to get back to their dwellings as best they could—and, having got home, left them with the uncertainty of wondering whether the services would be reestablished the following day.

They were not; they could not be. Every new attempt in that direction had provoked, after a short time, a further series of accidents worse than the first. Experiments were evidently made, during the night, and demonstrated that no clean-up operation or disinfection could clear the tunnels or the vehicles of the calamitous spores. It was necessary, until further notice, pending the discovery of an effective means of destruction, for people to resign themselves to the financial losses and the disturbance of social life that the cessation of economic activity would cause. The staff of the tramways and the Metro were put on temporary leave, on half pay; and each employee, being a germ-carrier, contributed—as the passengers had done—to the diffusion of the Lichen throughout Paris and the suburbs.

The contaminated zones were already very extensive. From what I saw before going home at 7 p.m., after wandering for a long time, the great boulevards were affected with a capricious distribution, as occurs in epidemics. Many electric advertising signs were still functioning tolerably well, but some had a number of their lamps "diseased." The luminous display in the Place de l'Opéra was only offering an illegible broken-toothed text. Several cinemas, in addition to the Paramount, had closed. On the terraces of cafés, even those with non-defective lighting, the faces were bleak. In spite of my lack of interest in external things, I sensed an atmosphere of consternation in the city.

And yet, the calamitous consequences of the cosmic invasion were only just beginning!

In my studio, on its easel, the initiated portrait was awaiting the sitting. At 8 a.m., already up and dressed, I started preparing my palette. A good night's sleep—unexpected, certainly, after those hours of torment—had settled my mind and restored equilibrium to my heart, reanimating confidence in the future and am accurate appreciation of the situation. It was only too probable that the game would be difficult to win, but my chances had tripled, increased tenfold, since the previous day. Good comrades, in appearance, so be it, to observe the protocol imposed by Aurore—but her confession of the day before gave me the true temperature of her sentiments. In the struggle that I had undertaken in order to cause her to share my love, she was my secret ally.

However, I feared losing my calmness and renewed confidence by virtue of overmuch reflection before the arrival of my model. When the concierge brought me the post, with the *Excelsior* and the *Matin*, I gladly let the old woman ramble on.

First, she thanked me for my advice; since lighting the candle, the lodge remained tidy and her husband's itches had disappeared. I was curious to know what she thought of events, though. She was informed, since her husband was a power-worker at the Metro, but from her comments I understood that the previous day's accidents were only tragic for those involved in them. Those things could not reach the domicile, so there was no need to worry about them unduly. For Madame Taquet, it was an annoyance mainly because her man had been laid off.

"But it's only for a day or two, of course—otherwise the Company wouldn't have given him half-pay. It'll be fine today, and he'll take advantage of it by going for a stroll. He'll go to the Eiffel Tower with his mates to collect zebi."

"What?"

"Zebi. You haven't see it? They started selling it in the neighborhood yesterday evening, on little carts. It's like jam and grows on the antennae of the Tower. It's said that it tastes

124

good, but I wouldn't want to touch it myself, even so. If Antoine's right, it can all be eaten. Have you eaten any yourself, Monsieur Delvart?"

I remembered young Frémiet's "raspberry jelly."

"My word, yes, Madame Taquet. Why not? One must take the benefits of science along with its inconveniences. If the police haven't forbidden its collection, that's because zebi is harmless."

The worthy woman shook her head, unconvinced. "That's not right—I have a suspicion that it can't be healthy."

Parenthetically, I ought to say right away that the repugnance manifested by my concierge was manifested at first by many people of the lower classes, who ought rather have welcomed as celestial manna that edible variety of the Xenobiota, a cheap foodstuff that compensated to a small extent for the inconveniences of other forms of the Lichen. The little handcarts that I saw later that day, in my neighborhood and elsewhere, attracted crowds of curious housewives to the gelatinous ruby-red accumulations quivering in the tin-plate buckets, but few yielded to the solicitations of the sellers and the placards: *Top quality raspberry zebi. Eiffel Tower jam. More nourishing than beef, according to the analyses of the Laboratory for the Suppression of Alimentary Fraud. 2 francs a kilo, 25 centimes a quart.*

Had the said Laboratory given its authorization, as the Crainquebilles[25] claimed? Or were the police turning a blind eye, during those days of relaxation? I don't know—but the fact is that the newspapers declared the substance to be harmless to the consumer, if not genuinely nutritious. From time to time, a housewife held out a faïence bowl or a jam-jar, which the merchant filled on the scales with a wooden spatula for stirring sauces, but business was slack. The low price of the product caused some disdain in the beginning, so long as its

---

[25] A name borrowed from a classic short story by Anatole France, which became generic.

collection was free, but once a syndicate had monopolized it the price rose and zebi became the object of a popular fad.

"And anyway, it can't be kept," Madame Taquet concluded. "You have to eat it fresh or it turns, like milk."

When the concierge had gone, I cast an eye over the papers. I've already mentioned the complete stoppage of services on the Metro and the tramways. On the electric railways, État, Orléans, complete disorganization and traffic from the capital virtually suspended. At the P.L.M., numerous aerial telegraphic wires had been broken between Paris and Villeneuve-Saint-Georges by a surcharge of the Lichen. The Midi expresses were running two hours late, at present, and down south between Marseilles and Nice, in the zone invaded by the Xenobiota, the disruption was even worse.

I had just read that the Conseil des Ministres was meeting to discuss the situation, and that the new parliamentary sessions had been brought forward to October 25, when the tubular carillon standing in for a bell at the door of my apartment rang.

Aurore already? A quarter of an hour early? I ran...

It was Luce de Ricourt, with her brother.

I must have let them see my lack of enthusiasm with regard to that visit, as untimely as it was unexpected, and Luce seemed to take a malign pleasure in it.

"You weren't expecting us, eh, my dear Tonton? Are we disturbing you?"

"Not at all. Come in. What brings you to Paris? I thought you were in Cassis until October 30."

It was only then that I noticed that Géo was carrying a voluminous parcel. He gave it to me.

"Your canvases, which the manager of the Hôtel Cendrillon entrusted me with the responsibility of bringing to you, at my request. I thought that more prudent than letting him send them."

My irritation eased before this service, rendered with such good grace, and I bore the intrusion with greater indulgence. Meanwhile, Luce had gone ahead into my studio like a gust of wind. She came to a halt in front of the recently-begun portrait.

"Hey, Tonton! That's the 'pretty young astronaut,' as Messieurs the journalists put it. And I'll wager that you're waiting for her, for a sitting?"

"Yes, but..."

"But now that we're here, you won't throw us out? Thanks. We'll leave you soon—but before then, do you know what you ought to do if you were kind? Introduce us to Mademoiselle Lescure. Ever since I saw her in the distance in Cassis, on your arm, I've been dying to make her acquaintance."

Impossible to refuse. While dreading some trap on Luce's part, whose mild tone was uncharacteristic, I resigned myself to introducing her to the person who must appear to her to be a triumphant rival, and against who she must be nurturing a solid antagonism.

At the precise moment when I acquiesced, someone else rang: Aurore.

In spite of Luce's affected effusions, there was a moment of embarrassment. To put an end to it, Géo explained their exodus from Cassis. On the very day of my own departure, October 17, the lights of the hotel had begun to manifest contamination. On the 18th, there had been no bread, for half a day, the bakers of Cassis all using electric kneading-machines whose motors had mysteriously broken down. Moreover, Madame de Ricourt had a pathological horror of fleas, and after having scratched herself two nights running, her complaints and lamentations had forced the decision to return...for the newspapers were only advertizing the invasion of Marseilles by the Lichen as yet, and they imagined that Paris was unaffected. Having left on the morning of October 19, they had arrived yesterday afternoon, Luce taking turns with her brother at the steering-wheel. They would have made the journey in considerably less time, had it not been for repeated breakdowns due to the formation of lichen on the headlights.

"It was hardly worth the trouble of changing abodes!" Géo concluded. "But you need to speak to our friend the doctor. The nurses must have talked—Madame Alburtin too, no doubt—and the Cassidians quickly held him responsible for the perturbations of the electric lighting and other accidents. The attitude of the population had become so hostile, by the time we left, that the brave fellow hardly dared show his face any longer. People were refusing to work for him; he had all the difficulty in the world finding someone to pack up and transport Mademoiselle Lescure's apparatus to the station."

"Poor Doctor!" murmured Aurore. "When was that?"

"The evening of our departure, I think—the 18th. The crates ought to be waiting for you now at the Gare de Paris. Anyway, the damage was done; Cassis no longer had a single unaffected house. The hoteliers are furious and heartbroken; the foreigners have all left for La Ciotat, Bandol, Saint-Cyr…and it was only after Chalons that we realized that we'd find the same thing in Paris. Just as bad—and worse! For what was only a petty inconvenience down there, in a village, risks turning into a catastrophe in a big city, where everything depends on electricity."

"In sum, dear Mademoiselle," Luce interjected, with a perfidiously affable and pitying expression, "Professor Nathan was spot on—you've made a sad gift to humanity there. We were already beginning to suspect, since the War, that the discoveries of science aren't all good…but tell me that you've brought back lunar gold by way of compensation."

Aurore shivered. "Indeed, I ought to be considered as a criminal…"

Was that allusion to lunar gold an involuntary gaffe on Luce's part, or a spiteful remark? Given the haste with which Géo interrupted, I inclined to the second hypothesis. Alburtin must have told them that the Rocket hadn't reached the Moon.

"Personally," said Géo, "I don't think public opinion will be tempted to accuse you, Mademoiselle. People do know, thanks to the revelations of the Press, that the initial seed-germs of the Lichen were brought back from space by Mademoiselle Lescure's Rocket, but the great majority of average Frenchmen don't 'realize' the connection. For the greater number, the cosmozoans are an impersonal myth, one of those book-learned givens that interest people without them thinking too much about it, as with so many articles popularizing science—and even those who remember something about them only retain the memory parrot-fashion.

"All things considered, it's fortunate that Monsieur Nathan's fine article has been little understood by the masses. People believe in cosmozoans as an act of faith, but they remain devoid of any measurable relationship with the Lichen, a material fact that they only know as a natural calamity, similar to an epidemic, a food or an earthquake. The Lichen that's blocking the tunnels of the Metro and the gracious astronaut they've seen on the screen or in portraits, can't have anything in common, in popular opinion. Only educated people like us succeed in establishing a causal relationship between the abundance of Xenobiota and the meteorites harvested by Mademoiselle Lescure, but they couldn't possibly think of holding you 'responsible'—and we know better than anyone else how futile it would be to hold it against you."

"You talk like a book, Géo," said his sister, deadpan.

Aurore looked at her defender gratefully. "That's reassuring, Monsieur. I feared hostile manifestations when my father and Lendor J. Cheyne arrive this afternoon."

Luce had been waiting for that. "My dear Mademoiselle, you must introduce me to Monsieur Lendor J. Cheyne, whom I'd very much like to meet. His American speculation on...lunar gold"—her tone was as if she had added: *which doesn't exist*—is utterly intoxicating. What time, then, is he arriving at Le Bourget?"

"Three o'clock."

"You're willing to do it, aren't you?" Luce insisted.

"Yes—but how?"

Géo cut in. "There's one thing we can do. My boss, Hénault-Feltrie, who has just phoned me, will be at Le Bourget this afternoon to welcome Messieurs Cheyne and Lescure on behalf of French Astronautics. I'll take you in my turbo, and even with the four of you, we'll still have room to bring them back to Paris. In spite of everything, that will be doing them a favor, for I don't think the Parisians, without being precisely hostile, will have a warm welcome reserved for them..."

I hoped that Aurore would turn the plan down, but she nodded her head silently—and Géo concluded: "That's settled, then. And we'll have lunch together."

I hoped to see the intruders leave, which would leave us alone, but Luce hadn't finished. She wanted to choose a few canvases from the "coves" her brother had brought back. She had a coup on the Bourse under way, which was certain of success, and was in haste to invest some money.

The discussion of the choice of paintings took place with Aurore's collaboration. She took so much pleasure in it that I suspected that she was glad of the opportunity that deprived her of a tête-à-tête with me, in spite of the promise she had made the day before. She wasn't sure of her good comrade!

When the interminable discussions were concluded, by the purchase of four canvases—for which Luce paid me by check—it was half past eleven. Aurore and Luce seemed to be on the best of terms. That annoyed me, but I experienced nevertheless a secret pleasure in considering them thus, in confrontation with one another.

Returning to her speculative projects, Luce said to her new friend: "I've taken a position on electrics going down and a rise in oil...on account, unfortunately. If I had a few hundred thousand available, I'd buy up all the oil shares on the market. You don't keep track of the Bourse? Nor you, of course, Tonton? Well, Royal Dutch went up to 400 francs yesterday, and Shell went past 700."

As she made these wretchedly venal statements, Luce became excited, taking on the supreme and complete expression of her beauty. More than ever, I understood why I had been taken in by her for so long; I detested the baseness of what she was saying, the sentiments within her...at the exact

130

moment, when the resplendence of her physiognomy and expression, forced me to admire her, with an artist's emotion: Titian's red-haired Danae beneath the shower of gold!

And Aurore, as disdainful as me of those contingencies, took refuge in a politely indifferent smile...Aurore, whose ingenious, supple and simple grace enchanted all the antennae of my humanity!

That little game of contrasts, savored in secret, helped me again, a little later, to put on a good face for our hosts during lunch...and then again, can a painter be surly toward the collector who has just bought four of his canvases, at a good price, and whose check is in his wallet?

XI. At Le Bourget

The "turbo," flat out on the Route de Flandre. An ingrate suburb of country inns. A Sunday crows on the pathways. Zebi-carts surrounded by samplers. No trams. Taxis and buses trailing their raged goiters of lichen. And since the Porte de La Villette, so many cars broken down by the roadside!

"Failed spark-plugs, all that," Géo tells us, with a dexterous twitch of the steering wheel to avoid a Cadillac that had just come to a stop in front of us, without signaling. "Personally, I've got a funnel that Alburtin gave me—to sprinkle the spark-plugs with salt water...sodium chloride...that slows down the growth of the lichen and renders breakdowns less frequent. It's only a palliative, though. You'll see—cars will end up blocked, like everything else...and aircraft too.

Between the enormous grey hangars that we pass on the left, the first glimpse of the leprous plain of the airport, where planes, near and distant, are taxiing along the ground, or landing with the graceful agility of ballerinas. An enormous crowd is piled up along the railings. At the gates, Republican Guardsmen on foot or on horseback. It's necessary to stop, to give the password.

Having parked the turbo, Géo guides us toward the Aero-Club pavilion. The cock shows ten to three. A loudspeaker announces that the aircraft carrying Messieurs Oswald Lescure and Lendor Cheyne has just flown over Mantes and will be here in a quarter of an hour.

In front of the pavilion, two groups are waiting. One, consisting of about 20 journalists, cameramen and photographers—almost all of them young men in soft hats and trench-coats—seems sharp and purposive. The other comprises a dozen earnest gentlemen, almost all old, sporting red ribbons or rosettes in their buttonholes, and two or three ladies, similarly decorated.

"My boss, Monsieur Hénault-Feltrie," Géo announced in a low voice, directing Aurore's gaze toward a solid quadragenarian who is chatting with Professor Nathan. "Under what name shall I introduce you, Mademoiselle?"

My companion straightened up. "Under my real name, Monsieur!" Aside, she finishes: "Enough lies!"

At the name of Aurore Lescure, Monsieur Hénault-Feltie, celebrated aviator and president of the Ligue Astronautique de France, bowed mutely and, as if getting ready to ask an embarrassing and delicate question, hesitated for two seconds with a smile in which I thought I can detect skepticism and irony—a smile that humiliated me, reminding me of a scrap of an article that I had read, signed Hénault-Feltrie, demonstrating the impossibility of reaching the Moon in Rocket MG-17, especially in five hours.

Monsieur Nathan, in his turn, greeted my companion, and said, in a prim tone: "I was expecting you yesterday, Mademoiselle."

Relieved by the diversion, she told him the story of our Metro accident, while Luce took possession of Monsieur Hénult-Feltrie.

Detaching themselves from their group, however, journalists were dispersing themselves around us, all ears. Objective lenses were aimed at Aurore and Nathan, pens blackening notebooks or pads—and on their faces, half-smiles, sly and conspiratorial. In one of the reporters, I thought I recognized the fake *valet de chambre* from the Hôtel Métropole, who was whispering in his neighbor's ear while looking at me. The latter approached me and said to me straight out: "Monsieur Gaston Delvart? Would you like to give me a few words about yourself...and Mademoiselle Aurore Lescure, whom you've been escorting in Paris?"

Should I get upset? No—better to improvise a few vague banalities...

The metallic drone of the loudspeaker announced that the plane from Cherbourg was in sight. Two large biplanes, one red and one blue, were converging on the airport, the red one from an English Company—the London mail—the blue one, ours.

The blue airplane touched down, taxied, came to a stop less than 30 meters away. The mechanics ran forward, wedging the wheels and positioning the stepladder. Almost intermingled now with the crowd of reporters, our group remained in suspense.

At the door of the passenger-cabin an unmistakable Yank appears, bare-headed, his physiognomy reminiscent of the famous Lindbergh, but with features less frank and less open, without that juvenile charm. Having disembarked, he helped a white-haired old man with a waxy complexion and the luminous eyes of genius to get down.

"Father!" cried Aurore—and heedless of protocol, she ran to meet him, amid the *Hip, Hip, Hurrahs!* launched by the most boyish of the journalists, amid the clicking of shutters and the rattle of "rolling" cameras capturing the passionate embrace of father and daughter...and then the ostentatious handshake, vigorous but devoid of affection, that she exchanged with her fiancé.

A flurry of introductions, names thrown out by Hénault-Feltrie, Nathan, Géo: Madame Camille Flammarion,[26] Madame Curie, Mademoiselle de Ricourt, Monsieur Lequin of the Air Ministry, Monsieur Dusautoy, President of the Press Syndicate...

The reporters, insinuating themselves between shoulders, added to the hubbub and the confusion. In the distance, against the railings of the enclosure, the crazed crowd howled...cheers or boos; it was impossible to tell. People only began to greet

---

[26] Camille Flammarion died in 1925, but it is entirely appropriate that his widow should be present on this hypothetical occasion to represent him. Whether or not Varlet was a member of the French "rocket society," he would undoubtedly have met Flammarion and had probably visited his telescope at Juvisy.

one another once assembled in the Aero-Club Hall, around glasses of champagne.

Official toasts: welcome to French soil the valiant champions of American astronautics…everyone, in turn, added his petty couplet.

The phlegmatic Lendor J. Cheyne, bowed like an automaton and emptied his glass every time. He excused himself, in an implausible gibberish, for "not speaking French very well" and handed the floor to Oswald Lescure, who thanked everyone collectively and individually with a few phrases learned by heart. He was not very fluent in French either. Then the individual conversations began, laying bait for the advantage of the journalists, some of whom had sneaked into the room.

Aurore had taken her father's arm affectionately. He was radiant, gazing at her fondly. She undertook to introduce me once again to him and to Cheyne, making me almost her savior on the occasion of the accident, which she described. But I did not know a word of English—she translated for me as she went along—and that was doubtless one of the reasons that alienated me from their good graces. In spite of the old man's accolade and protestations of gratitude—also translated, which rendered them slightly ridiculous—and the Yank's pump-like handshake, I sensed immediately that they were not sincere. I had indeed been Aurore's savior; I had captured her trust and amity—and for the father, as for the fiancé, I was also the enemy, capable of getting in the way of the jealous affection of the former and the plans and interests of the latter. There were unmistakable premonitions in that. Aurore must have sensed it too, for she darted a pained and disappointed glance at me.

Luce, similarly introduced into the intimates' corner, was considering Lendor J. Cheyne with an evident admiration. To begin with, he confronted her with his traditional insensitivity to feminine homage, but he melted when she began speaking to him in English at close range, in a voice that was contained but warm. All I could understand was the word "businessman."

How I regretted my ignorance! Judging by the Yank's interested expression and Luce's volubility and conquering smile, I divined that he was saying important things within range of my hearing—but I did not suspect the importance that the association of those two individuals was to have on my own future. Luce was resplendent in the perfection of the beauty that came upon her when she talked about business. The Yank manifested a slight anxiety on seeing a reporter prowling around them with ears pricked, who apparently understood English, and they both began to talk in whispers. At one moment, Cheyne started in surprise, but after a few tense seconds, a reply from Luce caused his face to clear, and he grimaced a mute smile, as if he were half-admitting some enormous joke.

Aurore, who allowed her father to become absorbed in an animated conversation with Nathan, was alone, and, like me, close enough to hear. She was listening, her nostrils flaring in disdain. A little later, she filled me in: Luce had just demonstrated to the Yank that she was as "American" as he was, by congratulating him on his lunar hoax...

Meanwhile, the officials had disappeared one by one, as had the journalists, with the exception of one last reporter, who was pursuing me doggedly. No one else was left but Nathan, who was deep in conversation with Aurore and her father. Cheyne had just accepted the offer mode by Géo to take them in his car, when an individual came forward whose entrance had passed unobserved.

"Aha! Monsieur Guyon!" whispered my reporter. And, seeing that the name meant nothing to me, he added: "The deputy director of the Sûreté." And he fell silent, waiting for the policeman to speak.

Monsieur Guyon made no attempt at secrecy He had only waited until now in order to express himself more at his ease. Addressing Aurore and the two Americans, he gave his name and title, and then said:

"Have no fear, Mademoiselle, we've known for two days who you are and where you were staying; I only regret that you did not have more confidence in the courtesy of our procedures. Your passport, if you would care to entrust it to me, will be returned to you this evening, properly authorized, at your hotel.

"And you, Messieurs, I regret to inform you that, by order of the Ministry, you have been placed under our surveillance. The government of the Republic does not intend to hold you criminally responsible for the calamitous accidents caused by the Lichen, and ultimately resulting from the landing in France of the apparatus constructed and launched by you. Nor will any impediment be placed on your financial activities, so long as they remain within the limits of legality—but an absolutely prohibition has been placed on your carrying out, at the Champ-de-Mars or elsewhere, the astronautical trials whose imminent exhibition you have announced. To facilitate your respect for that ordinance, I warn you that Rocket MG-17—which is to say, the crates that contain it, sent from Cassis by Dr. Alburtin, have been seized at the Gare de Paris-P.L.M. and placed in sequestration. They will be at your disposal again on the day when you leave French territory. Mademoiselle, Messieurs, I have the honor..."

Although he spoke French badly, the Yank obviously understood it better. He replied to the policeman with a mocking bow, while Aurore and her father seemed reconciled to the inevitability, and gave a definitive acquiescence to Nathan, who seemed triumphant. I became anxious. What decision had provoked this measure on the part of the police?

The English sentence that Cheyne addressed to the father and daughter between two mastications of his chewing gum had a tone of cold humor, and I remained in doubt as to whether he meant what he said even after the obliging Géo had given me a translation.

"He said: 'Come on—after this, the wisest thing to do is to return to America,'"

Nevertheless, the Yank allowed himself to be guided to the turbo, in which we took our places. Nathan accompanied Aurore and Oswald as far as the car-door, and left them with a last: "Until this evening, then," in order to return to his own car.

Géo gripped the steering-wheel as if he were holding our fate in his hands and beneath the acceleration-pedal. At the airport gate, however, the crowd, which had been compact ten minutes earlier, shouting and leaping up and down on the roofs of the hangars, was reduced to a single line of obstinate curiosity-seekers, and the Republican Guardsmen watching the entrances did not have to protect our flight against the slightest attempted hostility. Had the demonstration taken place prematurely, during the passage of some automobile carrying official personages, mistaken for the Americans? Or had the consumption at the little carts of the cheap and succulent zebi assuaged the sentiments of the laid-off Metro and tramway employees? I don't know. In any case, there were confused cheers, saluting indistinct names—I thought I heard "Hurrah for Madame Curie!" addressed to Luce or Aurore—which our car received at the exit, as it plunged through the gateway and headed for Paris at top speed along the Route de Flandre.

Fifteen minutes later, after only one brief breakdown and without ten words being pronounced inside the car, it stopped in front of the Hôtel Métropole. Aurore, her father and Cheyne got out, and the last—named, with a "Thank you very much" and a conclusive handshake, demonstrated his firm desire not to be escorted any further. Aurore was just able to whisper to me: "I'll try to come to your apartment tomorrow; in any case, phone me at 9 a.m. before I go out."

I was about to get out too, but Géo, before returning with Luce to the Rue Legendre, undertook to drive me as far as the bottom of the Caulaincourt steps. During the brief journey, I had the further benefit of Luce's reflections.

"You're a pet, Tonton, for introducing me to your model and her fiancé. I'll pay you back. What a marvelous fellow that Cheyne is! A true American, that one, not like that old walnut Oswald, and quite different from his fiancée. With him and Rosenkrantz, we're going to do some first-rate business. All the same, that was a reception that clearly demonstrates the eternal foolishness of the French. Why be so chivalrous? If this had happened in America and the rocket-launchers had been French, you can be sure that they'd have been made to pay the injured parties—them or the government—a few million dollars in damages."

XII. France Under National Proscription

I spent a miserable evening in my studio, not wanting to go any further than the small local restaurant where I put on an appearance of dining. I wallowed in melancholy, while sorting out various drawings, sketches and studies. Certainly, I understood that Aurore felt bound to spend at least that first evening with her father, and that neither he nor Cheyne had the slightest desire for my presence, but would that situation last? Had I been virtually eliminated from Aurore's life, even if she remained in Paris for a little longer? What if Cheyne put his idea of returning to America into practice? Would I have any further opportunity to talk to her? To profit from her confession? Did she regret that confession to the extent of avoiding me as much as possible from now on?

After prolonged insomnia, during which I turned various plans over and over in my mind, the least crazy of which, again, was to follow the trio to America. I ended up falling into an agitated sleep filled with ominous dreams.

Telephone her at 9 a.m.? But waiting at home for that time to come seemed intolerable as soon as I got up at dawn. As soon as I was dressed, at 7:30, I went downstairs. As I passed the lodge I saw Monsieur and Madame Taquet at table, with two plates of the quivering ruby jelly of the edible lichen: the zebi brought back the previous day by the power-worker on leave, from is excursion to the Eiffel Tower. The portion that Madame was consuming by the spoonful was no less copious than her husband's.

Under the pretext of collecting my post, I put my head around the door.

"No letters for me?"

"No, Monsieur Delvart. The postman hasn't been past yet—but here's your *Matin*."

I affected envy of her plate. "*Bon appetit!*" I laughed discreetly. "So it's not so bad, the zebi? You've come round, I see."

"You have to take advantage of it while it's fresh, Monsieur Delvart; it will go off between now and this evening, and my husband brought back nearly a kilo. That saves money in a household...especially at present, while he's only on half-pay...and who knows how long it will last?"

Without bothering to ask what might not last—the savings, the zebi, the half-pay or the present situation—I made myself scarce.

At the shop forming the corner of the Rue du Mont-Cenis and the Rue du Chevalier-de-la-Barre I bought a couple more newspapers and, going past Sacré-Coeur, went to install myself on a bench on the edge of the square, where a few of the local children were already playing, before the giant panorama of Paris...

FRANCE PUT UNDER A BAN BY AMERICA

My heart beat hopefully...for in that case, there was no longer any question for Cheyne or Aurore of crossing the Atlantic. I read the article in the *Journal* avidly.

The grave peril created in Paris and in France by the brutal extension of the Xenobiota has incited America to take precautionary measures against a possible contagion of the scourge by means of an excessive and unprecedented protectionism. A decree by President Hogg, issued from the White House yesterday and taking executive effect from today, October 22, suspends maritime communication with France. Under the terms of his decree, every liner, cargo-vessel or other ship originating from a port in France or having, in the course of its voyage, called at a French port, will be forbidden access to American ports. As a direct consequence, the only vessels, passenger-carrying or otherwise, authorized to leave America for destinations in France are those making return journeys. The Prohibition police, with its special armed fleet, will be responsible for the strict enforcement of the decree.

This decree, which so manifestly violates the rules in international law, and against which the head of the French government is raising a vigorous protest, reveals an astonishing alarm in a population as phlegmatic and well-balanced at that of the United States. It appears that the cold reasoning that is severing communications with France in this manner is clearly abusive. In the course of a five- or six-day crossing, the presence of the Lichen aboard the most rapid transatlantic vessel would have time to become evident. In consequence, it would be sufficient to establish a special sanitary inspection on arrival at an American port...

Among other consequences of this draconian measure, which will have a seriously injurious effect on our shipping companies and our great transatlantic ports of Brest, Cherbourg and Le Havre, as well as tourism, it is necessary to note that exports of American oil to France will cease at a stroke, since the tankers, if they cross the Atlantic and disembark their merchandise here, will be rendered incapable of returning to their home ports. There is no need to elaborate on the unfortunate results that this suppression of American oil imports might have at this point in time, when our need for that substance is increasing considerably, in consequence of the damage suffered by electrical lighting...

Desirous, on the other hand, of avoiding in the United States any risk of an adventure similar to that to which France is subject, President Hogg, by means of a complementary decree, has forbidden the preparation of any astronautical flight, the initiation or fabrication of any engine capable of crossing the limits of the terrestrial atmosphere. As a first application, this decree requires the confiscation of the laboratory of Monsieur Oswald Lescure and the astronautical factories of the Moon Gold Company, with the material that they contain. "All the gold nuggets that an expedition of this sort might bring back from the Moon," declares M. Hogg, among the considerations that motivated his decree, "will not compensate for the danger of possible causes of disturbance for our civilization being brought back from interplanetary space at the same *time, of which the scourge of the Xenobiota in France suffices to give us a redoubtable idea...and, in addition to the Xenobiota, who knows what other unknown and even more terrible perils interplanetary space might hold in store for us?"*

Let us hasten to add that similar prudent measures have also been taken in France. The American astronauts will not find here the facilities that are henceforth refused to them in their own country to realize their deadly experiments. An identical prohibition has been formulated, and communicated on their arrival at Le Bourget to Messrs. Oswald Lescure and Lendor J. Cheyne by Monsieur Guyon, deputy director of the Sûreté...

The example of the United States has been immediately followed by a number of other countries, the list of which is increasing hourly. At the time of going to press, we can cite, as having cut off all material communications with France: Canada, the Republic of Cuba, Mexico, England, Germany, Holland, Italy, Spain, Greece... With the exception of Belgium, which has declared itself associated with our destiny, the interdiction will soon extend to the entire planet. France is being treated as lepers and plague-carriers were in the Middle Ages! An excommunication such as the Church fulminated against heretics and schismatics! It is impossible to estimate, even approximately, the losses that this unprecedented situation will cause to commerce, industry and national life.

My personal concerns were dissolved in a vaster anguish, overriding my simple egotism. I let my gaze wander over Paris, which extended its giant panorama at my feet—the Paris thus isolated, along with France, from the rest of humankind...

Beneath the autumnal sun, jaundiced by the mist, that province of houses and edifices manifested its usual appearance...yes, except for the almost complete absence of smoke from the railway stations: the Gares du Nord et de l'Est to my left, the P.L.M. and the Gare d' Orléans further away toward the Seine, and to my right, much closer, the lines of the Gare Saint-Lazare.

I resumed my exploration of the papers. Ah, indeed, the railway stations: *Numerous cancellations of trains,*

The intensive exploitation of railways, as everyone knows, was only rendered possible by the complementary invention of the electric telegraph; conversely, even with the rolling-stock and the tracks in a good state, any impediment to the functioning of the telegraph and electrical signaling implies the impossibility of continuing the regular exploitation. The rupture of telegraph wires and signal controls having multiplied over the last two days on non-electrified networks, the companies have been forced to institute an enormous reduction in the number of trains, carrying passengers as well as goods, the maximum speed of which has been limited to 20 kilometers an hour.

We are, therefore, almost returned to the time of diligences—with the aggravation that we do not even have the resource of using those vanished antique rattletraps. Road transport services designed to increase or supplement the suburban services are still too embryonic to make up for the deficiency of the railways.

And for how many more days will automobiles still be usable? The failure of spark-plugs is multiplying with increasing frequency, and unshielded magnetos are falling victim to irreparable damage...

THE XENOBIOTIC INVASION INCREASES.

The secondary nucleus of infection, with Marseilles at its center, in which the situation is comparable to that in Paris, is gaining ground rapidly along the P.L.M. line. All the coastal towns between Marseilles and Toulon are affected. Further away, the appearance of the Lichen was observed yesterday in Saint-Raphael and Cannes. In the south-eastern region, Aix and Avignon have also been affected, as has Bordeaux in the south-west and Lille and Rouen in the north.

Yes, but what about Paris? On the preceding page, three columns of details of the various accidents, among others, some of a new kind "provoked by a variety of Lichen that eats away insulation and corrodes the metal of electrical conductors"—by virtue of which a number of short-circuits have occurred all over the place, in the open air and in subterranean channels: magnetos, dynamos and motors protected by iron grilles, wire and cables of every sort put out of service. Nothing astonishing in my encountering such sub-headings as *DAMAGE TO ELECTRICAL SUBSTATIONS, DAMAGE TO TELEGRAPHIC AND TELEPHONIC CENTERS*, but I won't read all that. Let's move on.

To summarize the situation in Paris, in addition to the 6th, 7th, 8th, 9th and 17th arrondissements, contaminated since the beginning of the invasion and where its progress has been less serious, the dissemination has reached the neighboring arrondisssements to varying degrees. At every moment, new nuclei of Lichen are observed in quarters not yet affected. One may consider, at present, the entire center of Paris condemned to imminent contamination. On the periphery, the 13th, 15th, 16th, 19th and 20th appear to be mostly spared.

The closest suburbs are affected, especially to the north and the south-west. In addition, nuclei have been found at Argenteuil, Taverny, Bessancourt, Enghien, Villeneuve-Saint-Georges, etc. Saint-Denis, contaminated since the 19th, is almost as badly affected as the capital. Versailles is also contaminated, to a lesser degrees.

The suddenness of the invasion of the Lichen and the abruptness of its development have surprised the public Authorities, and thus far, instead of immediate collective action, they have only taken fragmentary and belated action. If the electricity supplies have been cut off in the worst-affected buildings in Paris, it is only to the concierges or proprietors that we owe it, not the Company. The only general measure that has yet been taken by the Préfecture de la Seine has been to prohibit as from today the functioning of luminous advertising and informational displays.

In a few arrondissements, the Commissaires de Police are demanding notification of buildings affected by the Lichen, as with a contagious disease, which will be subjected to disin-

145

fection by the municipal services. Alternatively, the streets are being sprayed with solutions of bleach or salt-water, which kill the Xenobiotic spores. All of that, however, cannot have any great effect. Paris has fallen victim to the Lichen, as to a serious disease. If it is to be cured, it is necessary to take energetic and radical measures.

In some of the contaminated towns in the vicinity of Paris, and in the Midi at Toulon, local mayors have taken the step of forbidding the use of electric current in their commune, and that initiative has every chance of protecting the localities in question against the diffusion of the Lichen. The question of following their example to preserve the parts of Paris not yet contaminated, by forbidding the distribution of electric current throughout Paris and the département of the Seine is presently being discussed in the Conseil des Ministres.

Until this decisive measure has been taken by the President of the Conseil, nothing will have been done to safeguard Parisians. It is sufficient for a single lamp to remain lit in a single building to provoke the formation of the lichen around the light-bulb in question and the diffusion of the spores within and without the building by the inhabitants, who transmit it on their persons—but the Conseil dares not take the responsibility for issuing such a decree upon itself, which will be submitted to a vote of the Chambres, convened for October 25—three says hence.

What will be the probably duration of the scourge? Ought we to wait to see it decrease and cease of its own accord, as certain optimists have hastened to declare? The disappearance of the giant forms, growing in an ultra-rapid fashion, observed in the tunnels of the Metro is primarily due to the cessation of traffic and the current; it does not necessarily signify that the pressure of life is decreasing and that we no longer have to fear the emergence and proliferation of analogous or even more harmful forms in other electrical fields. Nevertheless, the eminent Professor Nathan is of the opinion that hope is authorized in that direction. In addition, it has been observed in the refrigerated chambers of Les Halles that

146

the lighted bulbs remain entirely clear of lichen, although the remainder of the building is badly contaminated. This observation confirms M. Nathan's assertion, in his article of the day before yesterday, that the spores cannot withstand a temperature below zero. This vulnerability of the enemy gives us, in any case, the certainty of being rid of it at the first frost...

Paris under snow? My painter's eye caresses the sovereign panorama that I discover from the height of the square. Instead of those glistening windows, those scintillations of gilded cupolas, that tenderly polychromatic Paris whose shades are delicately meting into one another in the autumnal morning, I evoke the infinite whiteness of snow, with blue shadows beneath an antimony sky.

I shrug my shoulders, pushing away the heap of crumpled pages. The first frost! And it's only October 22. Another month, perhaps two. That's a long way off...

Suddenly, I cease to be interested in events; I shake myself like a dog coming out of the water, casting off social consciousness in order to free my egotistical self: Gaston Delvart, the painter in love with the angelic astronaut.

Quarter to nine. Time to phone her. Abandoning all my newspapers to the old woman with the shopping-basket who is eyeing them covetously, having come to sit down on the other end of my bench, I return to a shop on the Rue de Mont-Cenis, where there's a telephone,

"Hello? Yes, Aurette here. Bonjour, my dear friend! Meet me? Alas, no—impossible for today. My father...I can't leave him. We have to work furiously: all the material to gather, transport to plan and organize. He has accepted on his own behalf and mine the proposals of Monsieur Nathan. No, my dear, we're not leaving! The borders are closed to us—don't worry, we'll have all the time in the world to see one another again. So, Lendor, in view of the prohibition on astronautical experiments, has set us at liberty, temporarily—he's going to form a cartel, I believe, with Moon Gold at its center; thanks to Mademoiselle Luce, he's due to meet the great businessman Rosenkrantz today...

147

"To get back to Monsieur Nathan, he had a long conversation with my father yesterday evening, and is so smitten with some of his views that he immediately offered us a fine situation: director of a technical research service concerning the Lichen. My father has accepted, and as he can't dispense with me, because I'm familiar with his working methods, he's contrived to have me named as joint director. See you this evening, you say, my friend? I'm afraid that I'm tied up...

"Well, if I find that I have an hour free during the evening, I'll send you a telegram—for you won't be able to phone me; I'll be away from the hotel all day...pardon me, my father is demanding me. Excuse me my dear Gaston...

"What? You think that I'm not...but yes! I have a great deal, a great deal of friendship for you...too much...no, no, shh! Not now. *Au revoir*. Perhaps this evening—or, if not, tomorrow..."

Certainly, I'm not very content; at first, I'm even furious—but after all, with the laboratory to install—where, though? she didn't tell me—I have to concede that she'll be busy and can't see me today.

And she hung up so quickly, damn it, that I wasn't able to ask her another question, which is going to torment me all day: since the association between Cheyne and her father is broken, have the interests that, as I understood it, led Cheyne to want to marry her, ceased to exist in consequence? Is the fundamental obstacle between us about to be lifted, sooner or later? If only she'd told me that clearly. I wasn't even able to make out from her tone what mood she was in. Joyful, or merely busy? These receivers distort the nuances of the voice so much!

Even without certainty, there appears to be a high probability of that. And on top of that hope, to enable me to be patient, I know that nothing is lost—on the contrary, that she isn't leaving. If I don't see her today, I'll see her tomorrow, and I can, at any rate, continue the battle, trying to secure the victory of my love.

In the meantime, in order not to think too much about myself, to act...let's see. To begin with, look after my material interests, utterly neglected since my return to Paris. I'm short of money. Deposit Luce's check at the Société Générale in the Boulevard Haussmann. From there, left bank, visit my dealers: Roussel, Lefort; collect my photos from my uncle's place...

Bus AM, which I went unhurriedly to catch at the corner of Rue Damrément, was packed with singularly bad-tempered people. I quickly ceased to be astonished, for we had no sooner reached the Pont Caulaincourt than an unscheduled stop immobilized us.

"That's the fifth breakdown since the terminus!" grumbled the conductor, leaping down to go and help his colleague, the driver.

A spark-plug failure, soon repaired—but which testified to the precarious state of the last means of surface transport. Chlorinated water was becoming impotent as a preservative against the Xenobiota. On the Pont Caulaincourt, another stoppage...ditto on the Rue d'Amsterdam. Five or six passengers, including me, got off to continue on foot.

At the Gare Saint-Lazare, I was curious enough to dart a glance into the waiting-room. Aspirant travelers were coming up against sealed gates. Sitting on their suitcases, others were waiting with the resignation of emigrants. Obvious Britons were jabbering recriminations at the employees at the check-in counters, who were refusing to weigh or accept their luggage and pointing at the posters: *No departures for England until further notice.* A handwritten notice stuck over the official timetables and superseding them, announced one or two "not guaranteed" daily departures of omnibuses for Le Havre, Dieppe and Cherbourg. In the background, between the deserted platforms, silent and dead, the rails were gleaming.

I went back into the street. From then on, the traffic was visibly thinner; for every two automobiles in motion, one was broken down along the sidewalk. The traffic-controllers with white batons were letting everyone go; the one-way system was no longer being observed, and—a significant detail—

mechanical circulation was mingled with horse-drawn vehicles, already numerous: antique coupés, prehistoric calèches, Urban Authority fiacres. So they still existed! Who would have thought that, outside of horse-butchers' displays, Paris harbored so many dung-producing engines?

Apart from that change, which rendered the retreat of civilization visible—and in which, I must confess, I rejoiced ironically, my painter's eye being avid for the picturesque—the moral atmosphere of the city did not seem to have altered much. The laid-off workers were staying at home, one had to assume, or at least not venturing into the vicinity of the Opéra, the Madeleine or the Champs-Élysées. The gas-workers, on the other hand, were hard at work. I saw some in the Rue Royale who were re-establishing gaslights on the pylons of electric street-lights.

Also along the length of the Rue Royale, violating highways regulations with impunity, zebi carts were stationed on the sidewalks, but the psychologically-aware merchants were selling two different grades—the difference was probably illusory—one at 10 francs a kilo and the other at 20. The dearer one was disappearing rapidly...

My dealer in the Boulevard Saint-Germain, who was also a "friend," invited me to lunch so that we could talk business at leisure. If Luce had seen me in such circumstances she would certainly have mocked the ease with which I allowed myself to be "rolled over" as soon as any appeal was made to my sentiments. The impression of having my wallet already garnished by the check I had just deposited in the Boulevard Haussmann doubtless contributed to it; I am unable to defend my pecuniary interests with the stubbornness that gives so many of my contemporaries the appearance of bulldogs ready to bite as soon as they start discussing a question of money to be given or received. I finally let my man have, at 30% discount on the price I had fixed, a canvas that he had on deposit and which he was evidently intent on keeping.

Even at that price, he affirmed, he was doing me a favor. The invasion of the Lichen was doing enormous harm to business. The art market had been hard hit by the world-wide blockade. For as long as it lasted, there would be complete paralysis.

My dealer in the Rue des Saints-Pères proved to be even more pessimistic, and not without reason. Two Americans had already come in, that morning, to cancel a 35,000-franc deal. He refused to buy anything from me, but agreed nevertheless to take a look "one of these days" at the "coves" I had brought back from Cassis,

On the Boulevard Saint-Michel, a few last motorbuses, taxis and automobiles, painfully dragging their clusters of lichen or broken down, were already inferior in numbers to horse-drawn carriages, whose good-humored coachmen seemed eager to take their revenge on the order of mechanical devices. What seemed strangest of all, however, at that time of year, was the sight sprinkler-vehicles sending sheets of water over wooden or asphalt pavements, as in the middle of summer. The strong odor of bleach denoted an attempt at sterilization and active opposition to the scourge.

Uncle Frémiet greeted me without his usual enthusiasm; he was slightly resentful because I had introduced the famous Aurore Lescure to him under a false name. The *Echo de Paris*—which I had not read—had printed my interview at Le Bourget. But he quickly took it as a joke, and his petty pique evaporated. He did not suspect, of course, that he owed to my visits the honor of being one of the first people in Paris to see the lichen manifest itself in his home, but if he had known, given that contagion was inevitable sooner or later anyway, perhaps he would have thanked me—for he found in that priority a sufficient compensation, in the free publicity given to his name and business by the interviews and the photos published in the daily papers. The advantage, however, was rather Platonic.

"I don't know whether it's a general measure, but they've cut off the current in the neighborhood. We've been able, in consequence to clear away the lichen, but it's vexing to see my lamps apparently intact, and to know that they're ready to function, but to be obliged to make use of magnesium flashlights to take a picture. It's true that I'm taking fewer of them; the clients are no longer coming. No one knows what the future has in store; everyone's abstaining!"

My aunt's first concern was to inform herself, with solicitude, about the guest of the other evening, whom she simply called "that nice demoiselle." Her second was to offer me, following a custom of Flanders that she still observed after 25 years in Paris, of offering me buttered scones and spiced bread with café-au-lait.

The dining-room was cluttered with jars of preserves and sacks of beans, peas, lentils and so on. I was astonished by their abundance.

"Are you expecting to withstand a siege, Aunt?"

"You can laugh, my lad, but it's necessary to be ready for anything, in this nasty business. I'm afraid of shortages, at any rate. Suppose the deliveries don't come any longer? Already, this morning, there was no milk. And the grocer's! At Potin's, a queue of 25 people…like the mobilization in 1914. Prices have gone up almost everywhere—but I managed to get these provisions at a good price, at a small grocer's shop that I often go to."

"Bah!" I joked. "You'll still have the resource of the strawberry jelly that young Oscar collects from his wireless set…"

"Alas, no! That's finished—and the scamp, who's gone back to school, explained to me, as he threw down his satchel in chagrin, that his radio, which is a model that can be plugged in to the mains, can't function any longer without the city's electricity supply. To replace it, it would be necessary to buy blocks of batteries."

"And Papa doesn't want to?"

"This is no time to make superfluous purchases," said the mother, trenchantly. "Come on, my boy, be good and eat up."

My worthy aunt also feared "the revolution" as the eventual conclusion of the adventure, and explained her reasons, in accordance with local gossip.

My uncle amused himself by letting her go on, and laughed at her fears—but only to explain his own. What worried him more than the lay-offs was the inertia of the civil authorities.

"What is the government doing? Nothing at all. It isn't even capable of organizing the battle. It's waiting for the Chambres to reconvene...talking-shops. If the President of the Republic, in France, instead of being a figurehead, had powers like the American one, at least..."

An hour passed in that family setting had distracted me, as usual. At half past five, on leaving my uncle's house, I found myself abruptly troubled by anxiety. Dusk was falling, and Paris was scarcely illuminated, as if regretfully.

No trace of the morning's optimism. Where should I go? What will become of me, deprived of any news of Aurore until the evening or the next day?

The words that she spoke to me that morning on the telephone come back, piercingly: "material to gather, transport to plan and organize." She isn't leaving France, no, but what if her laboratory is in the provinces? In her absence, who can tell me? Nathan? He'll send me backing, the boor! Ah! Géo. He must know something.

I'm lucky enough to catch him by telephone at Saint-Denis, at the Hénault-Feltrie factory.

"What's she been doing today? All that I can tell you, old chap, is that at 9:30 this morning she was anticipating a very busy day. I saw her for three minutes, with her father, in the hall of the Métropole, when I dropped Lucy off... Where's their lab? At the Eyguzon Dam, in the Creuse—you know, the central hydroelectric generating station that supplies part of Paris. Nathan's got some smart salaries for them—20,000 a month apiece. The 'new Edison,' you know...he'll find us a remedy for the lichen in five secs...

"Now, listen...I wish you'd been with us yesterday evening! We went to the Rat Musqué, Luce and I, with Rosenkrantz and Cheyne. That worthy son of Prohibition undertook a large-scale comparative study of the cocktails of the modern

Babylon—which didn't prevent him from talking business with Rosenkrantz, who was also putting them down. She's discovered her type, my sis—the complete American of her dreams. And Cheyne certainly thinks she's a business genius, for he listens to her like an oracle—but he persists nonetheless in declaring himself a misogynist, while affirming that he's going to marry Aurore Lescure before long. And those weren't the words of a drunken man; he had all his lucidity, cocktails or no cocktails…in the end, they went off together, seemingly to cook up some big business deal—and with Rosen on board, I wouldn't be surprised if it succeeds. I wonder, though, whether it will finish with a marriage, as desired…for Lucy might be very disappointed…"

And me too! How I would bless that alternative marriage, if it could be made! But Cheyne must have good selfish reasons for holding on to Aurore…

Meditation like a Scottish shower, in which hope and discouragement alternate their replies in the fashion of a Greek chorus, while I set off for the heights of Montmartre on foot, in the hope of finding a telegram from Aurore at home…

A walk as somber as my reverie, likewise traversed with fugitive glimmers of light. In conformity with the Préfet de Police's ban on luminous signs and informational displays, the intersection at the Châtelet offers a quasi-funereal appearance, with somber cliffs of façades instead of the usual flamboyant electricity. Here and there, on the Boulevard de Sébastopol, in islets spared by the contamination, a few electric lamps are still burning, windows dispersing their interior illumination, pink or blue, neon or mercury tubes, but at the junction of the Boulevard Saint-Denis, the perspective of the great boulevards is merely a black death-trap, a mall in some backward province, peppered with derisory gas-jets. The same on the Boulevard Magenta, which I go up, and where the zebi stalls, under their oil-lamps, aggravate the darkness. One the Boulevard Barbès, in the short journey from the Boulevard Rochechouart to the Château-Rouge, I find electricity again and walk briskly, but all the way from the corner of the Rue Custine to my apartment, depressing obscurity again...

No telegram from Aurore was waiting for me in the lodge, where the Taquets were playing bezique by the light of a couple of candles fixed in the necks of bottles. A miserable Pigeon lamp[27] was burning in the stairwell...

---

[27] A non-explosive gasoline-lamp invented in the late 19th century by Charles Pigeon.

XIII. The Presses Stop

Dear Gaston,

Fate has decided it; I shall not see you again before my departure. I had resolved to see you one last time, but events have gathered pace. My father is intent on leaving tonight, in order to set to work tomorrow, and things that I counted on explaining to you at leisure, in person, I have only a few minutes to summarize for you in writing.

Firstly, our mission. The technical details of the research we are going to undertake in the laboratory at the Eyguzon Dam won't interest you, my dear artist, but this is it in a nutshell. By virtue of its particular radioactive properties, one of the species of the Lichen cultivated by Nathan will doubtless permit my father to solve a problem that he has been working on for many years, and which he considers, with good reason, to be the great work of his scientific life. That discovery, if he realizes it, as we hope, will be the greatest conquest that humankind has ever achieved over the forces of nature. Even if our patron takes all the credit and Lendor Cheyne, to whom we are still bound, reaps all the profits, it will nevertheless be an immortal glory for my father. And moreover, as the discovery will only have been realized thanks to the cosmozoans, its benefits will repair the damage that I have caused by importing the meteorites into the human world.

My father and I, as I say, are still bound to Cheyne by contract. As you know, he has given us our temporary liberty, but he does not mean to put an end to our reciprocal engagements. Now, I only made incidental mention of these engagements in Marseilles, when I told you that my father and remain dependent on Cheyne until my marriage to him. It is now necessary that I explain them to you...while abstaining from passing judgment on my father, who consented to sign them.

By the contract that binds us mutually, Lendor J. Cheyne appoints himself as my father's "manager," settles his debts, *furnishes a laboratory at his own expense, and assures him an annual salary of $10,000, as the technical director of the Moon Gold Company—in exchange for which the Company acquires the exclusive right to exploit, in general, all his patents anterior to the signature of the contract, in particular those relating to astronautics and synthetic oil. With respect to inventions to come, my father did the right thing, and it's to me that future patents will revert.*

Furthermore, there is between Cheyne and myself a reciprocal engagement of marriage. By this marriage, which will give me a 50% share in the benefits of the Moon Gold Company, of which I am presently only a salaried employee, I will cede to my husband in compensation 50% of the returns on my father's new inventions.

Although he claims to be a misogynist, Lendor is fond of me—and, I would have said before meeting you, my friend, fond enough for the marriage not to be solely a business arrangement and for the association perhaps to be, on my side, if not happy, at least tolerable.

Cheyne's side of the arrangement, even deducting the compensations that he accords us, already seems profitable, but he has every confidence in my father's genius and he will not let go at any price of the possibilities of his future discoveries. He has given us temporary leave, but we remain salaried employees of the Moon Gold Company.

I cannot see any possibility of his releasing me from that engagement of marriage. In any case, were he to offer to do so, I would hesitate, I spite of...what you know...for it would be against my father's interests.

"You will judge, I hope, my dear Gaston, as I do, that fate has acted in our best interests, to lessen our suffering, by preventing us from seeing one another in the flesh. That is better for both of us, for our peace of mind as for mine. I know that you love me; you know that my coldness is only apparent and obligatory; that beneath the camaraderie of which I gave evidence from the first day we met, a more tender sentiment has developed, involuntarily and almost without my knowing

157

it. I confessed that to you once; that is already too much. I do not want to expose myself to the necessity, to the danger, of telling you again, face to face, as would have been bound to happen had I come to see you today.

A few days of reflection will permit you to envisage the situation with more serenity, but I shall not renounce seeing you again—alas, I cannot. Until then, my dear, too dear, friend.

AURORE

P.S. I will have to come back to Paris before long. The exact date depends on the success of our research.

Standing before the easel, from which the recently-begun portrait as looking at me, lit by the wan daylight of the rainy morning of October 23, I reread the letter, written on the Hôtel Métropole's headed notepaper and bearing the postmark of the Gare d'Austerlitz at 22:19.

Having left yesterday evening, my beloved must now be at Eyguzon, in the process of setting up her laboratory...

A severe blow, that letter; but the Aurore I know, with her sharp and penetrating sense of duty and her moral conscience as un-American as mine, could not have acted otherwise, and I shall not think about her any more, wishing to respect her word, which considers it a blessing of fate not to have to see me again. Far from discouraging me, that rereading completes the rout of the anxious uncertainties against which I struggled all night. I have, in the reaffirmation of her love for me, too many motives for rejoicing and hope.

The firm intention that she attributes to Cheyne of demanding the fulfillment of the promise of marriage does not disconcert me overmuch. Aurore undoubtedly does not know yet what I have learned from Géo: that Cheyne has fallen under Luce's spell. Whatever Géo thinks about it, the question of financial interest will not weigh heavily in the balance, if Luce takes it into her head to marry him. However American he might be, Cheyne is not a polygamous Mormon—and besides, the Mormons are no longer polygamous—so, if he marries Luce de Ricourt, he will liberate Aurore Lescure from her promise, which will set her free...free to follow her secret penchant, free to marry me...

Given the accelerated velocity at which events are progressing, if that is to happen, it can't be long delayed...

And what if someone were to inform Aurore of the turn that relations between her fiancé and our friend Luce are taking...? But I reject the suggestion, which has emerged from perverse depths of the sector of infamy that even an honest conscience contains.

Wait, then, and hope. Well, so be it. I shall be patient. That will be easy: a few days without seeing her, and perhaps the recompense in the end...

Patience! It's not just me who will need that! The *Matin* brought up by the concierge with the post, which I unfold, demands it of Parisians, and the whole of France!

USE OF ELECTRICITY PROHIBITED IN PARIS... PUBLIC SAFETY DECREE... NEWSPAPERS WILL CEASE TO APPEAR...

The gravity of the situation no longer permits delay until the Chambres reassemble on October 25. Overcoming yesterday's hesitations, the Conseil des Ministres, which met again last night, has, without exceeding constitutional legality, issued a decree, immediately ratified by the President of the Republic, which will take effect at noon today. Under the terms of the decree, which will be found further on in extenso, *the use and production of electricity in all its forms are prohibited in Paris and the Département de la Seine, and in all parts of the region contaminated by the Xenobiota. The appearance of the lichen in any location whatsoever will automatically bring the immediate application of that measure into force. The only exceptions are the sources of electrical energy—including those alimenting the transmitters of the Eiffel Tower, the telegraph and telephone network, etc.—which the government deems it necessary to maintain in activity in the national interest. These electricity generators will be equipped* with special devices, such as refrigeration chambers, that will prevent them from posing any danger of contamination to the vicinity.

There is a temporary exception for the low-output batteries serving to power wireless receivers.

The declaration to the Mairie of contaminated buildings is obligatory within two hours of the appearance of the Xenobiota, under penalty of a minimum fine of 100 francs. The objective of this declaration has is to slow down the propagation of the epidemic to healthy regions. While awaiting the arrival of municipal employees charged with carrying out a more complete disinfection, the declarer is obliged to ensure the isolation of the infected building, vehicle or individual, and their provisional sterilization with the aid of one of the products thus far recognized as efficacious: a solution of bleach or simple salt water. The organized services, municipal and others, may make advantageous use of chlorine in a gaseous state, and vapors of bromine or iodine, and other products that will be put at their disposal in sufficient quantities by the authorities.

In Paris and the contaminated regions, this declaration will facilitate the operations of sterilization, which will be carried out on a large scale and methodically during the yet-to-be-determined period of time when the use of electricity will be suspended.

The original text of the decree submitted to the Conseil called for the prohibition of the use and production of electricity throughout France, without distinction between healthy and infected regions. The Conseil has retreated, with good reason, from the absolutism of this measure, but the difference of treatment applied to contaminated regions and others raises a serious problem with regard to communications. If it were practically possible to raise barriers around the contaminated regions analogous to those on our present frontiers, all would be well, but that is impossible. It is therefore necessary to realize the best approximation, by reducing to a minimum passage from contaminated regions to others. The enormous

160

diminution of motorized transport required by the application of the decree will facilitate the solution of the problem. Surveillance posts will be established on major roads at the exits from contaminated zones, in order to verify or ascertain the need for a disinfection and complete sterilization of vehicles or individuals.

At departure-points from Paris, in the railway stations, where a reduced train-service can be maintained, this sterilization will be assured by the vigilance of the railway companies.

A special police force is to be instituted for the struggle against the Xenobiota. While waiting this organization, the existing police and the gendarmerie, with the auxiliaries that they consider it useful to recruit, will be responsible for applying these prescriptions. The task will be difficult and arduous, and the government is counting on the patriotism of everyone to facilitate it.

The further extension obtained by the scourge in the last 24 hours permits an appreciation of the extent to which the Conseil's hesitation in not promulgating this degree a day earlier is regrettable.

Here, in fact, are the population centers in which the lichen has been observed since yesterday: in the south-east, Nîmes, Montpellier, Grasse and Mention; in the south-west, Bayonne; in the north, Amiens, Le Havre and Dunkerque. Around Paris the extension is no less evident, and the list of localities that it would be necessary to enumerate is a long one. African France has also been affected; the Lichen has made its appearance in Tunis and Oran.

In Paris itself, this measure, taken sooner, would have impeded the birth of a particularly harmful generation of Xenobiota, which became manifest yesterday in various places, including the electricity substations, where it attacks the coils of transformers and had resulted in short-circuits and considerable damage.

Let us repeat that the situation is serious—tragic, even— but not desperate. Before falling silent—for a few days only,

161

we hasten to say, for steam-engines will be installed with all possible speed to replace the electric motors of our rotary printing-presses—the Press has a duty to exhort the public to bear this stern ordeal with a patriotic calm and dignity.

The eyes of the world, which has broken off material communications with us almost in its entirety, are on France, and it knows from hour to hour, by courtesy of the wireless telegraph what is happening here, and what attitude the French people are adopting. Whatever each individual's political opinion might be, we must all form a sacred unity, in the superior interests of France and civilization entire, and submit without complaint, stoically, to the consequences of the decree. That is the only means of cutting sort the propagation of the scourge and rendering ourselves masters of it before the contamination is universal.

Instead of allowing national life to be impeded by a progressive, and ultimately complete, paralysis that will then be of long duration, it is a question of voluntarily bringing about an immediate, but partial and temporary, pause.

It is necessary to recognize, as has already been said, that in the last 50 years, electricity has already become, a trifle prematurely, the queen of our civilization, its essential motor. Everything in our present technology depends on electricity, everything is linked to the functioning of certain items of electrical apparatus. With the suppression of electricity, all of Paris will come to a stop.

The means of transport—the Metro, tramways, electrified railways—have already been virtually abolished. If motor vehicles have been able to circulate until this morning it is because the intensity of their sources of electricity—batteries, accumulators, magnetos and dynamos—are weak enough only to engender varieties of the lichen that lack exuberance and are relatively benign. These varieties, however, produce spores like the others, the descendants of which risk becoming calamitous. In a few hours, the streets of Paris will cease to be contaminated by this mode of diffusion.

As for aircraft, their case is special, and they might be tolerated without danger. As they circulate in the air, protected from any new contamination, it is easy to sterilize their dynamos immediately before departure. That is what has already been done for a day or two at Le Bourget and Issy-les-Moulineaux, in order to avoid the clogging of the engine's spark-plugs leading to mid-air breakdowns, infinitely more dangerous than those of motor vehicles can be on the ground of our streets.

Communications? Without the telegraph, we know, no more intensive rapid railway traffic. Telephone cables are still resistant, but since yesterday, the perforating species of lichen we mentioned above has been invading the relays, eating away the insulation and corroding the wires carrying continuous traffic. The suppression of the service—at least for the public—will avoid the destruction of those costly cables, whose planning and placement takes years. In Paris, the functioning of "pneumatic tubes" depends on pumps that maintain the void necessary for the propulsion of the capsules.

Industry? In modern factories, most apparatus for lifting and handling, at least, is electric. If they do not come to a complete halt, production there will be badly hampered and slowed down.

Without electricity, it is obvious, there is a more or less complete paralysis of the nervous and muscular systems of our social body.

And human thought, too, is affected in its living sources by the suppression of newspapers; it hardly matters, in fact, that linotypes will still be able to ensure the composition of text, and even their printing, as soon as the rotary presses are immobilized by the cessation of their motive force.

Without electricity, Paris and all the contaminated regions are deprived of lighting worthy of the name, deprived of means of transport, deprived of rapid communications with the external world, of newspapers and, let us add, of cinemas and theaters. That means another 200,000 inhabitants of Greater Paris reduced to idleness...

163

The article continued with a summary list of occupations that would be deprived of work, first completely—electricians, Metro and tramway workers, taxi and delivery drivers, cinema and theater staff and newspaper workers, from the editor-in-chief to the office cleaner—and second partly: railway employees, telegraphists and telephonists, post-office employees, metallurgists and workers in various industries...not to mention the suburbanites too distant from Paris to be able to get to work.

Furthermore, the initial favorable measure taken by the administrators of the Metro and tramways granting temporary half-pay to laid-off workers was not to be extended, for the expense would be too great...and how long would it need to be continued?

One question worried me. It was all very well to stop the machinery of civilization in order to slow down the development of the lichen, but how were all the nuclei of contamination to be destroyed? Bleach did not seem to be very effective, to judge by the Metro, where it had not been possible to prevent the lightning-fast growth of the Lichen. Even if the other methods were more effective, it would require weeks or months to sanitize the whole of Paris.

I searched the various dailies that still appeared that morning, but I did not find any satisfactory response to that enigma. Was the government keeping its effective means of combat secret? With what end? There was every reason to publish it. Was it counting primarily, as an auxiliary in the fight against the Lichen, on a reduction in the vital activity of the Xenobiota during its enforced dormancy, or on the possibility that the seed-germs unaffected by the disinfection would lose their ability to germinate after a few days, as Nathan had supposed in his *Intran* article, and that the cessation of electricity would automatically bring about the extinction in Paris of the cosmic creation? Was it hoping for an early frost? Or had the Conseil des Ministres, believing in the intrinsic efficacy of the decree simply by the fact of its promulgation, voted for it in a moment of irreflective enthusiasm, as the Convention and the Comités de Salut Public were once wont to do? One was tempted to believe that, on reading the detailed account of the tumultuous debates of the night sitting.

In that case, though, would the decree be obeyed by people who were asking themselves the same question as I was, and not finding any better response?

XIV. The Great Shutdown

The week of the Great Shutdown was a singular period for me too—a lacuna. Being deprived of the daily society of Aurore, who had transported me, in the space of ten days, to the Sinai of a new and marvelous life, her absence hollowed out a great void within me, as if she had taken away with her the only interesting part of my personality. Sentimentally, I was in a state of flux and uncertainty; my anticipations of the future succeeded one another, different from one hour to the next, with no fixed point to which I could cling.

I did not even have, to draw a ring around that inconsistency, the armature of exterior routine. I fell back into a social life as disorganized as mine, or even more so, in temporary suspense. I was uninterested in my personal future, my work. Even my resolution to continue Aurore's portrait in her absence, with the aid of the documentary photographs, evaporated...

I lived in the hope of receiving news or the return of my beloved. I became an impartial witness, a disinterested observer—and I think most people were experiencing, each on his own account and for reasons other than mine—an analogous impression. We were waiting...

For that period, as for the preceding one, I have no pretention of writing the history of the invasion of the Lichen. Others, better qualified, have taken responsibility for that with a literary talent that I do not have. I have talked about it thus far solely as a factor in my personal adventure with the importer of the cosmozoans. I shall continue to do the same—but my own fate, for the duration of the Great Breakdown, was immersed in the social scheme.

The decree, bright forth by everyone's wishes, was welcomed in Paris as a necessary evil. People resigned themselves to an inevitable obedience, as occurs in numerous cases when docility to laws results less from real respect for them and voluntary consent as from simple inertia, every new regulation, however absurd and incomprehensible, silently tightening the belt of social constraint girdling every citizen of a civilized state by one more notch.

Besides, deprived of the magnetism of the press, whose role is to polarize the currents of public opinion, the latter, left to itself, remained fragmentary and individual, scattered in crumbs of divergent expression that no longer succeeded in coming together or settling into a common formula.

Without asking questions, without wondering overmuch how it would end, people started out having confidence in the government.

They were disoriented by the rupture of habits, but they enjoyed, with surprise and timidity, the abrupt release from and suppression of technological tyranny. Even those who were not laid off felt liberated from a constraint that had previously gripped them without their being aware of it. And to be able to go anywhere without risking the customary itching in a locality invaded by lichen! The first three days, October 23, 24 and 25, gave the impression in Paris of an indefinitely-prolonged Sunday: a Londonesque Sunday, of gray and insipid—almost lukewarm—weather, with no other distractions than going for a walk, to the café and the sampling of zebi from ambulant merchants' carts.

The terraces were overflowing. As on a taxi-less May Day, crowds filled the streets, where the traffic was thin and moving to a new rhythm, with their muted flow. The usual noisy harassment of the immense mechanical herd, with its motors and blasting horns, had almost disappeared; it was necessary once again to become accustomed to the rumble of iron-clad wheels and the clatter of horseshoes on asphalt or wooden pavements. Calèches, tilburys, *charrettes anglaises*, coupés, landaus, victorias—all those names read in the *Larousse illustré*, emerged from the oubliettes of memory in order to label the antediluvian vehicles trotting along at six kilometers an hour. A few police cars, however, with engines hermetically armored and sterilized by special procedures, gave evidence, along with the multiple squads of agents on bicycles, in unsuspected numbers, and the overhead drone of aircraft with badges continually patrolling the skies of Paris, of governmental precautions that nothing seemed as yet to require in that amorphous flow of the sabbatical crowd, which had no idea what to do with its liberty. And people followed with an approving gaze the large tricks with magneto-less Diesel engines, rolling ostentatiously along the great boulevards, the sight of which reassured them about the regularity of deliveries to Les Halles.

But all that—that calm, that peace, that facile and harmonious obedience to the decree—was in the center of Paris. It did not extend at a sure pace beyond the perimeter of the Parisian zone: the new interior frontiers that separated us from the rest of France.

I did not get my first suspicion of that difference until the first evening, thanks to the gossip of Madame Taquet, whose husband had a comrade engaged as an auxiliary policeman in the special brigade responsible for verifying sterilizations at the departure of travelers from the Gare de Lyon.

Driven by the anxious and idle consciousness that had invaded my incomplete self, I resolved to get to the bottom of it. The memory came back to me of my old bike, dismantled and stored away a couple of years before in a cupboard in my studio. I took it out, reassembled it and, the following morning, rode as far as the Villeneuve-Saint-Georges exit, where two posts had been established, with their barracks, facing one another on opposite sides of the road: one forbidding entry to the Parisian zone to automobiles with imperfectly-sealed magnetos, the other ensuring the sterilization of vehicles and individuals at the frontier of the healthy zone. It was a mess: a traffic-jam of trucks and autos such as had never been seen at the gates of Paris in the days of the *bulletin vert* on race days.

It was there, too, in a defoliated country inn where I stopped for a while to drink a glass of white wine while watching the Seine flow by, that I heard talk of the illicit "trafficking" of the improvised police. On the roads more than at the railway stations, which were better supervised, numerous travelers were leaving Paris after nightfall in vehicles made up to simulate watertight cladding and penetrating into the healthy zone, avoiding the obligatory disinfection.

I believe, in truth, that outside Paris, the decree was only observed in an approximate fashion during the first three days. The provincial dailies that I had the opportunity to read gave me other evidence, by virtue of the further nuclei of Lichen that were still becoming manifest in France.

Their strangulation must often have been delayed by negligence and selfish calculations, and not only on the part of individuals; it appears that municipalities were too slow to cut off the electricity supply, waiting until half the commune was invaded before doing so. It required, moreover, a certain measure of abnegation to put oneself in quarantine and set up guard-posts at the crossroads obliging automobiles coming from healthy regions to go around the locality henceforth without going in.

If I had not taken the trouble to go and see for myself, however, I might never have divined that underside of the situation. We were walled up in Paris by an invisible but nevertheless efficacious partition, without rapid and reliable news of the rest of France and the world.

No more Parisian newspapers. Outside of a few little political broadsheets printed on hand-presses, but so evidently mendacious that they were not worth the five *sous*, all that was to be found in the kiosks were provincial papers. It cost too much to send provincial papers to Paris by air, however, and by railway, the speed of goods trains scarcely reaching 20 kilometers an hour, so the *Nouvelliste de Lyon*, the *Moniteur du Puy-de-Dôme* and the *Dernières Nouvelles de Strasbourg* arrived a day late, and only contained outdated information.

There were loudspeakers, forbidden in ordinary times on the public highway but tolerated in the circumstances, which bellowed the news to passers-by. Those of the great dailies, among others, claimed to be substituting temporarily for the printed editions, but a rigorous censorship must have been in

169

force, for the news was uniformly optimistic. According to them, the "electric law" was scrupulously obeyed throughout France and the scourge was thwarted. A little more patience…etc.

People felt more isolated from the true facts than by the official communiqués of the war. The desire to be informed, the hope of finding someone who had seen or learned something, trustworthy eye-witnesses, was driving people to seek out friends and acquaintances and to engage in conversation with anyone, on the slightest pretext or none at all.

As for me, I made the effort to see a few comrades, but they knew no more than I did, and I rapidly wearied of any conversation into which I could not soon introduce Aurore's name. Twice in three days I went to the Rue Legendre in the hope of talking about her, but Géo was at his factory in Saint-Denis and Luce had left in an airplane with Lendor J. Cheyne, who was to give a lecture in Bordeaux, according to Madame Ricourt. The old lady's gossip did not interest me, and I left her to her occupations.

The sympathy manifested toward "Mademoiselle Lescure" by my worthy aunt contributed more than anything else to draw me to the Frémiets, but I was not otherwise insensible to the affectionate welcome I received there. Besides, little Oscar's radio was working again, thanks to a set of batteries that his father had finally consented to buy him.

"What about the decree?" I asked him, when the excited boy told me the good news. "What are you doing about that, young wireless enthusiast? You're infringing it, for piles and accumulators if I'm not mistaken are among the sources of electricity whose use is prohibited."

"But everyone's doing it," Oscar retorted.

"The fact is," my uncle admitted, "that according to the strict letter of the decree, we're in contravention—but as the boy says, everyone's doing it, from the big newspapers with their loudspeakers to the meanest individual. The electricity police have other things to do than make domestic visits—

other cats to skin, with the disinfections and the automobiles. In sum, there's tolerance, as the newspapers have observed."

Another indication of the mildness with which the decree was enforced, in those early days of insouciance.

I dined with the Frémiets on October 25. That evening, the radio station in Lausanne, having offered the condolences of the Federal Government to the French people, so harshly tested, informed us that Belgium had fallen victim to its loyalty to France in not closing it frontier. The lichen had appeared in Brussels. On the other hand, the same misfortune had befallen Spain and Italy, which had cut off communications on the 21st. Barcelona was contaminated, as well as San Remo and Genoa, apparently thanks to smuggling operations— which did not prevent Italian opinion from being rather hard on us; there was rumor circulating in Rome, in certain imperialist circles, that French aircraft had come by night to sow lichen spores on the Ligurian Riviera!

My uncle laughed at that. "Oh yes, of course! They're crazy!"

I recalled the ridiculous rumors that had circulated in the beginning. "Here, it was a 'gift from the Boche,' remember?"

"Yes. All that's just words, fortunately. The worst of it is that this stupid accusation by a few Italian chauvinists, comes just at the moment when France, by virtue of the decree, is doing the right thing. For it goes without saying that, as a disarmament measure, it will go one better than Briand and the late Stresemann.[28] The Societé des Nations ought to congratulate our government, which has dared to issue such a decree!

---

[28] Aristide Briand, the French prime minister, and Gustave Stresemann of the Weimar Republic received the Nobel Peace Prize in 1926 for the Locarno Treaties, which reconciled France with Germany. They were both strenuous campaigners for universal disarmament, but Stresemann's death from a stroke in 1929 and Briand's in 1932 took a lot of the wind out of the movement's political sails…and the Nazis subsequently took Germany in a very different direction.

Ordinarily, my uncle only expressed his pacifist opinions very discreetly, but that evening he got carried away. His point of view surprised me; I hadn't yet thought about that. For the first time, I saw that awkward consequence of the de-electrification of Paris, the South-East and other contaminated regions: the country defenseless, incapable of mobilization.

"So," he said, "the case is being heard. It hasn't been done expressly for that purpose, but the experiment is no less conclusive for that: a nation can find itself in a state of disarmament without immediately provoking a shock attack, as the warmonger claim."

"A shock attack? Hmm? How do we know? Perhaps it's taking place right now, at the frontier."

"At the frontier? No, my lad, it would already have happened and not at the frontier: on Paris, by air, with the most up-to-date methods: gas projectiles."

I fund a response immediately. "The attacker would be too frightened of catching the contagion of the lichen. The whole point of a shock attack would be to take subsequent possession of our country, wouldn't it? To occupy it—and to occupy it would be to re-establish the communications that our good neighbors have hastened to cut off."

My uncle got out of it by means of a paradox.

"That's a great pity—for if France had not been isolated so quickly, the entire world would have been invaded by the lichen, and then, farewell to the matamores'[29] hopes of rapid mobilization. It would be the end of war."

---

[29] The term *matamore* [literally, Moor-slayer, although the intentional analogy with "matador" introduces an ironic note of showmanship] was popularized with reference to a character-type in Spanish historical plays—a person always boating about his supposed heroic exploits against the Moors—and was subsequently used in France to refer to unconvincing self-proclaimed "war heroes" in general.

"Yes, uncle, but you're not thinking about what would become of civilization if electricity were to remain banished from our world. You, as a photographer..."

"Bah! It's necessary not to think only of oneself. And one can take photographs with magnesium—people were content for a long time with sunlight. Occupational convenience apart, I'm not overly attached to it—to electricity. We did without it 50 years ago, and civilization, as you put it, didn't do too badly. If the loss were to be compensated by a durable abolition of war, I'd bless it with all my heart."

"But people would continue to kill one another by other means. It's a necessity of human nature."

As usual when my uncle expressed his subversive views, my aunt sighed silently and looked at me sadly. I took pity on her and didn't persist.

That same day, October 25, a few hours after that family evening, while I stayed in my studio to wait for the afternoon post and perhaps a letter from Aurore, I had received a visit from Alburtin.

"Left Marseilles on October 23 at 4 p.m., arrived this morning in Paris at 6 p.m.—yes, my lad, 38 hours in transit! And I had to submit to two disinfections in the course of the journey, on exiting from contaminated zones—the first at Orange, the frontier of the south-east region. Worse than going through customs! They made us get out of our supposedly-infected train, put on gas masks and go through a chamber full of bromide aerosol carrying our luggage—and then into another shed for a 'sporoscope' examination, to see whether we were still carrying spores. Then on to another train, reeking of bromine...same story after Lyons, an infected zone, at Villefranche. France has broken up into a patchwork of petty countries. It's true that with the slowness of present communications, it's as if it had become four or five times larger...

"Note, too, my dear Delvart, than on leaving Marseilles the day before yesterday, there was no question of the decree; otherwise, I wouldn't have started off. A bad blow for me, this 'electric law'—but I did well, even so, to come to Paris..."

What the Ricourts had told me about their annoyances in Cassis had only been a prelude for Alburtin. Holding him responsible for the importation of the lichen, the fishermen of Cassis, whose motor-boats were no longer working, joining forces with the workers at the factories of La Bédoule, electrically equipped and immobilized by short-circuits, had come to the clinic in force one evening, invaded it and sacked it, obliging the nurses to transport the patients to the nearby hospital.

"You see, Delvart, there was a band of 200 or 300 fanatics filling the Rue Droite and shouting 'Death to the Boche!' For, in their eyes, I was a spy in the service of a foreign power, who had poisoned the region deliberately! The policeman and the two guards couldn't do anything, and the gendarmes had been locked in the gendarmerie. I suspect my colleague Dr. Martin of having staged the coup in order to put an end to my competition. In brief, I was obliged to flee by night in my car with my wife and Madame Narisnska, and we sought refuge with friends in Marseilles.

"That happened on the very day when I discovered that an ointment of lead oxide radically reduces the itching caused by the radioactivity of the lichen sores. You know that radiologists wear lead-line gloves to protect their hands against radiation—but no one would have wanted an ointment, so I replaced it with a lead-based soap, with which it's sufficient to wash in the morning and the evening to achieve desensitization. In Marseilles, my product, launched by a large perfume-manufacturer, was bound to secure the contentment of the population. I saw the future smiling on me again, and in order to obtain a monopoly in Paris I came here to patent my invention."

"My poor friend, you're too late! No one here is scratching any longer, since yesterday."

"With your electric law, it's no use. And who knows when I'll receive the indemnity that I'm claiming from the government for the sack of my clinic? It'll be necessary to establish the responsibility for not having been able to stop that mob, which the town of Cassis and the State will try to pass off on one another...there's some good news even so. I've seen Nathan and he's given me a job as a laboratory assistant in his research facility at Eyguzon. In the name of his old friendship for his former pupil, he told me. Perhaps he also has some remorse about not even having mentioned me in his article for the *Intran*. But one has to admire the irony of things: out there I'll be under the orders of Mademoiselle Aurore Lescure...the person who made the world the jolly gift that cost me so dear!"

That announcement made me regret not being a scientist myself, qualified to obtain an analogous position. I would be out there beside her instead of fretting in Paris.

I envied the luckless Alburtin with all my heart.

As he was leaving that same evening for Eyguzon, I gave him a letter, already stamped, that I had intended to put in the post, in which I begged Aurore to specify the duration of her presence in the laboratory. That uncertainty alone, in fact, had stopped me from taking the train that day, or setting off toward her by bicycle. But to depart at hazard was to expose myself to the risk of making an unnecessary journey, and—worse still—of missing her, since she might be coming back to Paris on a regular basis. That letter, dictated by my heart, contained, I believe, words capable of touching her—and I had had the courage not to make any allusion to the Cheyne-Luce intimacy.

The demonstration of the workless on October 25 was a first indication of the increasing discontent and weariness that was about to put an end to the placid resignation of the first days of the Great Shutdown.

A certain quantity of the unemployed had been able to enroll in the special brigade of ant-electric police, improvised to ensure obedience to the decree. These detectives of a new kind set out under the insignia of red armbands with decorated with an X—for Xenobiota. The populace took to calling them "the Xs" or "the electrics." They were in the railway stations, on the roads at the frontiers of the Parisian zone, in the disinfection services. All of these were immediately put to work, but those who were seen wandering the streets, to check whether the rare automobiles in circulation satisfied the demands of the law, had so little to do on the first three days that people got used to joking about "all those idle Xs, who have an easy time of it." Their activity, and their attributions, were to extend singularly, however, and confer a sad celebrity upon them.

A few hundred more of the unemployed had been absorbed by the gas companies, for the reinstallation of street-lighting. Others, ex-power workers, reverted to being coachmen, either of fiacres or the incongruous vehicles such as charabancs, mail-coaches, delivery carts and horse-drawn omnibuses, with the aid of which an embryonic public transport system was reorganized in Paris.

The greatest number of the unemployed, however, estimated at 200,000 or 300,000, remained on the street, with neither work nor pay, without knowing where they might find one or the other. Their discontentment was all the keener because the favor of half-salary granted by the tramway authority to the first employees put on leave had generated the hope that the measure might be extended to everyone. I know very little about politics, but it seems evident to me that the latter factor played a considerable role in the demonstrations of the unemployed, organized by the advanced parties. Their monstrous procession went along the great boulevards and filed passed the Chambre des Députés for two hours, which had just gone into session in order to approve of the decree. They demanded, to the tune of *Lampions*—"Give us pay! Give us pay!"—their full salary, or its equivalent in the form of a State indemnity, for as long as their unemployment might last.

Save for few minor scuffles with the police, everything passed off peacefully—but that demonstration, by its example, crystallized the discontentment and played the same role with respect to the public as a virulent newspaper article.

After having rejoiced for two days because the suppression of electricity had stopped the growth of the Xenobiota and permitted the ragged remains of the lichen to be swept into the sewers, the reaction set in. The capital was beginning to find the "electric law," previously demanded by the clamor of horns and cries, too harsh. The quarters that were still clear claimed that they were suffering injury without sufficient reason; why not do in Paris as in the provinces, where healthy regions retained the use of the current? In buildings already disinfected, people wanted to be able to switch the lights on again immediately. The passage of the disinfectants was dreaded because some—chlorine, in particular-damaged the furniture. At the same time, people railed against the slowness of the operations, carried out indolently. What was the point, anyway, in continuing them? To all appearances, all the arron-dissements seemed sanitized. No one was scratching any long-er, anywhere. What was the matter, then? The "Zenobia" was finished. How long did they have to wait to get the electricity back, to reestablish normal circulation, and everything else?

That evening, under the makeshift lighting, gas jets in the main roads and acetylene in the cafes, there was no longer the calm relaxation of a Sunday but an effervescence of disgust and discouragement. No cinemas, no theaters, no music halls. Everyone was fed up with the low-key life imposed on the capital; tempers were flaring, in the sentiment of the futility of such a life...

On October 26, that state of mind intensified, and there was a revolt against the decree. Ten times over, while cycling to the Ricourts at about 11 a.m., on the short journey from my apartment to the Rue Legendre, I saw agents of the anti-electric brigade dressing down motorists who had simply set out in their unprotected cars—and in almost every case, the denunciatory growth of lichen at the rear of the chassis proved that the spores were still adrift in the air of the capital. The latent nuclei were merely waiting to reveal themselves.

In the Rue Legendre, in response to my ring, Géo came in person to open the door. He held out the tip of the little fin-ger of a hand black with grimy grease.

177

"Excuse me, old chap, we've been without servants since yesterday. Put your bike here. As you can see, I'm in the process of getting mine in shape too—but there's a broken gear-plate; I need to repair it. This afternoon, to go to the factory, I'll risk taking my old banger...giving a bribe to the X who's watching the garage. Once outside, the worst I'll end up with is a 100 franc fine for the contravention."

"Do you think the danger's over, then?"

"Me? Not at all! But whether there are a few spores more or less in Paris, it won't change anything. Sterilization seems to me to be a utopia, as long as it's not carried out at a stroke, by drowning Paris—evacuated in advance, of course—in a cloud of gas...and I'm not going to go eight kilometers on foot."

"Is your mother well? Your sister?"

"My mother's gone to the employment agency, to try to find a maid. My sister's off on her provincial lecture tour with Cheyne. As he only speaks English, she's speaking on his behalf and introducing herself—she has some nerve!—as the intended pilot of the next rocket. They're in Brest and Rennes today. The enormity of it is that the ban on astronautical flights isn't holding them back at all, and the issue of the European shares will be fully subscribed in a matter of days.

"It's true that Rosenkrantz has joined forces with them. Cheyne has ceded him the proceeds of the fabrication of synthetic oil in exchange for Standard supporting the Moon Gold share issue. Cheyne's jubilant. He's found a suitable match. Goodbye misogyny—I'm beginning to believe that it will end well, in a marriage. Personally, I'd like nothing better, but it's our noble mother who'll find the insult hard to swallow. Think of it: an arch-plebeian Yank, the son of a road-sweeper! She's already down in the dumps knowing that her daughter's 'showing herself off like a mountebank and dragging the good name of the Ricourts in the mud of speculation!'"

I was buoyed up by joy at this favorable news. I experienced so much affection for my old friend Géo that, when he invited me to dinner that evening, I accepted enthusiastically. Before leaving him, though, a thought occurred to me.

"What if your mother hasn't found a maid?"

"Don't worry about that, old man. We'll go to Wepler's in the Place Clichy. Agreed? Come and pick me up at 7:30."

XV. The Ardent Lichen

The materiality of the facts has not, of course, been con-
tested by anyone, and could not be, except in systematic bad
faith. The official figures are there: 450 dead, 882 wounded;
1332 victims in all. Such is the frightful tally, in Paris alone,
of the incursion effected on that evening of October 26 into
the center of the capital by the creatures that were called the
Monsters of Saint-Denis, the Cosmic Chimeras or the Ardent
Lichen. Only one or two chroniclers of varying degrees of
intelligence, such as Monsieur Clémentel-Vault, dared to cast
doubt on their reality when the dailies reappeared three days
after the event, and attribute the victims to a communist riot.
One serious historian, Monsieur Raymond Valescure, in his
exceedingly well-documented work *In the Time of the Xenobiota*, even invokes by way of explanation a crisis of collective hallucination and "gregarious insanity," born of the mental tension of those days of terror. He appears to forget the fact
that that minds were not tense on the 26th, that the menace had
almost been forgotten, that people were beginning to sneer at
the decree in an illusory sentiment of security, and that the
communist riot and the Electric Terror were only manifest
after the incursion of the Chimeras into Paris. It is with reasoning analogous to Monsieur Valescure's that it has already
been "demonstrated" that Alexander the Great and Napoléon I
never existed.

Without taking into account the unanimous belief of the
time, however, or the opinion of Professor Nathan, who formally admits the authenticity of these monsters, there is the
official inquiry, which came to the same conclusion, based on
the depositions of more than 700 witnesses. There is the destruction of the power-station at Saint-Denis by military aircraft. Would the latter have received orders to destroy plant
and equipment worth several hundred millions if there had not

been certainty that it was a matter of something other than a collective hallucination?

As for me, I did not see the Ardent Lichen, but less than an hour after the event, I heard the testimony my friend Géo, who had narrowly escaped them.

He had told me once about an aviation accident in which he had first almost been burned and then nearly crashed into the ground, his parachute only having opened at the last moment—and that episode, he evoked with a smile. When talking about the Chimeras of Saint-Denis, however, his face was a mask of tragic horror; he had endured the most anguishing moments of his life...

On the morning of October 26, the communist municipality of Saint-Denis, obedient to directives from Moscow, had judged that the moment had come to inflict a defeat on the government by flouting the law and forcing the engineers at the electricity generating station on the Quai de Saint-Ouen to resume production.

At 2 p.m., from a distance, Géo, having evaded the slack surveillance of the Xs, saw thick smoke coming from the blast-chimneys of the power-station and a red flag with the hammer and sickle flying high. Like the others, however, the Hénaul-Feltrie factory was profiting from the restored current and work there, languishing the day before, had resumed its normal regime.

Nothing abnormal happened until 6 p.m. The workers having left ten minutes before, and the big boss having departed too, Géo was getting ready to return to Paris when sirens began blaring and a great clamor rose up in the distance...

But I shall hand over the floor of Géo.

"And then, here comes a young boy of 15—the son of the factory's night-watchman—pedaling his bike like crazy, and he leaps to the ground in the yard, shouting: 'Close the doors! They're coming! I've seen them. They're running after me! They've scoffed everyone at the power-station...'

"Who was he talking about? A band of communist harpies? No: 'balls of green fire!' Impossible to get anything co-

181

herent from him. The little chap was out of his mind, mad with terror. And to get further information, not so much as a cat outside, in the streets lit by electricity again. Except, toward the Quai de Saint-Ouen, the blasters were still smoking. For the people who'd been 'scoffed,' the personnel weren't doing a bad job. I gave up trying to understand and set off for Paris with my headlights on, at low speed to avoid a breakdown—for my car was 'making' lichen again.

"As you know, the Hénault-Feltrie factory is situated on the edge of Saint-Denis, 500 meters east of the national highway. As I turned on to it, heading south, I heard someone hailing me from the north. Under a street-light, I made out a barricade of carts and barrels across the causeway, and behind it, men with rifles. Communists or gendarmes, I thought they were after my rattletrap, and I accelerated, heading for Paris.

"Something significant had obviously happened...a drama. The road, ordinarily so busy, was absolutely deserted...deserted by the living, that is, for almost immediately, I had to serve round a corpse lying on the ground: a frightfully burned cadaver...then another, and others still: police cyclists, lying beside their machines...then a half-consumed cabriolet, still smoking, lying on top of its stricken horse.

"Explanation: a communist mob? But a mob, the passage of a revolutionary column marching on Paris, wouldn't have left that absolute void of living creatures behind it!

"It's true that beyond the junctions, on the side-roads, there were groups of people, who hailed me, waving their arms, as if I were running some danger—but they were too far away and I couldn't understand what they were saying to me. And still the deserted road, still strewn with cadavers, for kilometers...

"I went on slowly, rather nervous, I confess. The young lad's incoherent words came back to me involuntarily. I thought vaguely about some infernal machine, a terrestrial motor-torpedo. But the approach to Paris, encased between the houses of the Avenue des Batignolles, was full of people at the windows on the upper floors, and I was finally able to make out a few distinct shouts: 'Not that way! Save yourself! Be careful—they'll kill you!'

"Finally, at the crossroads of the Porte de Saint-Ouen, I saw 20 men and an officer on the Boulevard Ney, with an armored car. Just then, my engine started misfiring and dying. And there I was, broken down in the middle of the opening of the Avenue des Batignolles, facing the Avenue de Saint-Ouen.

"The officer, revolver in hand, seemed to hesitate. Positioned in the middle of the crossroads, he inspected both avenues one after the other. He called to me: 'Hey, you, motorist! Are more of them coming?'

"'I've only seen cadavers on the road. I don't know what you're talking about. Was it a mob?'

"In the distance, toward La Fourche, explosions crackled, then the rattle of a machine-gun. That lasted 20 seconds and suddenly fell silent. A clamor went up, and cries propagated: 'They're coming back! Every man for himself!'

"The officer left me to return to his men. They were disposed as sharpshooters to the right and left of the armored car, which had been set in the middle of the road, the muzzles of its machine-guns aimed at the Avenue de Saint-Ouen.

"Standing on the footplate of my car, ignorant of that danger, I was only thinking about seeing what would happen.

"A luminous dot at the far end of the ill-lit avenue was advancing with nimble little bounds...like a football that was rolling along on its own without anyone to push it. It grew in size and came closer, following the axis of the train-lines—and behind that first ball, there were others: one, two, three...ten...a whole string in single file...large balls of green light...like pharmacist's globes...but these balls were a meter or two in diameter.

"Have you read that story by Rosny Aîné called *Les Xipéhuz*? It made me shiver in my youth—when I still had time to read. These Xipéhuz, an aberrant creation born on Earth in prehistoric times, were beings endowed with intelligence, in the form of cones, gliding at ground level, provided with a single flamboyant eye....

183

"The frisson I experienced on reading that in the past gripped me again, but real, multiplied tenfold, in confrontation with those monstrous phosphorescent balls. I was still broken down at the crossroads, watching them come, lost in an immeasurable and perverse curiosity...in a fascination, like a bird in the presence of a serpent's maw...the Monsters born in the Saint-Denis power-station, progeny of the alternators and the comozoans...which, after a brief excursion to Paris to test their strength and reconnoiter their domain, were returning to their birthplace, perhaps to take a rest, and to graze on the current...

"Hypnotized, perceiving in two seconds and by means of a sort of panoramic intuition the thoughts that I've just put into words, awkwardly, I watched them come straight toward me, in single file: luminous emerald green globes, large and small...exactly like a joyful family coming back after a trip to the country...

"'Fire at will!'

"The Lebels crashed and the machine-guns sputtered. Flames were ripped from the first green ball by the bullets; it seemed to be agitated by violent palpitations, as if someone hidden inside were struggling, launching blows with his fists and feet, which were making the envelope of the balloon bulge. But it kept coming, straight toward the armored car, which ended up hiding it from me. I didn't see the impact, but a great flame suddenly emerged from the car, which was enveloped in smoke.

"The other balls of green light, large and small, had accelerated, as if enraged by the gunfire, charging the soldiers, who were still firing. They fell: one, two, three...the others, their weapons empty, took flight.

"Leaping and bouncing, the balls had gone past. Paralyzed by stupor and horror, I watched them come toward me, the machine-gunned ball in the lead, reduced to half its size and leaving a trail of fluorescent substance behind it...

"With a desperate surge, I tore myself from that catalepsy, leapt to the ground and fled along the Boulevard Ney...

"When I turned round, I saw that my car was in flames, like the machine-gun carrier..."

The incursion of the Chimeras had been stopped in the Place Clichy, thanks to the presence of mind of a motor-cycle policeman, who had stopped the firemen from the Carpeaux station, returning from a call to some chimney-fire. Two large hoses, set up in parallel at the entrance to the Avenue de Saint-Ouen, had succeeded, with their powerful water-jets, in making the fulminating globes retrace their steps...but not all of them. Two of the troop, forcing the hydraulic blockade, crossed the square, where they killed 100 idlers, and, emerging from the Rue d'Amsterdam, continued their hecatomb as far as the Boulevard Haussmann. They were annihilated at the Carrefour Drouot by the flame-throwers of a detachment of engineers sent in a truck from the barracks at La Pépinière...

At 8 p.m., when Géo took me to dinner at Wepler's, nothing remained in the Place Clichy as evidence of the event but a few pools of water at the entrance to the Avenue de Saint-Ouen. No trace of blood—the victims, taken away by ambulances, had succumbed to horrible burns.

But we saw the rise of that kind of siege-fever that was in the process of gripping all of Paris.

The illusory security that had reigned for three days gave way to an anguished consciousness of enormous and imminent peril. A rage, too, a despair that the work of the Great Shut-down had been compromised, and that everything would have to begin again, thanks to the sin of the Communists of Saint-Denis—and it was the general anger against them, as much as the military and police precautions, that stifled the riot that had scarcely begun.

The starting up of the electric power-station was a provocation, a ruse to attract repressive forces to the suburb. It was in Paris itself that the insurrection was in preparation. The leaders charged with giving the signal saw the arrival of the Chimeras as an unexpected, providential assistance, and the movement commenced at about 9:30 p.m. in the Place de la République, under cover of the confusion. But the Republican

Guard was alert; within five minutes, reinforcements were arriving from every direction, and the skirmish, limited to the edge of the square at the entrance to the Boulevard Magenta, was over before 11 p.m.

I was then in the Place de l'Opéra, on the terrace of the Café de la Paix, with Géo, and we saw nothing except for the passing of a few troop-carriers sent from the École Militaire. No one knew as yet that it was a matter of a riot; the rumor ran around that it was a new Chimera offensive—and that quasi-simultaneity made no small contribution to establishing the confusion between the two sets of facts.

A few minutes later, the *Echo de Paris'* loudspeakers announced the government's decision to destroy the Monsters of Saint-Denis.

"The criminal imprudence of the communists, who have violated the electric law and started up the power-station at Saint-Denis, has brought forth a new danger, with infinitely grave consequences. A generation of Xenobiota has been born, whose first representatives have sown death and terror in the capital. These creatures have returned to the plant, and measures will be taken to prevent them from effecting a further sortie. But, ignorant as we are of their possible scope of action, it is to be feared that, if they are allowed to multiply, these precautions might perhaps become ineffective. The plant at Saint-Denis will therefore be drowned in gas in the course of the night, by military engineers and aviators."

At the time, in the condition of mental aberration and high fever into which that terrifying adventure cast us, it was thought quite natural and straightforward that the bombardment had occasioned the partial destruction of the power-station, but on reflection, I wonder, along with many others—Monsieur Hénault-Feltrie, for example—firstly, whether that measure was not further justified by certain circumstances unknown to the public, and secondly, whether such damage could have resulted from simple gas-shells, or whether the Monsters of Saint Denis might have had far more to do with it.

Might they not, despairing of their cause, have destroyed their own lair?

It was claimed the next day, in fact, that the Ardent Chimeras' raid on Paris was only mounted by a small fraction of their total number, and that the larger contingent, entrenched in the plant, had taken possession of the controls in order to maintain its activity and provide alimentation to the entire tribe. The skeptics, however, made the observation, firstly, that the power-station, being equipped with the latest improvements in automation, would have continued to function just as well by itself until the coal stocks were exhausted; and secondly, that the burning of the plant could be explained by the mere presence of the vagabond fulminating globes, and that there was no need to attribute rational intelligence to them.

It seems probable, at least, in spite of the silence of the newspapers on their reappearance, that the 20 Chimeras seen in Paris were not the only ones to emerge from the plant. Another band of similar size must have headed northwards. It must have delivered somber blows during the night in Chantilly and Creil; then their excursion must have continued through a healthy region, deprived of current on their approach. Starved, without nutritive electricity, decreasing in size although still redoubtable, their last survivors might have been seen in the vicinity of Longueau, where all trace of them was conclusively lost...

Even taking into account only the facts duly certified—the march on Paris and the return to the plant at Saint-Denis, the behavior of the globe, the deliberate choice they seemed to make of their victims in order to strike them down by contact—scientists such as Professor Nathan, Dr. Charles Richet and the philosopher Henri Bergson have concluded that it is necessary to see the Chimeras as thinking beings, the first-born of a higher order of Xenobiota, something equivalent in their special creation to humankind in ours—and Monsieur Bergson has even deplored the fat that their destruction interrupted the experiment prematurely...

It is true that other scientists of no less great repute, such as Dr. Gustave Le Bon and M. Jean Perrin will not consent to see the mobile globes as anything more than simple electrical phenomena, concentrating within themselves a formidable reserve of energy, akin to "ball lightning," an aberrant form of the classic zigzag flash.[30]

The attempts of Professor Nathan to reproduce that particular variety of the Lichen in the laboratory having been fruitless, the question has every chance of never being elucidated.

---

[30] The fact that Varlet not only invokes these individuals as peripheral characters but attributes definite opinions to them is suggestive of actual acquaintance. Gustave Le Bon, a physicist turned social psychologist, hosted a weekly dinner-party for many years, of a kind that partly replaced the broader *salons* of the 19th century, to which—following a precedent set long before by Camille Flammarion—he was careful to invite intellectuals of every stripe, poets as well as scientists. If Varlet was an occasional guest, he would almost certainly have met Henri Bergson there, and very probably the physiologist Charles Richet (who signed his literary work Charles Epheyre) and the physicist Jean Perrin, and perhaps Madame Curie too. Varlet was certainly very familiar with Le Bon's ideas—the latter's pioneering work on atomic physics is cited later in the text, and the influence of his equally pioneering work on "crowd psychology" is very evident in Varlet's account of the evolving Parisian reaction to the Great Shutdown.

XVI. The Electric Terror

Whether they were intelligent or not, the Chimeras were redoubtable beings, and their appearance was a decisive reply to those who thought the continued observation of the decree superfluous.

Given such a terrifyingly conclusive example of the unknown dangers the Lichen still harbored, there was everything to fear from the resumption of the functioning of the smallest source of electricity.

There was an immediate and absolute reaction. The notion of the latent danger, which had weakened and had been replaced the previous day by a presumptuous confidence, flared up again, brutal and excessive, and became a panic terror, a virulent phobia which was maintained in a sharp state during the two days that historians have baptized "the Electric Terror."

On October 27, Paris awoke prey to that species of rage which derives from fear of an invisible and omnipresent menace that might explode at any moment. The official exhortations to increase vigilance diffused by the loudspeakers were superfluous. The terms of the decree seemed too moderate. No one any longer admitted that there were inoffensive sources of electricity. Even from a pocket electric torch, people almost expected to see an ardent lichen or something worse spring forth.

The new powers conferred on the anti-electric brigades and the new orders they were given stimulated them all the more because the agents, previously mocked and unpopular, now felt that they were supported by popular opinion. Puffed up by their importance, the Xs made arrests like other policemen, and entered houses, on the invitation and with the encouragement of citizens. Everyone became a benevolent auxiliary, and, if necessary, informer. The neighbor who possessed a radio set became a public enemy if he did not surrender his batteries of his own accord.

All motorized vehicles, including those with Diesel engines, became suspect. They were stopped on the strength of any denunciation; at the slightest trace of lichen on a poorly-shielded motor, the driver had to take to his heels to escape a beating, and if there was no policeman there to take the vehicle away to the pound, the exasperated crowd set fire to it. Detachments of boy-scouts were circulating on patrol, armed with real Brownings, of which they threatened to make use if a vehicle did not comply with their order to stop. Well-off motorists, in order to circulate freely, hired an X for the day, installing him permanently in the front seat.

More considerable sources of electricity still remained in Paris, however.

There was no emotion of astonishment, during the initial indifference of the Great Shutdown, at the knowledge that the telegraph and the telephone had only been suppressed for public use, and that a few lines continued in operation for official uses. It's necessary that a government governs, isn't it? And since the desired precautions were taken, there was no harm in those few items of electrical apparatus, appropriately protected from the lichen, continuing to function on a much-reduced scale. During the panic, however, this sage judgment was forgotten. A band of demonstrators gathered and went to the central telegraph office, declaring its intention of destroying the apparatus.

They did not destroy anything; the building was guarded by a squad of machine-gunners, the mere sight of whom sufficed to cool their zeal, and the two water-cannon summoned to reinforce the barracks at Château-Landon did not even have to be brought into play to disperse them.

A few historians have described that little group as a communist mob. That is, I believe, an error. The defeat of the mob that had begun to form on the evening of October 26th, amid the general hostility of the population, had discouraged the communist leaders, who were counting on a mass rising of sympathizers to support their troops. The demonstration at the central telegraph office, and two or three others of the same sort, had no political character; they were spontaneously-improvised movements in which everyone, regardless of parties, was only demanding one thing: the integral observation of the decree. In the day of the Electric Terror, far from wanting to overthrow the government, even its grimmest opponents expected salvation from it, and were glad that the governor of Paris and the prefect of police were men with "firm hands."

Under the influence of the morbid horror of the ardent lichen, even the inoffensive zebi was boycotted. The first carts that ventured on to the street on the 27th to sell their merchandise were attacked by exasperated housewives, who abuse the poor Crainquebilles and emptied the pails of "radio jam" into the sewers. The original source of the product remained, however: the transmitting station at the Eiffel Tower. The neighborhoods of Grenelle, the École Militaire and the Invalides, which believed themselves to be directly threatened by that proximity, supplied a column of volunteers brandishing axes, howling that it was necessary to cut the antennae and demolish the machines in the Tower. There too, precautions were taken and the assailants forced to retreat. For want of anything better they fell on the shed where zebi was being potted and stored on behalf of the syndicate, and destroyed or looted everything.

For fear of seeing their premises invaded and devastated, the great dailies abandoned their loudspeaker broadcasts, and from then on there was absolute silence with respect to all public news. That lasted throughout the afternoon of October 27 and the morning of October 28, until official public information posters were put up.

But none of that seemed serious to me on the 27th, while I remained in a state of suspense and the vacancy of my personality—while I awaited a reply to the letter sent via Alburtin...

It arrived the next day, on the 28th.

191

Stamped "air mail," addressed in Aurore's neat and upright handwriting, I take it from Madame Taquet's hands with a shiver of intoxicated joy and carry it off like a prey.

The end of the famine, the Ramadan of news!

I am obliged to pull myself together twice in order to finish opening it; my fingers are trembling, and I can only succeed by tearing the envelope apart.

Eyguzon, October 27
Dear Gaston,

> *My father is sending me to Paris for two days. I shall arrive on the 29th, at 6 p.m. Meet me at the Gare d'Austerlitz. If I don't see you on the platform or at the exit I'll come directly to your apartment.*
>
> *Your*

AURORE

It's nothing, those three lines, and perhaps the final formula is no more than a formula in her mind—but I see it as a testimony of half-confessed love.

Hope! Gratitude! A hectic vertigo of affection! "Good girl! Good girl!" I repeat, over and over again. How can I bear this tension of impatience that is driving me mad for all those hours? How many hours still separate me from her arrival? Thirty-three! That's terrible!

But I am henceforth immunized against the contagion of the unanimous folly, which I have allowed to invade me; here is my personality re-extended, reinflated...

And it's with a smile that I welcome the grievances of Madame Taquet, who stops me as I pass the lodge. She tells me that she wanted to talk me just now, upstairs. There's talk of evacuating Paris and cleansing it by means of gas. What do I think? She's asking my opinion, as she likes to do in difficult or awkward circumstances.

"Pooh! Yes, Madame Taquet, there is, indeed, talk of such an evacuation in places, but it doesn't mean anything."

"Yes, yes, Monsieur Delvart—it's quite serious. A commission has been appointed; the project will be discussed in the Chambre today or tomorrow; I know that from an usher at the Bourbon Palace, who confided it to the sister-in-law of one of my husband's comrades. The only chance that we still have, it appears, to get rid of it, is if there's a freeze within three or four days…but you must have heard the bells of Sacré-Coeur ringing for the last half-hour or thereabouts? That's for public prayers—to ask the good Lord to send us cold weather. Otherwise, if we don't get any frost, the evacuation will be on the second of November. Then what will become of us? We'll never find enough carriages to move house, will we, Monsieur Delvart?"

"Oh, you won't be moving house, Madame Taquet. If this ever happens, this evacuation, we'll all leave with our hands in our pockets, for 24 hours at the most—just time to go to the suburbs to eat a couple of fritters."

"Oh drat fritters! And what will we find when we get back? Nothing! The apaches will have stolen everything!"

"Police will remain in Paris, I assume, to keep watch in gas masks. But let's hope it won't come to that, and that the frost will come."

"In this weather! It's as warm as it was in September…and even in September…"

"That might change. Let's go—*au revoir*, Madame Taquet."

I set off for Paris, at hazard. I walked, elevated by a joyful excitement, already living the future, imagining my meeting with Aurore, the hours that I would spend with her…going much further than that first meeting, seeing our definitive union, later…our life together, according to six different scenarios. I let my imagination get drunk on all the possibilities, which it passed in review one at a time, by mean of long sweeps of a spotlight over the most various perspectives of our future happiness…

Unless…

193

But the moments when obstacles block the horizon did not last long, and I quickly recovered my hopeful course...

All these cinematic dreams were superimposed on the living reality of the street: a feverish and anxious Paris full of policemen with red armbands and gilded Xs, agents on bicycles, motorcycle couriers, Republican guards on horseback, trucks packed with uniforms...and black Senegalese troops grouped at junctions, laughing, beside stacks of Lebels...a Paris in a state of siege.

Where did I go that day? How many tens of kilometers did I cover? It seems to me that I had lunch somewhere near the Trocadero, the silhouette of which remains on my retina, associated with a restaurant table...

The weather was mild and gray, almost lukewarm. At a given moment, I noticed that I was sweating under my gabardine, and took it off to carry it over my arm.

The day was declining when I stopped, mechanically, with a group of idlers that has rapidly grown in front of a billboard, where a municipal poster was just finishing sticking up a white official sheet of paper.

ADVICE TO THE POPULATION IN CASE OF FROST

The Meteorological Office forecasts the arrival of an area of high pressure and an anticyclone that has formed over the North Atlantic and is advancing rapidly toward continental Europe. A considerable drop in the temperature thus seems imminent.

In case of frost appearing in Paris, in order that it might take maximum effect and lead to the complete and definitive sanitization of the capital, the Parisian population is requested to conform to the following instructions:

Firstly, as soon as the frost begins—which will be advertised by the ringing of church bells and the sounding of the sirens on public monuments, proceed in all dwellings with the extinction of fires, for cooking or other purposes, especially central-heating boilers.

Secondly, open all the windows in the building, including bedroom windows, and leave them open for at least four hours. It will be sufficient, in order not to risk any inconvenience to health, to remain in bed, well-covered. As for invalids and delicate individuals, who need warmth, take care to transport them into another room, already sterilized by the cold, in order to be able to aerate their...

The joyous exclamations around the poster were increasing. Finally! Deliverance! Oh, to be sure, no one would fail to carry out the recommendations of the poster—and people would make certain that their neighbors complied with them. Only too glad to have cold weather, if that providential frost materialized and people were thus able to escape the nightmare, without being obliged to have recourse to grand remedies and evacuating Paris! And they booed one bad citizen who dared to suggest that the story of the frost was nothing but a government maneuver, a trick to calm the citizens down...

Personally, I didn't care whether there was a frost or not. The true deliverance was the advent of Aurore. Her presence would be sufficient for everything to be for the best in the best of all possible worlds.

Nightfall caught me outside the Jardin des Plantes. That badly-lit Paris, in which the deployment of police and the military was taking on a sinister aspect, countered my anticipations of joy. I wanted to take refuge in my studio, where I might dream at my ease and sleep—for I felt suddenly exhausted. I had achieved the result that I had sought to achieve by walking: to dissipate the trepidation of expectation, to numb myself with fatigue, to reach tomorrow in the forgetfulness of sleep...

A horse-drawn omnibus, Bastille-Madeleine, carried me, passively, as far as the Opéra; then one last pedestrian effort, which seemed interminable, to get to the Rue Cortot...

"Monsieur Delvart!"

One foot already on the foot of the staircase, I came to a halt.

The concierge had come out of the lodge to say something to me—but she had a contrite and embarrassed expression, and could not bring herself to speak.

"Come on, Madame Taquet, what is it? Tell me."

"Well, this is it...it's very annoying, but you mustn't hold it against me—it's not my fault. You know that I waited as long as possible to declare the presence of lichen in the building. But yesterday, an agent came to collect the form and I had to give it to him. Then, this afternoon, about 4 p.m., the Disinfection Xs came, with their vehicle and all their gas-pipe equipment, and they did the entire house. I had to open your apartment for them, and Monsieur Noguès, who wasn't here either; otherwise, they'd have broken down the doors...

"You know how strict they are at present, the Xs...and to think that there might be frost tomorrow! It's a blow of fate, this disinfection. I'm afraid they might have done some damage in your apartment, and Monsieur Noguès'..."

They had. The curtains and my clothes weren't too badly damaged by the bromine gas, the odor of which persisted in my studio in spite of the windows being left open, but on a dozens of my canvases—the most recently painted—the whites had turned black, because of some chemical reaction.

A genuine catastrophe—but my physical weariness paralyzed any violent reaction. I remained stunned for a moment, under the oil-lamp, contemplating the ruined paintings; then, postponing indignation and anger until the next day, I went to bed, mentally bathed in the helpful thought of Aurore, and went to sleep almost immediately.

XVII. Aurore's Return

The misfortune seemed less grave—almost insignificant—when I awoke. Like a hymn of joy, I repeated: "She's arriving this evening, my darling girl! In ten and a half hours, I shall see her!" What importance could those petty blots on my canvases have, after that? If a restorer couldn't contrive to neutralize the bothersome chemical reaction with another that would return the whites to their original condition, I'd just have to retouch them myself—two or three days' work, that's all!

And to prove to myself that I was unconcerned about that contingency, I set about shaving, while humming the leitmotiv from *Die Walkure*.

The concierge rang twice, as was her habit when she had mail for me. With the left side of my face shaved but the right still smeared with shaving-soap I ran to open the door, fearing some snag. What if Aurore…?

"*Le Matin*, Monsieur Delvart! *Le Matin*'s back!"

Thank God that's all it is! "Thank you, Madame Taquet."

And very politely, I close the door in her face. To hell with her gossip! She's already scared me, with her idiot doorbell-ringing.

All the same, the paper will help me to pass half an hour…let's finish dressing and install ourselves in that armchair…

Let's see…editorial dithyramb, eulogies to the staff, the workers…

The prodigies of celerity that it has been necessary to accomplish to replace the electric equipment of the rotary presses with steam power…we have suspended publication for only five days, and we are the first to reappear today, at least 24 hours ahead of the fastest of our competitors…

That was a premature boast; the *Intran* reappeared that afternoon, at its usual time.

Summary of the events that occurred in the "interregnum of the Press." Charming! They're not kicking themselves! Yes, we know all this...nothing new: *Demonstration of the unemployed on October 25... Imprudent infractions of the decree at the Saint-Denis power-station: the ardent lichen...* Not many details. *A particularly dangerous species of Xenobiota...* It's not here that I'll find the truth of that dark tale; they judge that it's not the time to frighten the public... *Communist riots and criminal activity on October 26 and 27...* The communists have broad backs! *Attack on the central telegraph office...* I know—let's move on. Exhortation to calm: *All that is needed is a few more days of patience...the lichen has exhausted the first fire of its new creation and is decreasing, according to Professor Nathan. The resistance of the spores is in inverse proportion to the advancement of the forms from which they emanate. The most tenacious are those of the inferior species, always capable of reproducing themselves in their descendants in favorable conditions...*

The present situation in France. Map, with the contaminated regions shaded. Well! It hasn't changed much. The decree has done some good, then? Paris and the Seine, with a part of the Seine-et-Oise still form a kind of lop-sided crescent. The gray patch in the south-eastern region has reached Sète and Carcassonne. In the south-west, Bordeaux and Bayonne, as before. It's in the north that it's extended furthest: the zone now forms an irregular triangle from Dunkerque to Le Havre and Le Havre to Amiens...

Abroad. Spain has not yet taken serious measures against the lichen. In addition to Barcelona, Valencia, Madrid and Burgos are affected... In Belgium and Italy, similar decrees to France, since yesterday. In the United States... Ah! Well, well! Honestly, I can't help finding that funny. The ones who gave the signal to put France in quarantine! *In New York, the Xenobiota are making rapid progress. It is assumed that bootleggers...* Bootleggers, obviously. I'll read that later...

Uh oh!

EVACUATION OF PARIS POSTPONED

198

FROST FORECAST THIS EVENING

Discussion of the plan to evacuate Paris, which was to have been submitted to the Chambres yesterday by the Special Commission responsible for its formulation and finalization, has been adjourned. It is improbable that the government will be forced to have recourse to that extreme measure, for the Meteorological Office is forecasting the arrival of a cold front, which has every chance of reaching Paris this evening... And: *the population is exhorted...* Yes, as in yesterday's poster.

But in the other column, I catch with the corner of my eye: *Eyguzon*—that name now familiar and dear...

Professor Nathan informs us that the discovery anticipated by him is on course for imminent realization at the Eyguzon laboratory. The study of certain radioactive varieties has yielded to "the new Edison," M. Oswald Lescure, the secret of provoking atomic disintegration at will—which is to say, the liberation of the energy that the atom contains in a degree of extraordinary condensation. Dr. Gustave Le Bon, the French scientist to whom the glory belongs of being the first to occupy himself with this question, in 1910, has, in fact, calculated that if one were to succeed in liberating all the energy contained in a gram of matter with sufficient rapidity, the power furnished would be sufficient to propel a goods train comprising 40 ten-ton wagons around the world. There is no need to emphasize the importance of such a discovery. It represents industrial omnipotence and global hegemony for the country that has the monopoly on it. Let us only hope that another prognosis issued by Dr. Le Bon will not be verified. "The person who makes that discovery," he says, in his book L'Évolution de la matière, *will undoubtedly not see its realization; he will be destroyed, along with his laboratory, by a formidable explosion..."*

Someone's at the door! Who can it be, at this hour?

Unexpected...just like the other morning, the day we went to Le Bourget, so close and yet already so far removed into the past, when Luce arrived unexpectedly with her brother...

It was Luce again, but with Lendor Cheyne.

A Cheyne more American than ever, in his suit with Cubist shoulders: a Cheyne with a rictus smile, his jaws contracted by an implacable businessmanlike will, jabbering a worse French than on the first day. But he had stopped chewing gum, and I deduced from his brick-red complexion that he had been assiduously pursuing his comparative study of cocktails.

Luce, in all her red-haired Danae splendor.

With a mischievous expression, as if she has a surprise in store for me, she tells me that she...that Lendor...or, rather, he and she...have come to buy a few canvases from me—"coves," if possible.

Bad luck, then! Yesterday's accident becomes a calamity again, doubtless ruining the sale...and I tell them the story, displaying, to either side, the series of spoiled canvases propped against the walls.

"The very coves that you would have wanted, my dear. The restoration will take several days..."

She examined them, stroking her chin—but instead of the movement of recoil that I expected, I see her neck stretch, her eyes blink, and finally, she straightens up, saying: "Astonishing! Splendid! You're an idiot, Tonton, to talk about restoration! That would be committing a crime, spoiling these chiaroscuro effects; the disinfection apparatus has wrought a stroke of genius; this has a powerful originality...as beautiful as African Art. I'll take the canvases just as they are..." And, addressing Cheyne: "Aren't they lovely, my dear?"

The Yank opined, confidently: "Oh yes! Capital. Take the whole lot..." And, taking out his check book, he asked: "Combiène, Guéstoine?"

It was Luce who quoted him a price, authoritatively—double the one that I might have dared to propose.

That deal completed, my visitors sit down, and Luce starts talking about business...their business. In technical terms, in which I'm immediately lost, she explains astounding projects, vertiginous schemes, of which I can only grasp scraps: an oil cartel... synthetic fuels... cracking... dividends... shareholders. She gets around to the subject of the Moon Gold Company.

"I can tell you, Tonton... thanks to me, my dear Lendor"—and, like a lion-tamer proud of her pupil, she strokes Cheyne's arm, demonstratively, while he swells up, purring and rolling the comical eyes of an amorous hyena—"has come to understand that he's too young to believe in the utility of realizing a voyage to the Moon some day. He knows now that it will be sufficient to see in lunar gold a simple symbol of Credit. That has been evident to me from the beginning. And the proof that I'm right is that the new issue of shares in the European Moon Gold Company has been fully subscribed since yesterday, in spite of the deplorable condition of the financial market; the banks have all come in; the only opposition is from the electricity groups..."

Animated and triumphant, she was in the full glory of her beauty. I caressed her with my painter's gaze, as I would have admired an Old Master... but the sight of Cheyne tamed enabled me to anticipate a further revelation.

Suddenly changing her tone, Luce declared: "What's more, old chap, I have the honor of announcing my imminent marriage—on November 113, a fortnight hence—to dear Lendor. It's to begin to furnish our gallery that we've just bought your canvases..."

I must have gone pale, or red, with a flabbergasted expression. A vertigo of joy whirled within me. Tears of happiness, I think, came into my eyes.

She misunderstood. Truly, Danae didn't suspect a thing. After my distancing myself from her, and with the proof before her very eyes, in the portrait, that I was in love with someone else, she still believed—God's truth!—that I was weeping for my lost hopes...for regret at seeing her marry someone other than me! She imagined that I still retained a secret weakness for her!

"How emotional you are, Tonton! I wouldn't have believed...anyway, it's your fault; you're too timid. I'd never have guessed, myself. Then again, think—it would never have worked, the two of us. While, with that nice little astronaut..."

I didn't want to leave her under any illusion.

"No, Luce, don't be deceived. It's not that, simply surprise..."

"Don't defend yourself, Tonton—I don't want that. On the contrary, they suit you, those romantic tears. Don't worry, we'll remain friends Anyway, we have to talk business again...to regulate the disavowal of their contract, Lendor and his ex-fiancée, who'll become your future wife...for you'll marry her, won't you?"

"That depends on her..."

"She desires nothing more. That leaps to the eyes. So, there are questions of interest to discuss with her and her father. Don't worry—I'll make sure that Lendor conducts himself like a gentleman."

For a second, I wondered whether Luce might have come to see me, in reality, to obtain a compromise with respect to Oswald Lescure's invention, announced by the *Matin*, the rights to which would belong exclusively to Aurore, if Cheyne did not marry her—but I realized that I was overestimating her Machiavellianism.

And what did it matter? I would have forgiven her all her petty roguery, my dear beautiful enemy, Luce! Thanks to her, the last obstacles had been removed; thanks to her, Aurore was free, my beloved was mine!

"What do you say, then, Tonton? Are we still friends?"

With the warmest and most sincere effusion, I shook her satin-clad hand, as firm, full and healthy as that of a living statue.

At 5:30 p.m., wrapped up in a thick winter overcoat—for the weather had grown noticeably colder, I was feverishly pacing back and forth on the platform of the Gare d'Austerlitz at which Aurore's train was due to arrive at 6. Impatiently anxious, I was rehearsing what I would say to tell her about Cheyne's marriage; I was savoring I advance her joyful surprise, the renewal of her confession of love...

At 5:55, feeling someone tap me on the shoulder, I started nervously, and even uttered an exclamation. I turned round.

"Monsieur Nathan!"

In my optimism, in my benevolent goodwill toward everyone and everything, I greeted the great biologist spontaneously, forgiving him wholeheartedly for all his impoliteness, past, present and to come, happy that he had done me the honor of recognizing me. The imperious familiarity of that tap on the shoulder astonished me, though; it did not fit in with the memory I had of his Olympian attitude. The old scientists had to be deeply troubled, not in his normal state of mind.

Immobile in his fur-collared overcoat, he considered me pensively, his thick white eyebrows frowning...

How can I put it? Some high-tension concern radiated from his contracted features.

Finally, with a leaden and almost absent-minded gesture, he offered me his hand. "Monsieur Delvart, you're also waiting, I suppose, for Mademoiselle Lescure? I'm glad to find you here, and that you're friends. Let me say...I don't have much time...her train will be here in less than four minutes...I need to charge you with a delicate mission, which you'll fulfill better than I could with regard to her...

"Something terrible has happened...which is also a great misfortune or science. Her father is dead. The news has just reached me by telegraph from the Eyguzon Dam. Mademoiselle Lescure had only been gone two hours this morning when an explosion destroyed the research laboratory. A very violent explosion—nearly two kilometers away, the telegraphy post at the dam received a rude shock. It's the proof, Monsieur, the atrocious and definitive proof that the new Edison has just realized his discovery...it was, alas, almost inevitable, as Dr. Gustave Le Bon foresaw in 1910... In spite of everything, it astonishes me, though, in a first rate experimenter like

Oswald Lescure. Would he not have taken all the precautions indispensable in such a case, including the first and foremost one of only using an infinitesimal parcel of matter?"

I was scarcely following the scientist's reasoning; his voice arrived indistinctly, as from a distance. A lamentation of dolor filled my skull, drowning the triumphal song of a few moments before. Aurore! How could I tell her the frightful news? How could I talk to her, at the same time, about my egotistical joy?

The whistle of a locomotive...

The hall vibrates to the rhythm of the rain that advances along the track, slows down, stops...

In the crowd of disembarking passengers, I perceive her lacy capeline, her beloved face, her eyes, searching for me. Leaving Nathan behind, I run toward her...

Here we are, stopped face to face, a double reef in the midst of the flowing wave, battered by elbows and the corners of suitcases.

A mysterious divination of feminine and amorous instinct? Telepathy? What do I know? In my words of welcome, spoken feverishly, in the grip of my hands, in my anxious, avid, imploring gaze, which dedicates my pity to her whole-heartedly, she has read the terrible news that I was kneading in secret, searching for the best way to offer her the dolorous essence without causing her too much suffering.

She takes my hands again, having released hem. "Gaston! What's the matter with you? No—what's happened? Tell me, quickly. It's not you that it concerns?"

The temptation, for half a second, to begin by liberating the joy of my love, trapped beneath the mountain of sadness...while I suppress that desire, the other, calamitous news melts, escaping from me under the pressure of her gaze.

"No, beloved, you. Your father. He's..."

She suddenly freezes, into a frightening calm. She has seen the biologist, who rejoins us, and who stands before her, hat in hand, his baldness respectfully inclined. She fixes her ardent eyes upon him. She doesn't want to learn from me the misfortune that she has deduced, of which she is now intuitively sure.

In a strange, quasi-automatic voice, she asks: "The catastrophe has happened, Monsieur Nathan?"

The member of the Institut raises his head, then nods in a gesture of assent. "Yes, Mademoiselle, the new Edison has joined the most glorious martyrs of science in immortality."

"Oh! That's why he sent me away at the decisive moment...that he sent Dr. Alburtin and he laboratory assistants away. He foresaw...he knew..."

And as she falls silent, pale and absent-minded, her eyes wide with mortal sadness, he goes on: "My car is at your disposal, Mademoiselle...and yours also, Monsieur Delvart, if you wish..."

But I only just have time to catch her. She has fallen into my arms, sobbing—and between the sobs, I perceive words that open within my sympathetic sadness a trench resplendent with happiness: "My beloved Gaston, I'm yours; I have no one but you in the world..."

Magnificent moment! I have not had to tell her that Cheyne's marriage has liberated her. Of her own accord, she has renounced the interests that still bind her, she believes, to her ex-fiancé. She is throwing overboard the contract that would make her rich; she is sacrificing her fortune for me. She is giving me proof of a love that is the only thing capable of overcoming filial affection...

In strictly logical terms, I could end my story there, since that gesture, in assuring me of Aurore's love, closes the era of uncertainty and opens that of happiness, which is story-free by definition. For the sake of completeness, however, I shall give a synopsis of the rest of that day, since the predestination that had made my adventure begin with the story of the lichen and had linked the two together in such a narrow fashion, manifested itself again, in cutting short the effective reign of the Lichen on the day when I concluded the conquest of my beloved.

At the exit from the Gare d'Austerlitz, Nathan showed an awkward but touching concern for Aurore. That bachelor, with a sentimentally arid life, having sacrificed everything, even simple domestic bliss, to science, revealed a paternal soul. While supporting my companion by the other arm, he murmured words of encouragement to her.

On the sidewalk, beside the limousine guarded by a chauffeur and a Xenobiota policeman, he asked: "Where should I drop you?"

In her distress, Aurore turned to me. She put herself in my hands.

My decision was made: to surround her with an illusion of family life. I gave the Frémiets' address. The ever-ready benevolence of my uncle and the assured compassion of my aunt permitted me to hope that Aurore would not spend the night in a hotel. At the very least she would spend the evening among friendly faces.

I had not counted in vain on my aunt's good heart. As soon as she spoke, she took pity and made me the expected offer.

"No, no, Gaston—you can't take the poor girl to a hotel. We'll put her in the guest-room."

Aurore accepted gratefully. She allowed herself to be enveloped by an affectionate compassion that softened her grief. My aunt, having obtained information as to her tastes, busied herself between the kitchen and the dining-room, in order to prepare us "a little light dinner." My uncle was perfect; making no pretence of eloquent consolation, he muted his thunderous voice, talked about the imminent frost, and communicated his observations of the thermometer in the yard, which had gone down from three-and-a-half degrees to one degree above zero in an hour. Even young Oscar attempted to distract "the demoiselle" by showing her a box of Meccano and building a superb monoplane "for her." And I, while she was wiping her eyes, was thinking about the most serene future and dreaming of another child, who would have her eyes and mouth...

As we were sitting down at the table, an immense rumor rose up over the city; bellowing sirens, church bells ringing at full volume. The Meteorological Office forecast was coming true...

At 9 p.m., the thermometer outside indicated minus two degrees. In the course of the night, it fell to minus five. The frost lasted for 36 hours and extended over the entirety of France, without sparing the Côte d'Azur.

On the morning of October 31, in a Paris clear of lichen, the electric current was restored. The Metro, trams, taxis and motor-buses were running. Life resumed its normal course.

Our marriage, celebrated at the Mairie of the 18th arrondissement in the Basilica of Sacré-Coeur, took place on November 15, one month to the day after the landing of the MG-17 Rocket at the Belle-Fille pass.

The witnesses were, for the bride, Monsieur Marcel Frémiet, art photographer, and Professor Nathan, member of the Institute, and for the groom, Monsieur Géo de Ricourt, engineer, and Dr. Tancrède Alburtin.

Luce and her husband—Mr. and Mrs. Cheyne-de Ricourt since the day before last—and Madame de Ricourt were in the front row of the audience, with other notable persons who were listed in the newspapers but are unimportant to us.

The fusillade of photographers having been endured at the church door, Géo, shaking off the reporters, took us in his brand new Reinastella—which had replaced the Renault burned by the Chimeras at the Porte de Saint-Ouen—to the Pacific, where there was a private dinner.

At 6 p.m., the express to Marseilles left the Gare de Lyon, with a young couple aboard who were going to spend their honeymoon in Tunisia.

It was that evening, between Dijon and Lyon, that Aurore, tenderly nestled against me in our solitary sleeping-compartment, talked to me again about her father and the intuition she had had of his death, on seeing me with Nathan on the platform of the Gare d'Austerlitz.

"I suspected it, I had a presentiment of it," she had limited herself to replying, when I had asked her about it in the preceding days.

This time, she finally explained.

"When he came close to success in his discovery, my father seemed worried. He did something he had never done before, becoming preoccupied with the fate of his invention: 'Am I really working for the good of humanity?' And he explained his doubts. I reminded him of the principle that he had inculcated in me: 'Discovery alone is important; the scientist does not have to worry about the applications that will be made of his science.' He shook his head without replying. An article in the *Orléans Républicain*, which I read to him, affected him profoundly. It was signed by a certain Lieutenant-Colonel Verdier, who extolled the military utilization of intra-atomic energy for the construction of destructive engines capable of annihilating entire armies, 10,000 men in ten seconds.[31] 'There's no doubt about it—that's what will become of my discovery!' said my father, sadly. And he spoke to me in an entirely new fashion. 'Oh, if it could only be limited to the hands of sages—initiates—as in antiquity. Scientists ought to be able to use a special language, more hermetic than Sanskrit, to transmit their knowledge...' And he deplored the inevitable diffusion, in our democratic times, of applied science.

"His intimate imperative to seek obliged him to carry his invention through to the end, but he visibly regretted that his success was imminent and inevitable. He said something terrible, which ought to have made it clear to me: 'My child, if a catastrophe were to destroy me along with my discovery, that would be a stroke of luck!' But he smiled as he said it, and I

---

[31] Although I have not been able to trace it, this article was probably real. Numerous Verdiers served in the French army in the course of the 19th and 20th centuries, several of whom rose to the rank of Lieutenant-Colonel; there was definitely at least one active in 1930.

thought it was a joke. Only, in Paris, Gaston dear, when I saw in your expression, and Nathan's, that something bad had happened, those words came back me, and I understood that he had sent us away—Alburtin, me, and the laboratory assistants—under various pretexts, that day, because he expected...what happened. That he had voluntarily provoked it, no! That would be too horrible, I don't want to believe it...but he had undoubtedly neglected to take precautions...

"You know, beloved, how grieved I am to have lost my father, and you won't suspect my heart if I tell you this, but I can't help agreeing with him. It's a good thing for humanity that an almost-infinite source of energy has not been handed over to do the work of destruction. It's already too much to have brought the Lichen."

Comforting her with a kiss, I replied, thoughtfully: "Who knows, my love, whether the gift will not be more profitable in the end than you think, and that it presently seems. The adventure of the Lichen has given humankind mistrust and modesty, with a salutary dread. People believed that they could juggle with the forces of the universe with impunity; their pride has been dented. The new state of mind, which Nathan calls neophobia, is perhaps the first step toward a future higher wisdom, which will include a consciousness of comic harmony and the duties it imposes..."

XVIII. The New Life

Two years have passed, and facts have proved me right.

People no longer believe in the infallibility of material progress. Machines have ceased to be considered as sovereign and invulnerable to contingencies. As the plague of the Middle Ages imposed on humans a sense of their fragility, the Xenobiota have come to attack and put them in check. And like the plague, the Xenobiota might reappear.

Seemingly eliminated by the frost of October 29 and 30, the new creation remains present on the Earth, in a latent state. Even when no local epidemic breaks out, it is impossible to forget its existence, for a special brigade of Xs remains, and an Under-Secretary of Xenobiota.

The lichen has gradually invaded almost all inhabited land, in spite of the closure of national frontiers, which was recognized to be futile and quickly abandoned. Not a month passes, and hardly a week, without an epidemic of lichen being announced in France or abroad, which has to be immediately combated by a severe famine of electricity, isolation and disinfection.

In hot countries, in particular, the Xenobiota have become endemic.

It is true that the vital drive to great expansion has almost entirely ceased, that the spores have lost much of their reproductive power and that the ideal sterilizing agent has been discovered in iodine vapor, but the danger has not disappeared, and will probably never disappear.

Those of us who lived through the vicissitudes of the Great Shutdown retain a certain mistrust of electrical apparatus. Those who saw the Chimeras at close range scarcely dare to use a telephone or flick a light-switch. That phobia has attenuated and has not affected the younger generation, but they, like us, will have to "live dangerously." The cosmic enemy, implanted on Earth, holds us under its perpetual menace.

Another consequence: prohibition continues to weigh, in all countries, on astronautics. That is, as Nathan declares, a retreat of scientific curiosity, an entire realm condemned. In renouncing any attempt to leave their planet, human beings are setting limits upon themselves. They are saying to progress: no further!

My wife, of course, joins in with the chorus of regret, and adds her own to it, at having to renounce piloting rockets and one day making the journey to our satellite.

In spite of this embargo, the Moon Gold Company is highly prosperous. It liquidated its primitive goal to memory on the day when it obtained the lavish indemnity that Luce and Cheyne finally succeeded in obtaining from the government in Washington for the confiscation of the astronautical factory and laboratory. Lunar gold, a simple symbol of Credit—do the shareholders understand that? At any rate, they're very satisfied with the dividends.

Aurore has renounced her disapproval of that line of conduct, which has, she recognizes, become inevitable. She contents herself with not exercising her voting rights at meetings—for she has the largest shareholding. Luce kept her word, and Cheyne behaved properly; he gave my wife, in global indemnity for those of her father's patents that he exploits, 1500 shares of the European issue—the synthetic oil alone is worth that. At an average dividend of 8%, less taxes, that leaves us with an income of more than 50,000 francs a year.

With that and the sales of my paintings, whose prices are rising, we already have enough for our needs. We both have simple tastes, and Aurore didn't even want us to look for a better apartment than the one I had in the old building in the Rue Cortot; as it is vast, it makes a very agreeable abode. But she can't bear idleness, and would judge me criminal for confiscating an intelligence like hers. Nathan who testifies a paternal affection for her in his surly manner, has appointed her as his assistant in his laboratory at the Institut, where she works with him. The service is not over-demanding, and we are never separated for more than half a day. She benefits from four months' vacation.

Last summer, Nathan came to spend a fortnight at our villa in Brittany, when I got to know him better, and almost to like him; beneath his Olympian exterior, the scientist is a man like any other. I've seen him laugh several times, when I beat him at chess, which he plays with a lack of skill that amuses him—and those petty victories have contributed a great deal to making me less timid in his presence. It wouldn't take much to make me think myself his superior what I checkmate him more rapidly than usual—but I still admire the perfect ease with which Aurore converses with him as one equal to another.

And the meteorites? They're in the Museum, in a glass case in the bolide hall: a little pile of black dust in a glass saucer, beside the other saucer that contains the similarly black but slightly larger granules collected by Nordenskjold on the glaciers of Greenland. Nothing attracts them to the attention of the public but a label with a simple catalogue-number.

Sometimes, Aurore and I go to spend five minutes looking at them dreamily, and I recall that, although it's through them that the world has lost its former sense of security, I owe them the happiness of my new life...

SF & FANTASY

Henri Allorge. *The Great Cataclysm*
Guy d'Armen. *Doc Ardan: The City of Gold and Lepers*
G.-J. Arnaud. *The Ice Company*
Cyprien Bérard. *The Vampire Lord Ruthwen*
Aloysius Bertrand. *Gaspard de la Nuit*
Richard Bessière. *The Gardens of the Apocalypse*
Albert Bleunard. *Ever Smaller*
Félix Bodin. *The Novel of the Future*
Alphonse Brown. *City of Glass*
André Caroff. *The Terror of Madame Atomos; Miss Atomos;*
The Return of Madame Atomos
Félicien Champsaur. *The Human Arrow*
Didier de Chousy. *Ignis*
Captain Danrit. *Undersea Odyssey*
C. I. Defontenay. *Star (Psi Cassiopeia)*
Charles Derennes. *The People of the Pole*
Georges Dodds (anthologist). *The Missing Link*
Harry Dickson. *The Heir of Dracula*
Jules Dornay. *Lord Ruthven Begins*
Sâr Dubnotal *vs. Jack the Ripper*
Alexandre Dumas. *The Return of Lord Ruthven*
Renée Dunan. *Baal*
J.-C. Dunyach. *The Night Orchid; The Thieves of Silence*
Henri Duvernois. *The Man Who Found Himself*
Achille Eyraud. *Voyage to Venus*
Henri Falk. *The Age of Lead*
Paul Féval. *Anne of the Isles; Knightshade; Revenants; Vam-
pire City; The Vampire Countess; The Wandering Jew's
Daughter*
Paul Féval, *fils. Felifax, the Tiger-Man*
Charles de Fieux. *Lamékis*
Arnould Galopin. *Doctor Omega*; *Doctor Omega & The Sha-
dowmen*
G.L. Gick. *Harry Dickson and the Werewolf of Rutherford
Grange*

Nathalie Henneberg. *The Green Gods*
V. Hugo, P. Foucher & P. Meurice. *The Hunchback of Notre-Dame*
Michel Jeury. *Chronolysis*
Octave Joncquel & Théo Varlet. *The Martian Epic*
Gérard Klein. *The Mote in Time's Eye*
Jean de La Hire. *Enter the Nyctalope; The Nyctalope on Mars; The Nyctalope vs. Lucifer; The Nyctalope Steps In*
Etienne-Léon de Lamothe-Langon. *The Virgin Vampire*
André Laurie. *Spiridon*
Gabriel de Lautrec. *The Vengeance of the Oval Portrait*
Georges Le Faure & Henri de Graffigny. *The Extraordinary Adventures of a Russian Scientist Across the Solar System* (2 vols.)
Gustave Le Rouge. *The Vampires of Mars*
Jules Lermina. *Mysteryville; Panic in Paris; To-Ho and the Gold Destroyers; The Secret of Zippelius*
Jean-Marc & Randy Lofficier. *Edgar Allan Poe on Mars; The Katrina Protocol; Pacifica; Robonocchio; Tales of the Shadowmen 1-7*
Xavier Mauméjean. *The League of Heroes*
José Moselli. *Illa's End*
John-Antoine Nau. *Enemy Force*
Marie Nizet. *Captain Vampire*
C. Nodier, A. Beraud & Toussaint-Merle. *Frankenstein*
Henri de Parville. *An Inhabitant of the Planet Mars*
J. Polidori, C. Nodier, E. Scribe. *Lord Ruthven the Vampire*
P.-A. Ponson du Terrail. *The Vampire and the Devil's Son*
Maurice Renard. *The Blue Peril; Doctor Lerne; The Doctored Man; A Man Among the Microbes; The Master of Light*
Jean Richepin. *The Wing*
Albert Robida. *The Adventures of Saturnin Farandoul; The Clock of the Centuries; Chalet in the Sky*
J.-H. Rosny Aîné. *Helgvor of the Blue River; The Givreuse Enigma; The Mysterious Force; The Navigators of Space; Vamireh; The World of the Variants; The Young Vampire*
Marcel Rouff. *Journey to the Inverted World*

Han Ryner. *The Superhumans*
Brian Stableford. *The New Faust at the Tragicomique;The Empire of the Necromancers (The Shadow of Frankenstein; Frankenstein and the Vampire Countess; Frankenstein in London); Sherlock Holmes & The Vampires of Eternity; The Stones of Camelot; The Wayward Muse.* (anthologist) *The Germans on Venus; News from the Moon; The Supreme Progress; The World Above the World*
Jacques Spitz. *The Eye of Purgatory*
Kurt Steiner. *Ortog*
Eugène Thébault. *Radio-Terror*
C.-F. Tiphaigne de La Roche. *Amilec*
Théo Varlet. *The Xenobiotic Invasion*
Paul Vibert. *The Mysterious Fluid*
Villiers de l'Isle-Adam. *The Scaffold; The Vampire Soul*
Philippe Ward. *Artahe*
Philippe Ward & Sylvie Miller. *The Song of Montségur*

MYSTERIES & THRILLERS

M. Allain & P. Souvestre. *The Daughter of Fantômas*
A. Anicet-Bourgeois, Lucien Dabril. *Rocambole*
A. Bisson & G. Livet. *Nick Carter vs. Fantômas*
V. Darlay & H. de Gorsse. *Lupin vs. Holmes: The Stage Play*
Paul Féval. *Gentlemen of the Night; John Devil; The Black Coats ('Salem Street; The Invisible Weapon; The Parisian Jungle; The Companions of the Treasure; Heart of Steel; The Cadet Gang; The Sword-Swallower)*
Emile Gaboriau. *Monsieur Lecoq*
Steve Leadley. *Sherlock Holmes: The Circle of Blood*
Maurice Leblanc. *Arsène Lupin vs. Countess Cagliostro; Lupin vs. Holmes (The Blonde Phantom; The Hollow Needle)*
Gaston Leroux. *Chéri-Bibi; The Phantom of the Opera; Rouletabille & the Mystery of the Yellow Room*
William Patrick Maynard. *The Terror of Fu Manchu*
Frank J. Morlock. *Sherlock Holmes: The Grand Horizontals; Sherlock Holmes vs Jack the Ripper*

P. de Wattyne & Y. Walter. *Sherlock Holmes vs. Fantômas*
David White. *Fantômas in America*

SCREENPLAYS

Mike Baron. *The Iron Triangle*
Emma Bull & Will Shetterly. *Nightspeeder; War for the Oaks*
Gerry Conway & Roy Thomas. *Doc Dynamo*
Steve Englehart. *Majorca*
James Hudnall. *The Devastator*
Jean-Marc & Randy Lofficier. *Royal Flush*
J.-M. & R. Lofficier & Marc Agapit. *Despair*
Andrew Paquette. *Peripheral Vision*
R. Thomas, J. Hendler & L. Sprague de Camp. *Rivers of Time*

NON-FICTION

Stephen R. Bissette. *Blur 1-5; Green Mountain Cinema 1;
Teen Angels & New Mutants*
Win Scott Eckert. *Crossovers* (2 vols.)
Jean-Marc & Randy Lofficier. *Shadowmen* (2 vols.)
Randy Lofficier. *Over Here*

HEXAGON COMICS

Franco Frescura & Luciano Bernasconi. *Wampus*
Franco Frescura & Giorgio Trevisan. *CLASH*
L. Bernasconi, J.-M. Lofficier & Juan Roncagliolo Berger.
Phenix
Claude Legrand, J.-M. Lofficier & L. Bernasconi. *Kabur*
Franco Oneta. *Zembla*
L. Buffolente, Lofficier & J.-J. Dzialowski. *Strangers: Homi-
cron*
Danilo Grossi. *Strangers: Jaydee*
Claude Legrand & Luciano Bernasconi. *Strangers: Starlock*

ART BOOKS

Jean-Pierre Normand. *Science Fiction Illustrations*
Raven Okeefe. *Raven's L'il Critters*
Randy Lofficier & Raven OKeefe. *If Your Possum Go Daylight...*
Daniele Serra. *Illusions*